Twenty-One Steps of Courage

Twenty-One Steps of Courage

Sarah Bates

For the 1st Battalion

3rd U.S. Infantry Regiment

(The Old Guard) Sentinels

who stand watch at the

Tomb of the Unknown Soldier.

Unbounded courage and compassion join'd,

Tempering each other in the victor's mind,

Alternately proclaim him good and great,

And make the hero and the man complete.

—Joseph Addison

The Campaign

Acknowledgments

Authors are urged to *write what you know*. In the case of this story, I largely ignored that advice. Yet the novel moves from start to finish, embracing the same dogged determination of its Army protagonist. With the help of the people listed below whose contributions made this book possible, *write what 'they' know* became my mantra. With gratitude and respect I thank them.

Fort Myer, Arlington, Virginia, US Army 3rd U.S. Infantry Regiment (The Old Guard): Major Joel Lindeman, Public Affairs Office. Captain Justin T. Michel, Commander, Delta Company, 1st Battalion. Sergeant Nancy Deweese, Public Affairs Office, 4th Battalion. Private Second Class John Baker, Sentinel Platoon.

Walter Reed Army Medical Center, Washington DC: Major Christopher Ballard, Infantry, US Army, former Commander Warrior Transition Brigade. Captain Darrick Gutting, US Army, Chaplain Corps. Gigail "Gail" Cureton, Media Relations.

National Training Center, Fort Irwin, California: John Wagstaff, Director of Public Affairs. Etric Smith, Public Affairs Office/Media Relations Officer. Specialist John Edward Davis, US Army.

Other Military Experts: Sergeant First Class Jennifer K. Yancey, US Army Public Affairs-NORTHEAST, New York. Chief Warrant Officer Bill Tuttle, US Army (Retired), Afghanistan. Sergeant Mike Durand, US Army, California National Guard. Specialist Dwan Link, US Army, Fort Lewis, Washington. Staff Sergeant Christopher Milton, US Army Rangers, 10-83 (Retired). Specialist Joseph Gracia, US Army, 1/158 Infantry Battalion, Balboa Naval Hospital (Retired). Major Jonathan R. Smith, USMC, Camp Lejeune, North

Carolina. Sergeant Jon C. Rehac, USMC, Camp Pendleton, California. HM1 Aaron Seibert, US Navy, Wounded Warrior Battalion, Camp Pendleton, California. Chuck Fuller, US Navy, 1st Class Petty Officer, Naval Patrol & Recon Squadron, VP-6 (Retired).

Medical Experts: M. Jason Highsmith, PT, DPT, CP, FAAOP, Visiting Assistant Professor, School of Physical Therapy & Rehabilitation Sciences, College of Medicine, University of South Florida. Steven Peterson, MS, PT and Marcia LaBruyere, RN, Director, Perioperative Services, Fallbrook Hospital, Fallbrook, California.

Fallbrook Professional Writers–Carmi Cosmos, Catherine Cresswell, Jen Hilborne, David Hubbard, and Kara LaRussa who listened to every word and made the story better, and Michael Wolf who edited the final manuscript to reveal the story buried in the facts.

Jim Bates, fine art painter and the finest of husbands, who inspired me, pushed me and always believed I could write this book.

A special thank you to all the Soldiers at Army posts Fort Irwin, Fort Myer and at Walter Reed Medical Center who shared their personal experiences with me.

FOREWORD

What you are about to read is the remarkable story of a boy becoming a man; and of his courage and tenacity whose ambition is to follow in the footsteps of his combat-fallen father in becoming a Sentinel of the Old Guard. You will feel the resourcefulness and dedication of this soldier's efforts to be a proud member of the oldest unit of the U.S. Army; and to guard the Tomb of the Unknown Soldier at the Arlington National Cemetery.

If you have ever witnessed the Changing of the Guard ceremony at the cemetery you would see the 21 steps taken each way on the black strip that silently represents a 21-gun salute to the Commander-in-Chief. This story will tell you about the unusual abilities and requirements for those Sentinel applicants who are accepted for this honored duty. This story is that of an unusually dedicated American soldier and the many sacrifices, pains and emotions he absorbed–and the joy of achieving that lofty goal!

You will seldom read a book with such emotional impact. Its author, Sarah Bates, has written a truly heartrending novel of sacrifice, dedication, and perseverance. To do this, she has embedded with the troops; interviewed many sources; and traveled widely; and that 'adventure' is worthy of a book in itself.

As a result of her unique and 'novel' skills, you will count with the soldier each of the 21 steps through training, deployment, firefights, rescue and wounding in Afghanistan and his final step into glory.

I believe that you will you will be a prouder American after you have read and reread this exciting story. I can hardly wait to see it as a major film.

Chuck Fuller, Historian, Fallbrook, California
US Navy, 1st Class Petty Officer
US Naval Patrol & Recon Squadron
VP-6, Korea

PREFACE

In 2006 I watched a 4th grade teacher captivate her students by describing the role of the Sentinel soldiers who guard the Tomb of the Unknown at Arlington Cemetery in Washington DC. As she talked about the training, patriotism and commitment of these troops I began to wonder, "What if one failed?" This novel started with that premise; a book about a young man who desperately wanted to become a member of The Old Guard–a Sentinel, but didn't make it. After starting the research, however, my personal feelings of patriotism began to stir and I realized the story must take a different tack.

With the written blessings of the US Army Department of Public Affairs allowing me to interview soldiers, the research began in earnest. No firsthand knowledge of the Army, and particularly The 3rd U.S. Infantry Regiment (The Old Guard), proved daunting, so I read books: twenty at last count. I surfed the Internet looking for active duty soldiers. This resulted in discovering two who became central sources for the story and another whose poignant experiences nearly broke my heart. I read training descriptions; watched documentaries and films; combed through the *Army Soldier's Guide* and sent hundreds of e-mails asking for clarifications. But that could only go so far. In frustration, I realized I had to experience a soldier's life first hand to get a sense of what it's really like. That decision led me to Fort Irwin, the military's National Training Center in the California Mohave Desert. Dropped into one of their role-playing Iraqi scenario villages to gather research, I slept on a cot in a metal packing container, ate field chow alongside the troops and ducked for cover when a *sniper* appeared on a roof. Most importantly, I talked to the young soldiers about their experiences; frightening, humorous, and in most cases, deadly serious.

With that rich adventure churning my thoughts, I flew to the 3rd Infantry Regiment Headquarters of The Old Guard in Arlington, Virginia. On a humid 90-degree June day, a Public Affairs Sergeant walked me to each setting depicted in the book. From the military war dog kennels to the Tomb of the Unknown, I was allowed access behind the scenes, asking questions and scribbling notes as fast as I could. A day later a taxi dropped me at the impressive entrance to the Walter Reed Medical Center in Washington, DC. I spoke to doctors, physical therapists, a chaplain, and officers and I interviewed brave damaged troops struggling to regain their lives.

On the flight home I realized that the decision to insure the young soldier in this story persevered against failure was the right one to make. This novel is about one man, yet it is also about all those still fighting to preserve American safety.

Sarah Bates
Fallbrook, California
March 2012

INTRODUCTION

With each step, the cold seeps into his shoes, an aching reminder of the hours he must walk this path. He counts the steps, turning precisely at 21 then continues, his weapon balanced perfectly on his shoulder. Beyond him the lights of Washington DC start to fade as dawn breaks, gray and windy. He thinks of America's fallen heroes he protects there and banishes all concern for his own comfort.

He is the Sentinel who guards the Tomb of the Unknown.

CHAPTER ONE

US Army Forward Operating Base Miracle,
Hindu Kush Valley, Afghanistan 2008

"Strong, Lieutenant King wants to see you," Sergeant Morgan said as she shouldered into the tent where Army Specialist Rod Strong and Murphy and Thompson, two members of his squad played Poker.

Rod hadn't heard the NCO approaching. At the sound of the Sergeant's voice, he jumped to attention. The hand of cards he held scattered on his cot.

"At ease," Morgan said.

He tried to read her expression but the woman's face held no hint of the reason he was summoned.

Rod glanced at Thompson and Murphy then grabbed his weapon and followed the NCO out of the tent. No one spoke as the two soldiers made their way to King's tent.

Sergeant Morgan held the tent flap open for Rod then followed him in.

"Specialist Strong, reporting as ordered, Sir," Rod said, snapping a salute.

"Sit," the lieutenant said.

Rod placed his weapon across his knees, yanked off his patrol cap and sat down. He looked at the officer expectantly.

"Strong, you got a brother Mike?" Lt. King asked.

"Yes, Sir," Rod replied.

"I've been notified he was reported MIA several weeks ago. You were informed back at Ft. Myer?"

"Yes, Sir." Rod began to feel uneasy about this meeting.

1

"We learned there are two troops named Strong in the vicinity. One of 'em is you; the other's your brother, Mike."

"Here, Sir? What do you mean exactly?"

Rod leaned forward, feeling blood rush to his head and the weight of the weapon on his lap as it began to slide. He grabbed it.

"Best we can tell, he and two other men from the 82nd had been holed up in an outpost near Jalalabad. They were returning to Kabul in a Humvee, traveling by convoy with Afghan National Police. About six klicks along the route north of us, their vehicle was struck by an IED and ambushed. Two of the ANP troops and two soldier's bodies have been recovered. No sign of your brother yet. I'm sorry, Strong."

The news left Rod dry-mouthed. In a flash of black and white, he saw Mike's face, and could hear his voice, warbling as the doves did at nightfall; one of their childhood tricks to fool Mom when they hid from her.

"He's not dead then?" Rod managed to sputter then felt a flicker of hope.

"Didn't say that. Just don't know his whereabouts," Lt. King emphasized. "The 82nd's sending a patrol, but they're hours away. Until they check in we won't know any more. Go on back to bed, I'll send word when I have some news."

Rod stumbled to his feet then pushed through the open tent flap into the night. The winds scoured the landscape, revealing the expansive encampment bathed in moonlight. He turned toward his billet, head down against the gusts and hurriedly retraced his steps, all the while processing the stunning news. Ignoring the rumble of convoys setting out for nighttime missions and the drone of aircraft landing nearby, he began to formulate a plan to rescue Mike. It's what his dad would do, he reasoned. He'd promised Mom.

"Well, what did he want?" Murphy asked glancing up from the hand of cards he held as Rod returned in a burst of dusty air.

Thompson had taken Rod's place in the Poker game. A pile of chips lay on the cot in front of him.

The two men looked at him expectantly.

"My brother Mike's here in Afghanistan someplace," Rod blurted. He slumped down on the cot opposite and explained the circumstances.

"Man, this is huge! He could be anywhere," Murphy said.

"I didn't even know you had a brother," Thompson said. "Fuck, man!"

"Yeah, Airborne. We learned he was missing just before I got here." Rod stared down at the floor, then looked back at his friends feeling a surge of helplessness engulf him.

After lights out, Rod lay on his cot struggling to get comfortable and wishing sleep would take him away. Memories of Mike kept popping into his head. He imagined hearing doves, but there were no birds left near the area.

Finally, he sat up.

"Murphy," he whispered, reaching across the aisle to shake his teammate's shoulder.

The soldier sat up with a start. "What?" he said.

"I'm going to look for my brother," Rod said as he quietly tugged on his boots.

"Shit, that's stupid man," Murphy said. "Let's just wait for the 82nd. Sarn't Morgan'll clear it I bet, and we'll have support."

Rod knew the procedure, but Mike was out there somewhere and his promise to find him for Mom overcame all logic. He shook his head and bent to tie his laces, then shrugged on his ACU jacket.

Murphy groaned as his feet hit the floor.

"I'm going with you," he said grabbing his pants.

"This is my problem," Rod protested. "I don't want to drag you in."

Murphy had already done a tour in Iraq with the 25th MPs when the earthquake drew him to Afghanistan along with Rod and the other members of the Search and Rescue troops. The soldier reached in his duffel bag and pulled out his Kevlar vest.

"Put it on," Murphy said, gesturing at Rod. "Hey, we don't got a *trip tick*, how we gonna get around that?" Murphy then asked.

Having one was the only legitimate way they could leave the Forward Operating Base.

Rod held up a crumpled one he'd received the last time he went to the earthquake rescue scene.

"Let's go," he said.

When they left the quiet of the tent bivouac, Rod's heart beat faster than he'd ever remembered. Fleeting doubts about venturing into enemy territory beyond the safety of the FOB bubbled up. Fighting down the growing fear in his gut he focused on his objective. *Just keep listening for the doves,* he reminded himself.

The two men trudged toward Jalalabad, keeping to the narrow shoulder of the gravel road that marked the route. With evening, the winds subsided, freeing the ground of trash now piled in grotesque shapes against the concertina wire and rubble. The clear sky unveiled a canopy of stars and a full moon brightened their path. Walking six klicks in an hour to the site of the accident would be easy. Yet the fear of an enemy patrol spotting them kept Rod vigilant.

In every direction, the terrain's rocky surface resembled photos of Mars. Beyond the valley floor rose the craggy Hindu Kush mountain range with its infamous Khyber Pass. Murphy walked ahead, pausing every ten minutes or so to scan the horizon.

The moon was high when they reached the site of the accident. The Humvee lay on its side across the road. Rod approached it cautiously, tracing the burned out carcass with the small mag light he carried. Every bit of debris from the blast had been picked clean.

"Listen!" Murphy said, holding up his hand.

The two men ducked into the protection of the blackened metal, their ears tuning out the sounds of the earth settling. Faint voices were coming from the hills beyond.

"Someone's laughing," Rod whispered. "Taliban or ANP?" he asked.

"Wanna find out?" Murphy asked then took a long swig of water from his canteen.

Rod nodded. The two men were almost totally visible in the light of the full moon, their shadows disappearing into the wreck. It had grown cooler, and Rod pulled his handkerchief up over his mouth to keep warm.

Rod and Murphy started in the direction of the sounds drifting from a copse of low trees nestled against the mountainside, carefully picking their way around the boulders and scrub that dotted the landscape. Soon the sounds of voices became louder, and the smell of horses wafted toward them. Beyond a low hill, the light of a small bonfire flickered, throwing shadows of many men against a wall of rock protecting their encampment. Murphy motioned for Rod to drop down, then waved him forward to crawl nearer on their bellies.

Standing close to a group of ten or so people in Afghan robes and baggy pants, a tall bearded man with his head wrapped in a black turban hectored loudly. Murphy frowned.

"Taliban?" Rod murmured.

"Think so." Murphy nodded.

Rod pulled out his binoculars and inched closer to get a better look. Off to the side, near a group of horses tethered to a stake, a soldier sprawled, his head down. A dirty bandana wrapped around his face hid his eyes but the top of his head glowed copper-bright in the light of the fire. The man's filthy Army uniform appeared torn, as if he'd been dragged.

With a shock Rod recognized the soldier.

He turned and motioned frantically for Murphy.

"My brother!" he whispered.

Murphy's mouth gaped.

"We gotta get help," he murmured.

Rod nodded, then looked again. Mike hadn't moved.

The two men scrambled back toward the road, keeping low to the ground, moving as silently as possible. They reached the wreckage of the Humvee in a crouched run, and then stopped to lean against it, their chests heaving from the effort.

"I'm going to call in," Rod said, grabbing his radio.

"Wait!" Murphy warned. "Who you gonna get? We're not supposed to be here."

"Sarn't Morgan. I trust her. She'll know how to contact the 82nd patrol. They may be near," Rod replied.

He began to speak into the radio, muffling the sound of his voice with his sleeve.

Before he got a response, Murphy grabbed his shoulder, spinning him around.

"Look!" He pointed in the direction of the road they'd just traveled.

Moonlight shimmering on a line of darkened vehicles indicated a convoy moving in their direction.

Rod punched the radio *OFF* and the two men knelt down in the shadows. Murphy flipped down his night vision goggles and motioned Rod to do the same.

Slowly the convoy rumbled closer. When the front end of the lead vehicle reached the Humvee, it stopped. Two men exited the vehicle, popped open a cyalume stick and held the infa-red light close to a map.

"Patrol. Maybe the 82nd," Rod whispered.

"Yeah, and if we can see them, Hajji can too," Murphy said, heading out of the shadows toward the convoy.

Rod followed. Behind the up-armored armament carrier Humvee in the front, three more of the 13,000-pound vehicles emerged.

Murphy nudged Rod.

"Lookee there, lots a fire power."

Rod stared hard to make out the silhouettes of the big machine guns. Looming low against the banked sides of the road, the battered camouflaged vehicles resembled craggy elephants on their knees. From a distance they could easily be mistaken for rock outcroppings.

"Who goes there?" Rod heard first, then the click of an M-16 safety latch releasing.

"Murphy and Strong, 25th MPs," Murphy called out.

When they reached the two men standing in front of the vehicle, Rod recognized their Airborne insignias.

"You looking for a missing soldier?" Rod asked.

"Affirmative. And why are you here?" The man who spoke moved closer. "Sarn't Devore. Corporal Emerson, my RTO," he continued, gesturing to the radiotelephone operator who stood beside him.

"The man you're looking for is my brother, Sarn't," Rod said. "We know where he is."

"I asked why you're out here," Devore repeated.

"Looking for him too," Rod admitted.

"Your Sarn't know where you are?"

Murphy broke in. "We're sort of on our own."

"I see," the sergeant said, shaking his head.

7

Murphy pulled the crumpled trip ticket from his sleeve pocket and flashed it quickly in front of Devore's face.

"Damn!" the sergeant said, and then turned to Rod. "You know where he is, huh?

"Over there," Rod said pointing in the direction of the rock outcropping. "Hajji's got him." Rod glanced quickly at Murphy.

Devore motioned Rod and Murphy into the shadows beside him and told the driver to kill the cyalume. At once the string of vehicles and men seemed to blend into the landscape.

In a hushed tone the sergeant questioned Rod and Murphy, focusing on specific details.

"Let me show you," Rod said, kneeling.

He pulled out his knife and drew a map in the soft dirt. In the moonlight, the rough lines cast shadows in sharp relief against the pale sand.

"Twenty minutes ago, tops," Murphy said.

"Weapons?" Devore asked.

"AK-47s, a few 74s that I could see," Rod said.

"Everyone had a weapon," Murphy added.

"There's probably a watcher keeping tabs on the camp," Devore said. "You see anyone near the trail?"

Murphy shook his head.

The ambient light surrounding the convoy grew brighter and Devore looked up at the moon with its bright halo and frowned.

He turned to the RTO standing by his side waiting for orders. "Radio the 25th MPs at FOB Miracle and let 'em know we've got their two *weekend visitors* here. Tell 'em we're short and we're going to keep them."

"You two stay up here with me," Devore said. "You'll scout." He turned his head and muttered into his radio. Within seconds two soldiers joined their small circle.

"Corporal Ruiz, Corporal LaRussa, team leaders", Devore explained.

Devore turned his binoculars toward the clutch of mountains where the Taliban hid.

"They've likely seen us," he said. "If they haven't scattered, we'll have to move fast."

Devore and the team leaders squatted to look at Rod's crude map.

"Alpha team," Devore said, pointing right, then "Bravo, there," he said, indicating his left.

Ruiz and LaRussa disappeared into the shadows. The whisper of desert boots rose as gunners scuffled to security positions at the trucks. The rest of the two squads, bristling with weapons, vanished in a tumble of activity. SAW Gunners and riflemen along with grenadiers shouldering M-4s with 40mm grenade launchers scattered into position.

"Move out," Devore said, motioning Rod and Murphy forward along with the radioman, like ducks in a row.

The troops advanced along the rocky terrain, crouched, keeping low, blending with the brush and scrub.

Rod's heart raced as he ran, open mouthed, gulping air.

The four men rolled onto their stomachs at the ridgeline where Rod and Murphy first saw Mike's captors.

Rod rested his chin in the soft dirt then pushed his helmet back to get a closer look.

"Some of the men and horses are gone, Sarn't," Rod said. Alarm tinged his voice. He swallowed hard. In the shadows he spotted Mike's crumpled form.

Devore leveled his binoculars and scanned the scene below, then motioned for the men to deploy their night vision goggles. Once again the landscape took on an eerie green glow.

Just then Rod spotted a glint against the rocky cliff above the campground.

"Look!" he pointed.

"Guard!" Devore murmured, nodding to the men behind him in the direction where Rod had seen a reflection off the barrel of a weapon in the green luminescence.

"Pull back," Devore whispered, then summoned his team leaders.

Rod scrambled back down the slope to find the two soldiers waiting.

"Okay, here's what we're doin'," Devore said. "Ruiz, put your Alpha SAW gunners beside LaRussa's at the south. LaRussa, you take your medic and one of the grenadiers, secure the rear. Keep your radio open. You're going to control the SAWS. I'll take six of your men with me; we'll sweep the camp from the west and go get our guy."

Ruiz and LaRussa nodded, then melted into the night.

A bullet screamed past them and ricocheted off a boulder behind Devore, followed by a loud crack.

Rod hit the ground, his helmet smacking a rocky outcropping.

"Shit!" he said, dragging his weapon up to his shoulder.

To his right, Murphy flattened against the ground, weapon poised.

"They see us! CONTACT! 100 METERS 12 O'CLOCK!" Devore yelled.

CHAPTER TWO

"Talking guns, Corporal," Devore shouted into his radio then shouldered his carbine and motioned for Rod, Murphy and the RTO to follow him.

Rod started out, then looked behind to see the six Bravo paratroopers move into line. Within seconds, Devore's assault team were hidden with Rod hunkered down behind a small bush. Now on his belly overlooking the camp below, sharp rocks ground against his knees.

Gunfire exploded in the east as the first SAW unloaded, then another, followed by a barrage of M-4 rounds. From their vantage point, Rod and Murphy watched the Taliban fighters scramble for their horses under protection of a spitting machine gun hidden on the mountainside. Dust and smoke from the enemy's fire rose around them in a swirl of flapping robes and sandaled feet. Bullets sprayed toward Devore's men, flying over Rod's head as the assault team moved over the small ridge and down into the clearing, taking cover where they could.

Rod zigzagged across an open area and lunged behind a boulder, his chest heaving, weapon at the ready.

The SAWs exploded again. At a lull in the gunfire, he raised his head to look for Mike and saw his brother still tethered to the stake. Face down. Rod felt someone crawl up beside him.

"That him?" Devore asked, huddling closer to Rod to use his cover.

Rod nodded, then shouted "Mike!" The man on the ground didn't move.

"He's dead, we're too late," Devore muttered, glancing at Rod.

"No, no, can't be!" Rod insisted.

"You did all you..." Devore said, reaching out to grab Rod's arm, but Rod wrenched away.

"*Coo...*" Rod called out, cupping his hands around his mouth to imitate the dove's voice. Still no movement.

"*Coo...*" Rod called again, louder.

"He moved his foot," Devore said. "I'm going after him."

"No Sarn't, let me," Rod yelled and started to rise then crouched back and raised his weapon.

Tracer rounds flew over their heads as a mob of Taliban fighters shouldering AK-47s swarmed into the clearing from the protection of the rocks firing wildly. The concealed machine gun began to strafe the ridge.

Devore grabbed Rod's arm. "Get down here!" he yelled, pulling him to the ground.

Rod dropped onto his belly and leveled his weapon at the advancing enemy. A man with flying robes took a bead on their location.

"Fire! Fire!" Devore screamed.

Rod squinted into the M-4 scope and with green chaos thundering around him, his brain quieted as he focused and emptied the magazine at black outlines rushing toward him like cards flipping on the firing range.

Devore's carbine barked and two Taliban fighters fell nearby.

The metallic smell of spent ammunition, wood smoke and the acrid odor of sweat thickened around Rod's head.

He fired again, then again, over and over, growing more confident with each empty magazine. In his own world now, one by one, he picked off the fighters desperately trying to overrun his position.

"We need help," Devore yelled. He thumbed the button on his ICOM, then leaned into Rod's shoulder and began to fire.

"Emerson, locate nearby TAC AIR our location, over," he said.

"Roger, that Sarn't," the RTO responded.

"Sarn't! On your left," Rod yelled.

Three fighters were scrambling up the slope toward them. Rod aimed and pulled the trigger. One of the men flew into the air, the bullet blowing his forehead off, his weapon firing uselessly. The second man dropped to his knees, pitched forward and slumped to the ground.

Rod looked down, struggling to force another magazine into his weapon. The explosive rush of a projectile erupted nearby. A grenadier had crawled up to their position and unleashed his 40mm, blowing the third Taliban fighter into pieces. Rod's head rang from the vibration.

"Roger that, over." Rod heard Emerson's voice crackle, as if from a far distance. The reverberation in his ears resonated like cymbals.

Once again the radio sputtered.

"Raven 114, two Apaches, 5 nautical miles north, Sarn't, over," Corporal Emerson said.

"Tell 'em, Raven 114, this is Red Two," Devore said. "I need some suppression just north of my position. Enemy dismounts behind a ridge. Danger close. I say again, danger close. Will mark target with infrared laser. Will mark friendlies with strobe lights. Say again, friendlies, strobe lights. Put it in north of strobes, 100 meters, over."

Rod's eyes widened. He looked around for Murphy, and saw him notched down nearby, flattened into a small hollow in the dirt, his carbine popping shells.

All the troops with Devore had bunched up together. Trapped.

Rod pressed his nose against the rocks at the ridge, eyes level and saw Mike struggling with the ropes. His guards had vanished.

"Sarn't! I gotta get my brother!" he yelled.

"Go for it. I'll cover you," Devore shouted, then leaned back and heaved a smoke grenade toward the campsite as Rod sprinted into the roiling white cloud that obscured his movements.

Moments later the men heard the high whine and rumble of aircraft.

"Apaches," Murphy yelled, pointing up with the barrel of his carbine.

Rod fell to his knees beside his brother, ripping at the ropes with his knife.

"Mike! Mike!" he yelled.

His brother's eyes fluttered open.

When Rod saw a glimmer of recognition he jumped to his feet, grabbed his brother under the arms, and began to pull him toward Devore's location.

White strobe lights danced from Devore's hiding place and sounds of the radio blared loudly.

"*Red Two, Raven 114, ahhh roger. It's your call, danger close. Enemy behind ridgeline, 100 meters north of laser. Rolling in with two Apaches hot. H-E in the gun-run. Coming in northeast. Thirty seconds. Keep your boys' heads down. We're bingo fuel, so we can't hang around for the rest of the party. Ahhh, wing and a prayer, Raven out.*"

At once the two Apache choppers blazed across the campground, tracer rounds strafing the disoriented enemy in a flurry of fire and smoke, then disappeared into the star-studded black above Rod. Chaos rocked the mountainside as a rumble of boulders and dust rose to hide the Taliban fighters scrambling away.

Within yards of Devore's cover fire Rod spotted the glint of metal against the mountainside a second time followed by an explosion that lifted him off his feet. His knee buckled as the fury of a mortar shell spun him around. His grip on Mike loosened and the weight of his brother's body pulled him down. Rod struggled to his knees, trying to stand. Blood spurted wet and sticky from the side of his calf and searing pain sent the contents of his stomach into his throat. In disbelief he grabbed his leg, then fumbled for the first aid tourniquet he carried. It fell from his hand, useless.

"Sarn't, I'm hit!" he screamed then clutched Mike's biceps and began to claw his way forward.

Enemy rounds popped and spun by him, kicking up dirt across his goggles. A trickle of blood ran down the side of his face. He licked his lips and recognized its metallic taste on his tongue.

Gotta keep moving, he thought, pushing the toe of his right boot into the dirt, over and over, inching forward while he dragged his useless left leg. His grip on Mike tightened as he got closer to the cover where Devore and Murphy lay firing overhead.

"Medic! Medic!" Devore shouted and raced to where Rod lay on the ground with Mike slumped beside him.

"Hang on Strong!" Murphy yelled.

Rod raised his head to peer into the green darkness, blinking to focus on the voices calling his name. His vision narrowed and in the apex he saw a familiar soldier extend his hand. The brilliant light silhouetting the troop's helmet seemed warm and comforting and Rod felt the beat of his pulse like a metronome rocking him. Beth called out adding her voice to that of the soldier, worried expressions on their faces. Mom stood alongside, wringing her hands, and beside her sat Tango, his sweet black face turned to the side in question. Images of Rod's life began to tumble and spin.

"Shock! I'm going into shock!" he mumbled, then felt his grip on Mike's arm release.

Rod looked up to see a medic kneel and rip off the Velcro tourniquet attached to his harness. He wrapped it around Rod's leg with a couple of quick turns tightening it, leaving Rod with the uncanny impression his left leg lay buried in snow.

"Mike? Where's my brother?" Rod whispered, straining to look beyond the medic's bulky body.

"Don't worry about that," the soldier said, then jumped to his feet and disappeared from Rod's line of sight.

Devore and Murphy looked down at him, their expressions grave. Then strong arms moved his body onto a stretcher.

"Lay his weapon alongside there," someone said.

"Take it easy troop, let's not lose this soldier to the terrain," another voice instructed.

Rod felt lightheaded but realized the sharp prick in his arm meant a line feeding drugs to the pain.

"Elevate that leg," someone called out, and instantly gentle hands lifted his left leg and cradled it.

He watched through rapidly blurring vision as the medic deployed a field splint, recognizing for a second the swath of bandages around his knee.

"Medevac! Medevac! This is Red Two, 82nd Airborne, we have one man down, one wounded. Six klicks northwest, FOB Miracle. Requesting assistance, ASAP!" a loud voice ordered.

What is that all about? Rod wondered, feeling warm and oddly comfortable.

He touched the cold steel of his M-4. "Got my *wife* here," he murmured.

"That you do, Strong, that you do," Sergeant Devore said.

From the encampment area, the sound of gunfire stopped, and as Rod's world grew black, he heard the sound of a dove calling.

CHAPTER THREE

Oceanside, California, 2006

"Mom, we've been over this," Rod Strong said, determined not to let his mother get to him today, of all days.

He poured detergent onto the stack of plates piled inside the kitchen sink then blasted them with hot water. Chocolate crumbs and the blue frosting used to write *Happy 18th Birthday* on his cake melted into a gooey mess. He scrubbed at the remnants, and then stacked the rinsed dishes in the drainer on the countertop.

Through the window he glimpsed a hummingbird alight on the red feeder outside, its wings beating furiously. Though June fog swaddled their tract home a mile from the beach, the cool mist did nothing to chill the heat of their discussion.

Donna Strong pulled a towel from a drawer and methodically began to wipe the dripping plates.

"Did you go see Doctor Mullin like I told you?"

"Yes."

"And?"

Slender, but sturdy in her green scrubs and nurses shoes, Donna looked pointedly at Rod, her eyebrows raised.

Rod smiled at the recollection of his conversation in the doctor's office when Dr. Mullin explained his obsession with order was mild. Lots of people had it. And so what if he counted things? He'd done that since he was little. Mullin said it would grow less frequent as he got older. He didn't have OCD as Donna suspected. That would have wrecked his plans.

Rod glanced at his mother. Her lips began to quiver.

"The doctor said 'Fine', just keep in touch if I want. It comes and goes, you know that."

"With Mike away, what's to say if something happens to you?"

"Mom, stop worrying about me."

His brother Mike's scant letters from Afghanistan and his infrequent calls troubled his mother. Every day it seemed, more troops were deploying to the Middle East. Each time a Marine from nearby Camp Pendleton lost his or her life or was reported injured, the local newspaper carried the details. Rod knew from the slump of his mom's shoulders that she'd read one of the stories. Mike joined the Airborne to fight, but not Rod. His Army destiny lay in fulfilling his father's dream. From the time he could walk, Rod mimicked John Strong, helping him spit shine his shoes, press his Army uniform and polish the brass buttons, happy in the glow of his easy smile. The first time he tried to match the 21-step cadence his dad practiced flawlessly, Rod knew what he wanted. Then John died in the Gulf War. Rod's mom raised Mike and him with a resolve dedicated to their father's memory, so John Strong's dream continued to exist for Rod. At times he saw a faraway look in his mother's eyes that puzzled him; the look of someone he didn't know. Theirs was a soldier's life, but as he grew older Rod suspected it might not have been the one she would have chosen.

It was that look that started the argument this morning.

"I don't care what your dad did. Or Mike," his mother said. She took an angry swipe at the kitchen counter with a sponge.

"It's your dream I'm afraid of. Who says you get to do what you want? Huh? Who says?" Her voice grew louder. "Not that recruiter who only wants to feed you to the war. He doesn't care."

"It's not the recruiter, Mom, it's me. I care."

"Why not college first?" Donna asked.

Rod heard the familiar pleading tone in her voice; she'd used it often to convince him her ideas were best.

"I can go to college later," Rod replied to placate her, trying to sound enthusiastic.

He hadn't considered school without the Army at all.

"But what about Walgreen's? I thought Big Ed had you in for a promotion."

"I don't want to stock shelves, I don't want to work at Walgreen's and I don't want to go to college now," Rod said, the volume of his voice rising.

At the sound, his black Lab Tango trotted into the kitchen to nuzzle his leg. Rod looked down at the dog and ruffled its ears, glad for the distraction.

"You tell Beth?" his mom asked.

"Not yet, but she wants what I want." His girlfriend would support him. Of that he was positive.

"Don't be so sure," Donna shot back.

"Mom, just stop! I know what I'm doing."

"This discussion is useless," his mother cried, then balled up the towel and threw it across the room at him, catching Tango's attention.

Rod grabbed the damp bit of blue and white cloth mid-air, flinching as she rushed from the room in angry tears.

He shook his head at the dog and turned back to the now cooling sink of murky dishwater.

The rear end of his truck fishtailed as he hit the gas pedal and gunned it down the street toward town leaving skid marks on the driveway. Now he regretted it. Mom didn't deserve that, but she didn't understand how much this meant. Only Dad could have. But now sitting in his truck drinking coffee from a paper cup and watching the stucco storefront office on Hill Street he'd calmed down. With it, his commitment grew stronger. Rod slid his eyes away from the *Closed* sign hanging motionless on the door.

"Relax," he muttered and began to tap his heel on the floor.

Around him, the fog started to lift. A shopkeeper fumbling with a ring of keys hurried past and glanced at Rod suspiciously. Two surfers in black wet suits ran past, holding boards over their heads. On the damp sidewalk, an old woman in a blue sweatshirt shuffled along pulled by a cocker spaniel.

Rod drummed his fingers on the steering wheel. On the seat beside him, Tango slumbered, oblivious. The rumble of waves hitting the beach and the cries of gulls swooping over the Pacific filled the gap.

He checked his watch then drained his paper cup and crumpled it, exploding in anger as drops of cold coffee flew onto his chinos.

"Dammit!"

Tango raised his head, yawned then closed his eyes and settled back.

Rod checked his watch again. The second hand ticked to 8:57 and a compact white Ford pulled into the driveway adjacent to the office. A bulky man dressed in the combat uniform of the Army climbed out, lifted a briefcase from the back seat, then closed the car door with a loud *thunk.* Rod heard the lock beep and felt his stomach churn.

He watched the man enter the office then turn the sign on the door to *Open.* One hundred three steps exactly, Rod calculated, judging the distance from where he sat to the office. He'd walked it before.

He thumbed through the documents in the envelope on his lap, rearranging them in alphabetical order for the fifth time.

"Birth certificate, driver's license, high school diploma, got it."

He glanced at the specks of drying coffee on his pants leg then checked his reflection in the rear view mirror and frowned. The trim above his right ear was uneven. The barber screwed up the Army reg haircut he got yesterday leaving a skim of brown bristles.

"Stay boy," he said to the dog as he locked the door to his truck.

Rod felt a shiver as he pushed open the door to the office and stepped inside.

"Morning!" the Army recruiter said, his hand outstretched. The soldier's black eyes drilled into Rod's. As if by instinct, Rod pulled his shoulders back, trying to stretch his lean six foot one frame another inch or two.

"Rod Strong," he said, grasping the man's hand.

"Joining this man's Army today, or just looking?" the recruiter asked.

His deep and pleasant voice sounded welcoming. The knots in Rod's stomach released and the turmoil of his decision to enlist was replaced by a sense of certainty.

"Yes... uh, joining," Rod's eyes went to the Infantry insignia on the soldier's chest, then the name plate on his desk.

"Sergeant Moon, sir."

Moon chuckled. "Don't call sergeants 'Sir'."

"Just being respectful, Sergeant Moon," Rod said, his face growing hot from the blunder. *Mike would have rolled his eyes and smacked him on the shoulder for that stupid mistake.*

Moon gestured to the hard metal chair facing his desk.

"Sit down, let's talk."

Rod took in the bare desk, worn and shiny from use, the GoArmy posters plastered on the walls. Eight posters. A calendar hung on the wall behind the recruiter's chair. Sgt.

Moon pulled a pen from his desk drawer, booted up his computer then punched a key. At once a sheaf of papers began to collate in the printer across the room.

The scent of the sergeant's after-shave stirred the stale air in the room as he retrieved them.

"You've thought this through, young man?" he asked, bending over the printed form on top of the stack of paper and beginning to write.

"Rod?" His penetrating eyes looked up.

"I have. I want to join up. Now."

"You eighteen?" Sgt. Moon asked, leaning forward to stare at Rod intently.

Rod pushed his birth certificate forward, barely able to contain the emotion that milestone meant.

"Here, fill these out, son," Sgt. Moon urged, fanning the printed forms across the desk and offering the pen.

Son? Rod hurried through the process, then paused.

"What's this about *occupation*?" he asked, scrutinizing the list of skill training offered by the Army.

His gaze stopped on *canine handler*. Certified to handle search and rescue dogs when he was an Eagle Scout, he helped with obedience training at PetSmart for two years. He scribbled in *certified search and rescue dog handler* on the line that asked for *other skills,* then hurried through the rest of the form.

"You gotta choice what you want to do," Moon said in response. "Have any idea?"

"Oh, yeah...sorry. The Old Guard."

Moon looked surprised. "That's not on the list," he said. "It takes a long time to get there. You sure?" he asked.

Rod nodded. He knew all about the route; he'd lived through it with his father.

"Hang on then." Sgt. Moon turned to a file cabinet behind his desk. "Here we go."

He opened a folder with *Infantry* printed on the tab then looked up at Rod.

"Well, you look like you meet the physical requirements," he said.

Rod grinned. "I know. I'm built just like my dad. He trained to be a Sentinel."

"Oh, yeah? When?" Moon asked.

"1991" Rod answered sitting up a little straighter. "One week before his first mission he deployed to the Gulf."

Rod fixed his gazed on the GoArmy poster on the wall next to Moon's desk. The soldier looked fit and brave, like his dad, not like Sgt. Moon whose belly stretched the front of his ACU jacket.

"He was killed."

Moon shifted uneasily in his seat, then turned back to the printed forms.

"Sentinels have to meet a special weight, height, measurements. You know that? Never had a soldier sign up to be one before. Course I can't be sure, you have to pass the physical and all..."

"I'll make it. I've planned it all out."

"Well, good, the Army needs soldiers with plans." Moon's voice trailed off.

Rod's eyes went back to the poster of the soldier resembling his dad. The man really did look like him, he decided.

"Yep, plans," he said softly.

"If you had a friend join up too, you'd be *Battle Buddies,* it's something the Army does for new recruits. Got anyone in mind?" Moon asked, his voice taking on a sly persuasive tone.

"No, just me," Rod replied.

"Well, then the Army will assign you a *buddy.* Let's see, what else do you have to know?" Moon asked, tapping his chin.

He scanned a list in his hand then looked up at Rod.

"You know it's Basic? Then Advanced Infantry...Army calls it *AIT*? Then, Airborne School..."

"My brother Mike's Airborne, 82nd," Rod broke in. "And, Ranger School, add that."

Moon raised his eyebrows.

"My dad was a Ranger."

"Okay...and if you want Ranger School, you sign up for it all at Fort Benning," Moon continued.

"Yeah, I read all about it on the Internet."

"We'll just put that down on the sign up form, right here." Moon's hand moved over the form as he recited Rod's requests then pushed it across the desk.

Rod signed his name with a flourish at the bottom.

"Now what?" Rod asked, settling on the edge of his chair.

"Where'd you get that?" Sergeant Moon asked sharply, pointing at the silver bracelet around Rod's wrist.

"A guy at work. Said he wore it in 'Nam."

"You take good care of it, hear?"

"I do Sergeant Moon."

Moon slicked his hands over the sides of his head and pulled his chair closer. When he did, Rod noticed the long stubble on the sergeant's *high and tight* haircut. *Probably missed an appointment.*

The recruiter ticked off the steps that would occupy Rod's days until his orders arrived.

"When do I go?" he cut in.

"Depends on when the next recruit class's called up."

"My brother went right away."

"It's 2006 kid. Army's changed a little bit in the last two years. You'll get a letter pretty quick, it'll tell you what to do."

Sgt. Moon rose to his feet. "Any other questions?"

Rod sighed. "No. I'm disappointed that I have to wait." His voice rose in frustration.

"Son, waiting is part of the Army."

Rod narrowed his eyes. *Don't call me SON,* he thought, then snapped to and saluted, hardly able to breathe.

The sergeant smiled. "Welcome to the United States Army."

CHAPTER FOUR

"On my way, Dad," Rod muttered as he sprinted for his truck.

Later, when he pulled into his driveway, Donna's faded red Volvo was parked on the street. Monday was bingo night at St. Peter's so she hurried home from her job at the hospital to make an early dinner.

Worry about facing her strangled the elation Rod felt earlier. Now uneasiness in his stomach replaced the excitement.

The front door screen slammed behind him as he waved Tango inside then ducked into his room and kicked off his shoes.

"Rod? Dinner's almost ready," Donna called from the kitchen.

"In a minute," Rod said.

He tossed his jacket on a chair and plopped down on the side of his bed. For some reason he thought the familiarity of the cocoon he'd arranged there would be different. The comforter thrown off in the night lay crumpled on the floor and balled up sweat socks filled his wastebasket. The contents of his backpack were still strewn about. But on the shelf facing Rod's bed, his dad's worn Army boots polished to a sheen rested beside the man's official photograph in his Sentinel uniform. Rod glanced at the photo then spotted dust settled on the boots. He jumped up, grabbed the front of his tee shirt and wiped the leather clean. *Nothing has changed but me.* He started for the doorway and then turned back to perfectly align the toes of the boots.

Rod found Donna peeling carrots and watching the evening news. With a somber expression, the announcer lowered his voice to relate details of the day's casualties in Baghdad. His mother's hands stopped, her attention focused on the images of camouflage-clad bodies dashing through smoke.

"Oh, Mike," she murmured.

The afternoon Mike enlisted Rod sat at the kitchen table, his Algebra homework spread all over. His brother burst in and just blurted it out. Mom couldn't talk for minutes. Mike didn't back down, though. If he joined the Army, she said, and something happened to him, the only man left in the family would be Rod. When they glanced at him, the look full of tension that passed between them weighted her words. Rod viewed his brother's decision as exciting and brave and wondered why Mom seemed surprised. Army life colored everything they knew.

Mike had been in for two years coming home at first with stories of combat that left Rod breathless. Over time, his exploits began to over shadow their dad's Army service. Sometimes when Rod replayed the memories, the roles of his father and brother blended in a confusing way. Even though his brother's eyes grew more tired and guarded and his stories more vague, by Rod's senior year, he knew exactly what his next step would be. And, Mom wouldn't be happy about it, either.

Now, dreading the encounter with her even more, Rod paused in the doorway. Emotions played across his mother's features. Donna sighed then picked up the dishtowel lying on the counter and wiped her eyes.

Rod bustled into the kitchen, opened the fridge and squatted to look inside, feeling the cold blast against his shirt.

"Mom?"

Donna glanced over her shoulder, her expression drawn.

"Your brother...they all look like Mike...."

Rod heard the break in her voice, but plunged ahead, impatient to tell her his news. Get it over with.

"That's Iraq. He's in Afghanistan now. Remember?" Rod stated.

"It's all the same."

"No it's not." Rod began moving milk cartons and plastic containers around in the fridge. "We got Cokes?" he stalled.

"In the back behind the orange juice," Donna said, turning back to her task.

"Mom."

"What?"

The refrigerator door closed.

Rod popped the lid on a can and leaned against the counter.

"I got something to tell you." His heart beat so fast he swore she might see his chest moving. "Would you look at me please?"

He reached out and tapped her shoulder.

Donna turned away from the pile of raw carrots and wiped her hands on her apron. Brown curls shot with gray framed her face now lit up with an expectant smile on her lips.

"I signed up." Rod held his breath, watching her face for signs of anger, but instead saw the smile falter.

"I knew it. It's useless to reason with you," she said, shaking her head. "Just like your brother."

Donna looked into his eyes then her gaze dropped as she turned away, picked up a knife and started to slowly cut into a carrot. She paused, and then began to chop furiously.

Rod watched as bits of orange flew into the air and scattered on the counter top. Finally Donna's hands stilled.

"It's my life, my call!" Rod said, his voice loud.

"Feed the dog," Donna said quietly, then placed the pan of vegetables on the stove and carefully adjusted the flame.

The argument was over.

Rod watched her familiar gestures, imprinting them in his mind. Now she had changed too and he loved her all the more.

———

On Monday, Rod's job at Walgreen's didn't seem as necessary as it had on Friday. Even keeping a mental record of the repetitive steps each time boxes were transferred from pallets to shelves didn't interest him as it once did. He took care to cinch up the black kidney belt he wore for stocking, and made sure his safety shoes were tied firmly. At last these precautions meant something. He suspected his coworkers in the warehouse noticed his attitude had changed too, particularly Eric Garcia who joined the crew the same week Rod did.

"Dude, s'up?" Eric asked.

Tall and handsome, with mischievous eyes, he didn't fit into the Walgreen's bunch any better than Rod. He claimed he wanted to be an accountant, but most often sat off by himself at lunch reading a soccer magazine.

Eric eased in line at the time clock, shifting his lunch box from hand to hand. "You're so happy-like today. You in love?" He drawled out the question, his voice lilting into a tease.

"Joined the Army yesterday," Rod said, watching the clock until it registered exactly 5 o'clock before slipping his card into the slot.

"No way! Thought you were a college boy. Don't you know the Army gets you killed?"

Eric's face split into a big smile. Rod knew Eric had considered joining up too; Navy, but his bad eyesight quashed that idea.

"Not me, I got other plans."

"Dressing up like a toy soldier and marching? That's not Army. Army's fighting. Killing bad guys, man."

Eric hooked his thumb and pulled an imaginary trigger then laughed. He took his car keys from his pocket and bounced them in his hand.

"I gotta go, my sister's cooking. Wanna come?"

"Nah, thanks, I got stuff to do," Rod said, heading for the door.

"Hey, Rod. Your mom's okay with this? I mean with Mike gone and all? My mother'd be on her knees crossing herself every ten minutes if I joined up."

Eric touched him on the shoulder stopping him.

"She doesn't like it, but no way I'll end up in Afghanistan like Mike. After a year at Fort Benning, I'm good to go. I checked it out."

A look of concern shadowed Eric's face.

"Yeah, well things can happen, dude..." his voice trailed off.

CHAPTER FIVE

Rod still hadn't told Beth Gooding, the girl he loved. He ignored her e-mails. He'd punched in her number on his cell phone at least five times, then hit *cancel* and drove by her house without stopping. She knew what his dream was. She bought into it from the first. So why was he stalling?

When he got home from work two nights later, Beth sat in the kitchen with his mother. A tray of strawberries lay on the table along with a bag of peaches. The room smelled of summer and ripe fruit. Tango bumped his leg, the dog's nails clicking on the linoleum floor as he danced around in greeting.

"Rod!" Beth jumped up and threw her arms around his neck. "I was so worried. Where've you been?"

Her anxious blue eyes searched his face. As she leaned close, her silky sun-streaked ponytail brushed his cheek. Over her shoulder he locked eyes with his mom, who turned away.

"I'm going outside to water," Donna said, then pushed open the back door for Tango who bounded out and disappeared into the waning light of dusk.

A moment later Rod heard the sound of the sprinkler hit the shrubs near the door.

"Beth I gotta talk to you. Sit down, huh?" Rod gestured at a kitchen chair.

He grabbed her hands. Looking into her face he saw concern and swallowed hard not to lose his courage.

"Look Beth, I always tell you stories about my dad, right? How he served in the Army, and how I thought I wanted the same thing?"

She nodded.

"Well...yesterday after my birthday party and all, I did it."
He took a deep breath.

Beth's eyes widened.

"But..." Beth started plaintively.

Rod thought she planned to argue but she stopped.

"When do you go?" she said, her voice thick.

Beth sniffed and seemed to grow smaller and fragile. She
pulled her hands away and stood to lean against the kitchen
counter facing him. For the first time since he'd known her, Rod
couldn't read her expression. She seemed to be processing his
news carefully, like the debate over good and evil.

"I brought the strawberries you like," she finally said,
turning from him to hold up the tray in her hands. "The peaches
are for your mom. My dad picked them this morning."

"Well? What do think?" Rod asked, anxiety coloring his
voice.

"Nothing. So you joined the Army. Here, taste this," she
said, handing him a strawberry.

Dismissing the subject so easily worried him.

Beth poured the fruit into a colander then set it under a
spray of cold water.

"I'll help," Rod said, jumping up to tumble the berries onto
the counter top.

He tried to relax, but realized her response came too
quickly. Engrossed, he began to count them out as the red fruit
piled high.

"So you're okay with this?" he called after her.

"Rod, it's you going, not me," Beth said, her voice sharp.
She whirled around.

"If you're asking me for permission, you don't have to. What
right do I have to say *no*? Because you're running off and
leaving me?" Beth's face reddened, and her blue eyes grew
flinty gray.

"Beth, please...."

"Well, what did you expect?"

She began to open and close cupboard doors, slamming them as she went.

"Where's your mom's plastic containers?" she demanded, peering into an open drawer.

Suddenly she wheeled around and faced him, her eyes filled with tears.

"Guys are getting killed there. What if something happens to you?"

"You *know* it's all I ever wanted," Rod said in desperation. He blocked her progress to reach into the space above the fridge then held out the stack of lids and boxes.

"*Fine*," Beth said, grabbing them.

"Besides, you start your nursing program in August. You'll be busy with school while I'm in training."

Rod regretted the whining tone in his voice immediately and reached out to her. She turned away from him.

"Beth, I love you," he pleaded.

Too late, he realized he should have picked a better time to deliver his news. And her concern for his safety went unacknowledged.

"I know." Beth sighed in resignation. "Just give me time to let this sink in, okay?" she said and began to fill the containers with berries.

"Okay, then. Fine." Rod said, but the huge weight he thought would lift from his shoulders remained.

Beth tapped on the window above the sink to get his mom's attention, then walked to the kitchen door and pushed the screen open.

"It's all right, Mrs. Strong, you can come back in now," Beth called through the open screen door.

He gathered Beth into his arms and held her trembling body.

"It's going to be okay, you'll see."

He kissed her neck and when she didn't pull away he rushed to explain he'd write every day, he'd e-mail and call so it would be like they'd never be separated. Yet, by the time Beth went home that day, Rod's face hurt from smiling.

————

Three weeks later, the letter arrived telling him to report to Fort Benning on July 17. The reality of leaving set in and his mother and Beth began planning a farewell party.

All the older guys at work regaled him with their own war stories. More than one wondered out loud about Rod's choice including one bitter old vet who'd been to Vietnam.

"Kid, they'll send you right to Iraq, you know. Why you signing up for that?" the man asked.

Rod's boss, Big Ed, tried to get the stories stopped; he'd served in the Army at the end of the Vietnam War and never saw combat. His wistful recollections bolstered Rod's decision.

"Why, when I signed up, all I got to do was walk guard duty at Fort Ord. Shut down now, you know," Big Ed said one day over his bologna sandwich.

Rod liked Ed; he'd been good to him. When he pulled the man aside and asked advice he believed Ed thought of him as a son. Of course, his dad wouldn't have gotten a beer gut, nor smoked like Big Ed did.

Rod spent most of the last day at home cleaning his room and rechecking the contents of his small duffel against the Army packing list. He planned to say his goodbyes at the party that night. Beth came over early to help Donna and brought her mom and sisters to put up decorations. The kitchen bulged with open containers, casserole dishes covered in aluminum foil, and in the pantry, cakes and pies fought for room.

Rod eased up to Beth and put his arms around her.

"You smell like chocolate chip cookies," he said, squeezing her shoulders.

With her tanned arms bare and simple blue shorts, Rod thought she'd never looked hotter. His body reacted immediately, and for a miserable second he considered their decision to *wait* until they were married.

"Stop it Rod," she giggled, and then kissed his cheek, leaving him distracted and uncomfortable.

By late afternoon, the June fog that plagued Oceanside rolled in from the Pacific muffling the sounds of music and noisy conversation coming from the Strong home. Rod's high school buddies snapped photos with their cell phones, a sprinkling of husky Walgreen's warehouse employees argued baseball, and everyone talked over each other in a steady stream of loud conversation. Donna rushed from kitchen to table, rearranging platters of sandwiches, fried chicken, too many potato salads, and appetizers donated by well-wishing neighbors.

In one corner of the room, Big Ed leaned over Rod's high school best friend Rascal talking motorcycles. Rascal worked for a motorcycle shop in South Oceanside. He'd promised Rod to look in on his mother and Beth while he was gone. Ed's voice grew louder as he gestured wildly with a bottle of beer. Eric and his girlfriend Marta flipped through Rod's CDs.

Rod caught Beth's eye as she came out of the kitchen with a platter of sandwiches. He grabbed it and handed it to her sister, then pulled Beth out into the middle of the living room that had been cleared for dancing. As music filled the room, he looked into Beth's eyes, folded her in his arms and began to sway to the rhythm.

He leaned in close, his mouth against her ear, and the scent of the sweet clean perfume in her hair teased his nose. For a moment, he thought his heart would burst. His beautiful girl. His dreams; all there ready for him to experience. *Tomorrow it starts,* he thought, letting his mind wander from the excitement.

Beth tilted her head to look into his eyes.

"Everything will be okay," she said, but Rod heard an odd note of uncertainty in her voice.

"Love you, babe," he whispered, and held her tighter.

"Hey, man, can I cut in here?" Eric tapped Rod on the shoulder.

Rod broke away from Beth and stared at his friend, puzzled.

"Just kidding, man, I got something to tell you." Eric smiled. "Got a minute?"

Beth nodded, so Rod grabbed Eric by the shoulder and steered him through the kitchen into the back yard.

"What's up?" he asked. The light from the kitchen slanted across Eric's face.

"You aren't the only one leaving Oceanside tomorrow," Eric said.

"Yeah? Who else?"

"I joined up too."

"You got in the Navy? But your eyes?"

"No, dude, I'm going with you. Army."

"No way!" Rod said in disbelief.

"I want to get an education. Something better than stacking shelves for a living. Army's a good place to do it, the recruiter told me."

"Yeah, but what about Iraq?" Rod asked, suddenly worried for his good-natured pal who seemed so tied to his family and ready to stay in a safe place.

"Ahhh, I'm not worried. I'm macho...no one's going to kill me, man."

Suddenly embarrassed that he might have caused Eric's hasty decision, Rod grabbed him in a bear hug.

He looked at his friend closely then said, "Come on back in, we've got to let people know. This party's for you too, now," Rod added and pulled Eric into the kitchen.

"Hey everybody, listen up," Rod shouted. "I've got something to tell you!"

CHAPTER SIX

"Mom, I'm out of here," Rod called out.

He stood in the living room, clutching his orders and the one-way airline ticket to Fort Benning, his black duffel at his feet.

Donna came in from the back yard wiping her hands on her jeans. A basket of tomatoes hung from her arm.

"Big mess in there," she said, cocking her head at the pile of dishes strewn on the counters in the kitchen.

"You know I could have taken you in the car," she said, looking up at her tall son.

"It's okay, Mom, Rascal offered, it's a long way for you to drive."

Rod gazed at his mother. He took in her slight frame and her blue eyes like his. He tried to memorize her appearance at that moment to carry with him along with the photo of his dad he kept in his wallet.

Just then Tango bolted in from the yard skidding to a sit in front of him, a spit covered ball in his mouth.

"Hey, buddy," Rod said, dropping to his knees to hug his dog, breathing in the scent of Donna's rosemary plants clinging to Tango's coat.

"Take care of Mom while I'm gone, now, okay?" The big dog dropped the ball at Rod's feet and nudged it with his nose.

"Can't play right now," Rod said, looking up at Donna. "I'll miss this guy, too," he said, surprised when the corners of his mouth began to quiver.

"You take care, Rod," she said softly, reaching for the familiarity of the dog's silken ears as Tango pushed against her. "Your dad would be proud."

Donna threw her arms around Rod and hugged him so hard he thought his ribs would crack. Just then a Harley thundered down their street and coughed to a stop at the curb in front of their house. Rod gently pulled away.

"That's Rascal, Mom, I gotta go."

He grabbed the duffel and bounded down the sidewalk before Donna could see the tears in his eyes.

Donna and Tango stood just inside the screen door as Rod straddled the bike's rear seat and settled a helmet onto his head. Donna tugged a tissue from her pocket and held it to her nose as he waved goodbye and the motorcycle pulled from the curb then roared down the street.

———

At the Delta Airlines counter, Rod spotted Beth standing with the Garcia family, her blond mane a beacon of light in the sea of shiny black. Among the crush of passengers waiting to enter the security area, knots of people surrounded other young men and women holding envelopes identical to Rod's orders. Eric started in his direction then paused as Rod pushed toward Beth through the crowd.

"Hi," he said softly, cupping her chin in his hands for a kiss.

Beth's face was a mask of confusion. She looked like she'd been crying, but Rod's excitement overcame any doubts he might have had about her concern for him.

"I'm glad you came," he said.

"Of course I'm here. I have something for you."

She reached into her purse and pulled out a small folded frame. "Look! It's you and me when we went to SeaWorld."

Rod flipped it open and gazed at two photos of them in front of the Shamu Show. They were wet and laughing, their mouths gaping at the insanity of being drenched by the whale on a cold February day.

"Thanks..." he said, turning away to bend over and unzip the duffel then poke Beth's gift inside.

Rod looked at his watch, then put his arms around Beth and hugged her to him. Across the crush of people he saw Eric glance up at the *Departures and Arrivals* monitor. He nervously shifted his weight from foot to foot as his brothers and sisters crowded around him, vying for attention.

At that moment, a loudspeaker crackled above the din of the noisy airport chaos.

Delta flight 32 to Columbus, Georgia now boarding Gate 10.

"That's me, Beth," Rod said, noticing Eric had left his family and started toward him after hefting a gray bag onto his shoulder. Beth held him tighter.

"Bye babe," he said, hugging her close one last time then lifting his duffel.

Beth walked beside him along the line. As they reached the agent at the security entrance she gave him a lingering kiss then stepped back to wave. Rod turned and raised his hand. His last image of her imprinted on his mind; smiling eyes filled with tears, her bottom lip trembling.

When he ducked into the aircraft's open doorway he felt a fleeting moment of uncertainty but dismissed it.

Eric slid into the seat beside him and pushed his bag under the seat.

As the aircraft lifted over San Diego and banked above the ocean, Rod glanced down, first ignoring its familiarity then wondering when he'd see it again.

"Well, here we are, man, two homies going off to war," Eric said, then smacked Rod's knee and laughed. The gold studs his friend usually wore in his ears were missing.

That wavy hair will be gone too once the Army barber gets him in the chair, Rod mused.

Still incessantly talking and joking, Eric kept up a steady stream of nervous conversation throughout the flight, even getting the flight attendant's phone number in the process. When the cabins lights dimmed for the in-flight movie, Rod fell into a restless sleep full of jumbled images. A uniformed man beckoned, his hand outstretched. Rod couldn't see the man's face, yet he knew who he was, he sensed his presence all around him.

"You're doing the right thing, son," the man said, his Army drab unmistakable.

"I know, Dad," he replied. "I know."

"Hey dude, you're talking in your sleep!" Eric shook his shoulder. "And get your head off me."

Rod opened his eyes to see the cabin lights on. From his window seat he looked down at ribbons of headlights on a highway below threading through the unremarkable sameness of industrial buildings. He watched the double beams grow larger as the aircraft descended, then felt the plane jolt as its landing gear engaged and dropped.

"Too late to turn back now, Eric said, jabbing Rod on the arm.

But the nagging sensation of uncertainty once again surfaced. "One, two, three..." he started whispering, drawing the numbers out to settle himself.

CHAPTER SEVEN

Rod and Eric pushed through the exit doors at the airline terminal to find a large white bus idling at the curb. In the sodden humidity of Georgia's night, a bunch of guys clustered near a corporal in Army Combat Uniform holding a clipboard.

"You Garcia and Strong?" he asked.

"Yes..." Eric replied, looking at the nametape on the soldier's chest, "Corporal Muskat."

"Get on the bus, smart ass," the corporal said, shifting his gaze to the next man in line.

The murmuring voices of the other young men standing nearby hushed. Rod jabbed Eric in the back with his finger then hefted his duffel and moved behind the other men who quickly formed up into a ragged line as Muskat called their names.

Rod sat beside Eric on the hard bench seat of the bus trying to catch glimpses of the Georgia landscape as it flew by in the darkness. Sweat dripped between his shoulder blades and he wished he'd grabbed a bottle of water in the terminal.

Conversation grew quiet and somebody complained about the windows being stuck closed. An hour later the bus pulled onto a parking lot beside a convenience store. The driver stood up and stretched. His black balding head slick with sweat gleamed in the overhead light.

"Ya'll ain't gonna have any brew for a long time, so if'n ya'll want some, better get out here and go buy it," the driver said.

At once a murmur of questions pulsed through the crowd and Rod saw the hand of the corporal shoot up and point at the door.

43

Eric started to rise, but Rod grabbed his arm, jerked him back and shot him a warning look.

"No," Rod said, looking at Eric, who rolled his eyes and smiled sheepishly.

A half hour later, the bus drove into a park beside a line of trashcans.

"Throw them bottles and cans in there, and don't miss," the driver said.

The men who'd bought the beer rushed to exit and return.

Corporal Muskat rose to his feet. "That's it, recruits," he said. "Now shut the fuck up!"

Shrouds of gray moss draped trees along the route that wended its way through slum after slum before emerging onto a highway lighted with bright overhead signs and direction markers. Finally, their vehicle lurched right onto a frontage road. The chatter that started the moment they left the highway stopped and Rod caught sight of a stone buttressed sign that read *Welcome to Fort Benning, Home of the Infantry.*

At last, they pulled onto a dimly lit stretch of tarmac and stopped. A cluster of soldiers in wide brimmed hats stood waiting.

"Drill Sergeants," someone whispered as one of the soldiers pulled away from the group and climbed through the open door.

Silhouetted against a line of floodlights, the man's campaign hat was pulled down low obscuring his eyes, leaving a jutting chin full of purpose.

"Gentlemen," he started in sharp crisp tones, "I am Drill Sergeant Badger. This is your home until 22 September. It's my job to see you become Soldiers who proudly wear the uniform of the U.S. Army. But more important, you respect the Army, its code of conduct", Badger took a deep breath, "and your soon-to-be band of brothers all over the world." His voice dropped to a rough whisper, "Now get your sorry asses off this bus!"

Rod and Eric fell into line behind a tall kid with red hair and ears that stuck out like cup handles. Sergeant Badger stood back and looked each man in the eyes as he stumbled down the steps into the humid night.

Finally, as the dust and exhaust from the departing bus enveloped them, Badger squared his shoulders and shouted, "Let's go, you bunch of mama's boys," and led the straggly line of men into the night.

CHAPTER EIGHT

After getting uniforms, shots, physicals, learning how to march, and the first physical training test, it was pick up trash and move his gear from place to place on the whim of a drill sergeant. *Is this it?* Rod wondered.

The second Sunday after he arrived, Rod stood in line to instant message Beth, hoping she'd be online too.

"Hey, it's me. How are you?" he tapped out and waited.

"I'm here, I miss you!" Her reply popped up and scrolled across the screen. Rod smiled.

Just then a recruit standing behind him touched him on the shoulder.

"You gonna be there all day?" he asked.

"Give me a sec here," Rod said. He began typing again. "I am so bored. I wish you were here."

"Me, too," Beth replied, the letters speeding across the screen.

"Me too," the guy behind Rod mocked. "Then I could use the computer."

Rod looked around annoyed. "Just a minute," he said.

His fingers flew, adding bits of information about his adventures so far, and then he waited.

"I have to go, Rod, it's time for church. I'll e-mail you later", Beth wrote. Rod groaned, then signed off.

"Okay, bye for now. Love you."

"Finally," the recruit behind him whined.

"Shut up," Rod responded, then got up and wandered back to his bay.

He felt anxious and out of sorts and even Eric's smiling face from the bunk across from him didn't cheer him.

One thing did break the monotony: the constant harassment from the drill sergeants who'd *correct* any little infraction with exercises. Getting *smoked* they called it, and no one escaped. Rod would silently count out the pushups with the recruit struggling on the floor, and yell them out loudly when he became the culprit.

The humiliation of being reduced to a zero in one's own mind caught a lot of Rod's platoon off guard. Some of the guys complained about it when the drill sergeants couldn't hear them, others handled the pressure with humor.

"I haven't heard my first name since my mom waved goodbye at the Greyhound station," the kid with the red hair complained.

"You mean your name isn't *asshole?*" another soldier joked.

Rod watched the sergeants carefully, trying to note the smallest details requested, figuring it meant staying out of trouble. Some of the time he judged right.

———

At the end of week three, he and Eric got the call. The 198th Infantry Brigade needed recruits, which meant fourteen weeks of Basic Combat then Advanced Individual Training ahead.

Once underway, the constant stress of classes, physical training and Change of Quarters or Fireguard duty in the middle of the night took its toll. Sleep-deprived, Rod stumbled through the days barely keeping up. It wasn't long before even Eric, whose macho act helped him in tough situations before, crumbled.

After a particularly long march down range for training on Improvised Explosive Devices, Rod glimpsed Eric rummaging through his footlocker after lights out.

"What're you doing?" Rod whispered loudly.

In the dim light he watched Eric toss shirts and socks onto his mattress, then a notebook, then a wallet.

"Nothin'", Eric whispered back.

"Hit the sack, Sarn't's coming in for bed check in a minute."

"Right!" Eric said, and then Rod heard the rustle of clothing, a locker lid slam closed and finally the creak of Eric's weight on his rack.

When he rose up on his arm to look over at Eric, he saw him nervously fingering his Rosary.

"You okay?" Rod asked, keeping his voice low.

"Yep," Eric responded, then turned his back to him and settled. "Goin' to sleep," he added.

Rod wondered about Eric finding a way to cope with the unexpected arduous routine. He came from a family of women who mostly took care of him. Basic Training devastated some soldiers, but Rod knew what to expect. His dad and Mike had told him, and then filled him in with their own stories of the Army's techniques for breaking men down before they built them back up again. That night however, staring up at the darkened ceiling of the barracks, his thoughts drifted and he felt a tiny crack in his resolve and wondered if he'd made the right decision.

I'll make it, though, he thought, then rolled over, punched his pillow and with that drifted off to sleep.

————

As they became a unit, the guys in the platoon were quick to tag each other with nicknames, especially after their last names became the ones they heard the most. As much as Rod hated it, he became *Hotrod*, probably for his obsessive zeal and orderliness the guys noticed. Eric Garcia, the only Latino in the platoon, got tabbed *Bean*, a label he resented from the beginning and now fused his temper each time he heard it. But none of the guys escaped. There was a *new* name for all of them, and each responded to *fuck head* when Sgt. Badger directed his scorn in the direction of an unlucky recruit. Rod's eagerness to get going each morning angered a few of the guys, especially Private Jones who vomited each night after chow. Rod wondered how a guy like that would stand up in-country. He knew a confrontation loomed with Jones, now tagged the *Sick Call Ranger*. He just didn't know when.

On Monday of week three at 0530 Rod's platoon lined up to begin a five-kilometer march in full gear. The rain forecast began with a drizzle, prompting the men to hastily wrap their ponchos over their rucks. By the time they stepped off, rain fell in sheets.

Rod saw Jones eyeing him as they trudged along Moye Road toward its intersection with Wild Cat. From there the platoon would continue into the sticky clay muck of the Georgia post.

"What you lookin' at?" Jones whispered over his shoulder.

"Nothin'," Rod replied, keeping his eyes forward and concentrating on his footing in the mud and the ruck balanced on his back. "I don't fucking care what you do," he said and began to count his steps to stay focused.

It was true. But Jones' attitude annoyed Rod. His incessant complaining and refusal to adapt disrupted the platoon. Rod couldn't figure out why Jones had joined up in the first place. He knew why the soldier couldn't keep any food down, it was fear, he ventured. Fear can kill a man, Rod's dad had said.

He thought back to that moment. He and Mike were fishing with their father at the Oceanside Pier, gigging for crabs when a kid fell over the railing and Rod's dad jumped in to pull him to safety. The kid's parents were so frightened they didn't move, just kept yelling for the kid to swim—a boy no older than he. When Rod's dad reached the boy, he grabbed him and began stroking for the beach in long pulls of his arms. Rod could see the anxiety on the boy's face melt as he clung to the man who had saved him. Later, Rod's dad told them what went on in his mind. About the fear and failure to do what's expected. About the feeling of keeping the boy from drowning.

"I knew what to do. The kid's parents weren't reacting fast enough. How to face fear. I learned that in the Army. You gotta do it when the time comes."

Rod recalled the earnest expression on his father's face, how intently he looked into his eyes then turned his attention to Mike in the same manner.

That night as the men climbed out of their muddy gear and headed for the showers, Jones caught up with Rod.

"You think you're such hot shit. I don't give a fuck about you or your brother or what your dad did. Just don't come near me with that patriotic crap about how you like being here, I don't want to hear it."

Garcia was right behind them. After Jones walked out of earshot, he caught up with Rod.

"Hey man, don't mess with that guy; he's got the evil eye. With all that heaving he does at night, I think he's trying to get out. Faking like he's sick or something," Garcia said.

Rod nodded. "Yeah, thanks..." Rod could avoid the man but Jones' menacing attitude meant trouble.

After chow, just before lights out, Rod pulled the photos of his dad and Beth from the bottom of his footlocker, and looked at them. The gleam in his father's eyes still urged him on and the joy of that moment when the camera caught Beth and him made him smile.

"Hey, Rod, whatcha doin'?" Garcia called over.

He lay propped up on the side of his rack and in the dwindling light Rod could see his big white grin.

"Oh, yeah, Hotrod, still looking at the pictures of your girl?" Jones called out in the dark. "I saw her once...at a bar...she was sooo happy to see me."

"Shut up," Garcia said, getting up and planting his feet on the floor.

"Or, what you stupid Mexican *bean*," Jones responded.

Rod heard Jones shuffling around trying to get his boots on.

"Or, vomit won't be the only thing coming out of you," Garcia said.

In the darkness, Rod didn't see it happen as much as he felt the impact of the two men colliding in a thud of fists and feet.

As they hit the floor, other members of the platoon rushed to goad them on. Rod started to wade in, worried that his friend would be punished instead of Jones.

Suddenly, the lights flashed on, bright and glaring.

"Ten-*hut*!" someone yelled.

"Get the fuck up off that floor, Garcia. Jones!"

Sergeant Badger's form filled the doorway. Behind him two other sergeants loomed in the darkness then pushed into the barracks.

Garcia's nose ran with blood, and a red bump began to swell over Jones' left eye.

"Get this shit cleaned up, you two, now! Then I want to see you both in my office. In two minutes!" Badger's voice boomed through the bay.

He stood over the two soldiers, the muscles in his jaw working. The rest of the men stood at attention, trying to appear invisible.

Badger turned and strode out. Rod threw Garcia one of the brown towels from his foot locker and watched him press it to his nose, then slowly rise to his feet.

"Shit," Garcia muttered, turning toward the shower room.

A few minutes later, Rod heard the abrupt blast of water on and off. Jones limped off to his rack, grabbed a towel and began mopping up the sweat and the blood on the floor.

The door to Sgt. Badger's office crashed open.

"WELL!!?? GET THE FUCK IN HERE!" he yelled.

At that, Jones and Garcia snapped to attention then marched into his office and shut the door.

Both men cleaned latrines in the bay for a week and Rod didn't see Private Jones at chow for the duration.

CHAPTER NINE

Five weeks into Basic Training the members of Rod's platoon were becoming a cohesive unit. Except for Private Jones and his shadow Wilson, a pathetic soldier who teamed up with him to cause problems, Rod liked the other men. Rumor had it that Wilson's family pushed him into the Army because they'd lost control of him. Anyone who wanted to buck authority could easily lead him. He worshiped Jones for his cruelty and the fear that he too had of the unexpected hardships of Army life. Wilson's short chubby stature made him a perfect slave to Jones' manipulation; as Jones went, so did Wilson and the two of them became a constant source of agitation especially to Rod.

When his platoon began endurance training he watched Jones and Wilson falter time and time again. It was never so obvious as the day the platoon faced the obstacles on the 900-meter course that meant nonstop physical movement in complete battle gear. Ninety-degree temperatures and the humidity from recent rains slicked their faces and drew mosquitoes from the ponds and marshes to buzz around their ears.

As Garcia took off, Rod stood fourth in line, his boots sucking at the clay. Blisters had formed on his heels and tops of his toes and he clamped down on his jaw to push the irritating pain away.

Sergeant Badger and the drill sergeants for other platoons in line ran beside the soldiers, keeping up a volley of encouragement.

"You sons of bitches better hurry up there, the God-damned enemy can't wait to shoot your ass off!" Badger shouted, his face angry and red.

Don't look at him, don't! Rod's brain warned. He shuffled his feet in place, watching for a gap, counting out the steps he needed to take to stay focused. Jones and Wilson fell in line behind him.

"Careful Hotrod, you might break something'," Jones said softly.

Wilson sniggered loudly, "Like your delicate ankle, heh, heh!"

"Wouldn't want anything to happen to our fancy little Hotrod, now would we?" Jones added, letting the remark slide into a hoarse laugh.

Rod glanced over his shoulder, then turned back quickly as Sergeant Badger came alongside.

"Go!" Badger yelled, hitting his shoulder.

Rod stumbled forward, vaulted over the three-foot wall, wincing when the rough surface of its cement blocks cut into his hands. He hunched down to race through the lane guide then dropped to his belly onto the rope ladder suspended over the ground. He took the rungs two at a time. With each move through the wet course his feet churned the red clay mud onto his ACUs, his face, and hands. When he reached the low wire crawl, he spotted Garcia on his stomach ahead of him thrashing helplessly. The poncho that covered his ruck had snagged on a barb.

"Garcia! Hold on man, I'm coming," Rod yelled, then flipped onto his back and began to crawl, pushing the low wire up with his M-16 and using his elbows and feet to propel him forward. The effort left long wet tracks in the mud. Overhead, M-60 machine guns blasted inches from his head, some sounding closer than blanks should be.

Demolition charges in nearby pits exploded at intervals and with each explosion he saw Garcia flinch and duck his head. By the time he reached him, his battle buddy's eyes were wide and each time he moved to free himself, he sunk deeper into the mud. The deafening noise obliterated the screaming voices of the drill sergeants.

"Stop!" Rod yelled, slapping the top of Garcia's helmet to get his attention.

He reached up to pull the fabric of the man's poncho off the barbed wire freeing him and the sharp point of the barb bite into his hand.

"Now, go!" Rod shouted, turning him over and pushing hard against Garcia's butt.

Garcia looked back. "Thanks, man," he mouthed.

By the time he reached the hurdles, gasping for breath under the weight of his gear, Garcia started to falter. Private Eric Garcia's weight had ballooned in the preceding weeks as his ravenous appetite kept apace with his exercise. While the rest of the guys like Rod lost weight by pushing up their PT scores through exercising, Garcia kept gaining. When Rod saw his friend slow down and hesitate, he sprinted forward and boosted him up, losing his footing and taking the full weight of Garcia's lunge as his boot bore down onto his shoulder.

"Oh, shit," Garcia puffed, the exertion straining his voice as he plummeted over the last hurdle with a thud and fell into the final trench sending up a flume of murky water over his head.

Rod helped him struggle to his feet, threw his own body over the window wall and finally, its 40-inch barricade beyond. By the time Garcia hit the five-foot jump, Rod stopped with his hands on his knees gulping for air. Before he cleared the course he felt the wet sticky sensation of raw skin in his boots.

When the platoon finished and collapsed on the ground, muddy and groaning, Sgt. Badger's voice barked orders over their heads.

"What the fuck do you think you're doing? Get up!" Badger shouted, leaning down to peer into Wilson's face.

When the man looked up, Badger yanked him to his feet by his harness, his mouth close to Wilson's ear. "I said GET UP! And that goes for all you assholes," he said, turning to face the rest of the platoon.

At once the men heaved themselves off the ground, staggering to their feet.

"Squad leaders, form up your men," Badger ordered, then watched each man with interest as the platoon slowly lined up in marching formation.

A hard steady rain began to fall, drenching the line of men dragging themselves back along Moye Road. Ahead of Rod, Wilson and Jones lurched under the weight of their sodden rucks. Jones limped along handing off his clips of canteens to Wilson who awkwardly tried to hook them onto his harness.

"Keep your fucking hands to yourself," Sgt. Badger yelled coming along side Wilson when he saw him humping part of Jones' gear. "You fucking pervert."

Wilson shook his head dismally then handed the gear back to Jones who wrenched it from his grasp.

"Candy-ass," Garcia whispered over his shoulder to Rod, nodding at Jones.

Rod poked his friend in the back with the butt of his rifle.

"Shut up, Garcia. Leave 'em alone", he said, fatigue slowing his words. "Don't get in that mess again."

Water poured off the lip of his helmet and as the energy of the day drained from his body, he marched, legs heavy, slowly counting each step, placing one foot in front of the other, feeling the weight of the dripping gear on his hips, the eight pound M-

16 and ammo belt stuffed with magazines straining his arms, the sleeping bag strapped to his shoulders, the ruck with his MREs and canteens of water thumping against his back and the constant buzz of mosquitoes swarming his face. A dark thought bubbled up. *Is this worth it?* Rod shook off the question and kept walking.

CHAPTER TEN

Now immersed in the final five-week stretch of Advanced Infantry Training, Rod anticipated its conclusion. Up next, *Exodus*, when he'd get to see Beth and his mom for two weeks before Ranger School convened. Everything going exactly as planned. Yet the process confounded him. And, rumors about a troop surge coming added uneasiness among the soldiers. He wondered if he'd ever get to The Old Guard.

His muscles hardened at Fort Benning and his weight dropped. Worrying about the 31-inch waist required for Sentinels no longer seemed necessary. The hours in the sand pit. Marching up the grueling *Stairway to Heaven* mountainous terrain. Regardless of the rain and muck, or sun so bright his eyes got burned, training had paid off. He'd become used to the red Georgia clay that oozed into his boots and dyed his socks and feet. When he sweated, the clay seeped through the seams in his uniforms and turned to slime in his armpits.

Finally in mid-October his platoon lined up to get their Class A uniforms. The guys in his bay were all smiles as they teased each other about the fit and the desire to look their sharpest, yet for Rod the importance of the green uniform eclipsed its appearance. It marked the next signpost towards his goal.

The needle hovered at 99 degrees on the thermometer outside and the Indian summer humidity rose over 80 percent. As the temperature climbed, so did the grumbling voices of the troops and the acrid odor of sweat and aftershave rose over the lines.

"Damn, it's hot," someone yelled.

"This ain't nothin, Dude, it's 125 in Iraq. Get used to it," a voice answered.

Specialists and civilians quickly measured the soldiers and handed them their uniforms, occasionally pulling a short soldier or a stocky one out of line for individual attention. Badger warned them to be quiet, but the constant buzz of voices never stopped.

Rod walked out of the fitting rooms, holding his uniform on a wire hanger over his shoulder. After an hour of adjusting coats, trousers, selecting shirts, shoes, ties and covers, his uniform felt right. He wiped the ever-present sweat from his neck and grabbed a water bottle from the case near the front door then continued down the sidewalk to his bay. He was deep in thought when a friendly smack on his back turned him around.

"I got a package from my sister," Garcia said, looking sharp in his ACUs with his new uniform draped over his arm. "Tortillas and a bottle of sauce. Want some?" he said.

His eyes flashed. Offering to share what little came from home was a big deal.

Rod nodded as they walked on.

"You worried about next week?" he asked Garcia.

"Live rounds?" Garcia glanced sideways at Rod. "Nah, I'm not worried now, gotta trust in my old battle buddy here, right?"

He threw an arm around Rod's shoulders.

"I'm not even sure where you are in maneuvers," Rod said. "Under all the green paint, with twigs stuck in our helmets, we all look the same."

"Yeah, I think that's the idea," Garcia said. "But man, if we eat those tortillas I can smell if it's you!"

As the two men approached the bay, Rod glanced ahead then laughed nervously. Sergeant Badger stood on the steps, his eyes were narrowed and a familiar scowl pinched his face.

"Garcia and Strong, I see you two shit-heads everywhere. You engaged?" Badger growled.

"No Drill Sarn't." Rod shouted, coming to parade rest.

He could hear Garcia's heels click into place beside him.

"Just picking up our *mess dress*, Drill Sarn't!" Garcia growled back.

"Either of you seen Jones or that shadow of his, Wilson?"

"No, Drill Sarn't," Garcia yelled, louder, his eyes avoiding Badger's gaze.

"You see those two assholes, you tell 'em I want to see 'em. Ya hear?"

"YES, DRILL SARN'T," Rod answered, hoping the sergeant would move on and they could relax.

The weight of his new uniform pulled against the wire hook curled around his finger slowly cutting off circulation.

Both men stood at attention a moment more until Sergeant Badger brushed past them and headed toward the chow hall.

"Quien sabe? What've they done now?" Garcia asked.

He pushed open the screen door to the bay and hung his uniform in his locker.

"Damned if I know. Maybe the *Commando* left a mess in the latrine and Wilson didn't clean it up," Rod ventured. "I hope we don't see 'em. I keep thinking you're going to get in a fight again. That Jones is a mean SOB, and Wilson's too stupid not to follow his lead."

———

Just before lights out, Sergeant Badger strode through the open bay door.

"Ten-*hut*!" a troop yelled.

Eighty-eight feet hit the floor as the platoon leaped to obey the command.

"At ease!" barked the corporal behind Badger.

The Drill Sergeant began to walk slowly down the center of the bay between the men, stopping every once in awhile to face one of them and look into his eyes. In a shuffle of feet, the soldier would snap to attention. Badger stopped at Garcia, and put his face so near his nose, Rod saw Garcia flinch.

"Garcia. You a troublemaker? You a fighter?"

"NO Drill Sarn't!" Garcia shouted.

Garcia's hands clenched.

"Jones says you and Hotrod here beat the shit out of him. That true?"

"NO Drill Sarn't!"

"Jones and Wilson say you and Hotrod are troublemakers. What do you make of that?"

"DON'T KNOW DRILL SARN'T!"

"Jones says his *delicate* stomach can't stand you two. That true?"

"YES, DRILL SARN'T!"

Out of the corner of his eye, Rod noticed the beginning of a smile crawl onto Badger's face.

"At ease men," Badger said and proceeded to tell them why Jones and Wilson wouldn't be back.

"A guy either fits or he doesn't. It's bad enough half of you'll shit your pants the first time you hear real gunfire, no need to have it comin' out of both ends."

Badger stopped short of a grin, then turned around and walked back to his office.

———

By the time Rod found out what had really happened to Jones and Wilson, Advanced Infantry Training was coming to a conclusion. He and Garcia were in their last training phase and deciding what their next steps would be.

Old Jones went AWOL, Beth, Rod wrote to his girlfriend. *Took his little slave, Wilson with him. The guys all thought Drill Sergeant Badger's explanation sounded weird. He said they 'transferred' but that doesn't happen. Too bad the platoon lost two men, but after graduation, we all split up anyway. Eric Garcia's thinking about staying with the Infantry. Who'd a thought, huh? You should see him now. That soft gut is gone. Are you coming to graduation? You and my mom? Would you call her about it? She didn't go to Mike's and I'd sure like her here, especially since I'm going straight into Airborne. Let me know, huh? I miss you so much. We marched today in full gear and I should be tired, but I'm mostly hungry. Don't seem to be gaining weight, though, for all I eat. Miss you. Love you. Please come to graduation? P.S. Give Tango a big old hug when you see him. P.P.S. Has Mom said anything about Mike lately? Rod*

He folded the letter, counting each turn of the paper, slipped it into an envelope and stuck a stamp on the corner precisely 1/8th inch from the sides, then pushed the letter under his pillow.

"Hey, Garcia...you asleep?" Rod whispered into the darkness of the bay.

"No.

"You hear from Marta yet?"

"No. But, my mom wrote she saw her with some girls going into a restaurant for lunch. She waved and said *Hi,* my mom said."

"Why isn't she writing?" Rod asked.

He'd seen Garcia moping when mail call rolled around and he didn't hear his name.

"I don't know, man, maybe she's busy or something." His voice softened into a whisper.

Two days later he told Rod he put in for Infantry in hopes he'd get to see action. Iraq. Afghanistan. Somewhere he could take his mind off Marta and why she'd fallen silent.

CHAPTER ELEVEN

Throughout AIT, deployment to Iraq colored everyone's conversations. Then one night at chow, Rod's platoon watched a CNN broadcast when the Director of National Intelligence, John Negroponte, stated "the Iraq war has made the overall terrorism problem worse." The men stared at the screen in stunned silence.

"Shut that damned thing off," someone shouted and a skinny private jumped up and hit the *OFF* button.

"Sarn't says General Casey doubts the Iraqis won't be ready to take over from us for another 18 months," Garcia said.

"Shit! I'm ready to go," a corporal sitting nearby claimed loudly, his voice joined by a roar of approval.

"You know what this means, don't you?" Rod asked after the broadcast.

He and Garcia sat on their bunks cleaning their weapons. They'd just left a loud and boisterous conversation in the chow hall about deploying; who would go where, and when. For Garcia, the prospect of fighting the bad guys took on importance he hadn't expected, and he told Rod so; but for Rod, the notion that the future of his career may be disrupted nagged at him.

"Yeah, I'm going to Iraq and you're not," Garcia said, an edgy tone of finality coloring his voice.

"Here," he said handing the jug of lubricant to Rod.

"Maybe, maybe not," Rod said.

The faint acetone odor bothered him at first, but now, after cleaning weapons daily, its familiar smell meant welcome routine.

"What if you don't go to Ranger School?" Garcia asked.

He held up the M-16's firing pin and inspected it.

"Won't happen," Rod replied. "It's not in my plan."

Outside, a platoon *smoked* on some Drill Sergeant's whim, ran by shouting out *When that left foot hits the ground, all I want to hear is that FOOT sound.*

Rod and Garcia exchanged glances and laughed, then an uneasy quiet settled over the two men as they industriously concentrated on their tasks.

Rod held his M-16 up in the air and squinted through the barrel.

"I'll go to Iraq for you," Garcia said softly.

"Sure you will. You take care of *Garcia*. I'll take care of me." Rod said, then looked across at his friend, slowly measuring single drops of lubricant into his weapon exactly as instructed.

Garcia had grown quieter with the deployment rumors and for the first time, Rod worried about him.

The two men worked in silence, until they'd wiped the weapons clean, reassembled them, and stowed their cleaning kits.

———

On the morning of the live fire battlefield simulation, Rod woke to a pillow smacked against his head.

He sat up with a jerk. "Shit, Garcia, what'd you do that for?" he grumbled.

The soldier sat across from him, dressed out in full *battle rattle.*

"I'm ready," he said with the dopey smile on his face Rod had grown to understand meant nerves.

"Take that shit off; we don't go till after chow. Rod squinted at his watch. "Crap, it's not even 0400. It's still dark," he said then closed his eyes and pulled his blanket over his head.

But Garcia persisted. "Let's get ready, man," he said then began to drum his feet on the floor.

"Oh, fuck," Rod muttered, rolling over to stand and pull on his pants.

Being picked as squad leader for the exercise had advantages; getting up this early wasn't one of them.

Two hours later, after a briefing on the maneuver against Opposing Forces, Rod crouched on the ground against a tree, his heart beating hard. Leafy branches and twigs protruded from his helmet and harness blurring the shape of his body. Green and brown paint obscured his face. The rest of his squad lay concealed nearby. Garcia chose a sprawling bush four feet away half hidden in shadow. Rod could hear him breathing and talking to himself.

"What are you mumbling?" Rod whispered as loud as he could.

"Nothin," Garcia replied, then resumed the low murmur.

"You sayin' your rosary?"

"No...yeah."

"Put it away, OPFOR'll hear you," Rod whispered and waved his squad forward.

In a rustle of tiny movements, the landscape shifted as the squad took new positions. Garcia didn't budge.

"Move!" Rod demanded, looking back at Garcia.

The limbs of the low bush trembled and Rod saw him poke his head out, then duck back into cover.

"I can't," Garcia whispered.

From beyond them a loud explosion shook the ground.

"Strong?" called a squeaky voice from a thicket of trees a few meters to his right.

As the squad leader, Rod knew he had to move the troops or risk losing squad leader points. On the perimeter, the drill instructors watched.

He jumped to his feet, arms raised in a *V* signaling the scenario training approach expected. He motioned the squad to move ahead and at once, in an almost silent rush, the soldiers took new positions flanking out and away from him as instructed with the team leaders on point. Each man seemed to disappear into the dense brush. Rod crouched and looked back. Garcia still lay hidden.

"Shit," Rod muttered, then flipped on his radio opening contact with the team leaders.

"Red Alpha, Bravo One, this is Hotrod. Stay in place till my command," he said then ran back, keeping low, darting from tree to tree.

When he reached Garcia's cover, he found him squatting on the ground, shaking and distracted, fumbling with his gear.

Rod grabbed him by the harness and pulled him out, then put his face as close to Garcia's as he could. The soldier's eyes flew open and deep inside them Rod saw tiny flickers of panic.

Rod's whispered voice turned hoarse with anger.

"This isn't about you Garcia. It's about the mission. Now get the hell up and fucking move or I will leave you here for the OPFOR to tie, bind and gag."

Nothing had prepared Rod for this situation. Earning squad leader points were important. It's one thing to get pissed at someone you didn't know, but his friend failing him?

Garcia nodded dumbly then struggled to his feet and fell into step behind Rod.

"Move your ass! The rest of the squad's fate is on you right now!" Rod called over his shoulder and felt a surge of relief as Garcia swerved ahead of him and fell into place behind his team.

The back of the soldier's pants was dark and wet and Rod forced back an ugly ripple of shame.

A second later his mouth brushed his radio. "Red Alpha, Bravo One, this is Hotrod. Move out."

"Roger that, Hotrod," first one, then the other team leader radioed back.

Slowly, Rod pushed ahead with the squad, scanning the dense forest, watching for activity beyond the scope of their formation. Nearby the team leaders took positions.

Trailing his team, Garcia plodded along, ducking for cover every two or three steps. Rod couldn't tell if the private's behavior meant he knew what to do or he had fallen into *robot mode.*

Just then Rod's radio crackled. "Hotrod, this is Bravo we got OPFOR ahead, 70 meters, hunkered down beside the dirt road."

"Roger that, Bravo."

Rod's arm flew up. He glanced around, spotted the squad's location points, then walked into a small clearing and stretched his arms wide.

"CONTACT!" yelled the drill instructor standing nearest the perimeter of their maneuvers.

"ONLINE!" Rod shouted, feeling a jolt of excitement.

Within seconds the team leaders had their men formed up in a raggedy straight line, weapons up, stepping out.

An M-16 engaged on his right with a staccato pop. Rod's heart jumped as a plastic OPFOR target silhouette toppled forward in a spray of pine needles.

"Keep your eyes open!" Rod shouted.

Sweat poured down his face, and the red Georgia dust swirling around his feet drifted up and clung to his lips.

Two weapons popped on his left.

"Watch your flanks. We don't want to lose anybody," he called out.

His heart began to beat faster and his breath came in short bursts.

"FOR'D", Rod yelled, sighting his M-16 and scanning the deep underbrush for targets. At once the landscape shifted again as soldiers hustled from cover to cover, crouching to shoot, lining up targets beneath tree limbs.

From the middle of the line, Rod could see his team leaders cautiously moving ahead, directing their teams to follow.

Two staccato pops blasted from over his left shoulder and he saw Garcia reload then drop to the ground, his weapon sighted on an OPFOR target barely visible in the green shade. Rod watched the target fly to the side, then heard Garcia's familiar low chuckle. He turned back to look and saw a wide smile on his friend's face and a quick thumbs up.

At the After Action Review, Rod kept his comments brief, omitting the confrontation with Garcia.

"Sure everything went according to plan, Squad Leader?"

"Squad's squared away and ready, Drill Sarn't," Rod lied, staring directly over the man's shoulder.

CHAPTER TWELVE

The day before graduation Rod woke up angry. Flights from San Diego and Donna's work schedule didn't jibe. So no Beth or Mom at his side for Family Day. At the Turning Blue ceremony before graduation, instead of family, it was Badger who fixed the blue cord onto his uniform shoulder. That night he could barely sleep for thinking about Beth's arrival the next day and seeing his mom's smiling face.

Graduation day dawned bright and warm. At 0500 when reveille blasted through the bay, Rod paced the floor, already up and dressed. The heat of Indian summer radiated off the ground and shriveled the remaining grass beyond the graduation site. Even the spindly trees planted along the perimeter seemed to wilt. Behind the troops the blue banner proclaiming *192nd Infantry Brigade, Take The Highground*, appeared to shimmer in the sunshine.

When his platoon lined up on the asphalt parade ground with the battalion, he scanned the sea of faces looking for Beth in the sea of civilians who'd arrived to celebrate. Rod peered into the crowd, shading his eyes with his hand. No mom waving madly. He saw Drill Sergeant Badger turn his way, the corners of his mouth straightened into a serious line. Ignoring the man's gaze, he worried, *Where are they?*

A moment later, Major General Longworth Shafter, the post commandant slowly walking down the line stopped, and looked at him quizzically.

"I know you," he said.

Rod stared straight ahead.

"You're John Strong's son, Mike," he said.

"No Sir, Mike's my brother. I'm Ramrod Strong."

"Well, hmmm. I knew your dad, Ramrod. Knew he had one son. Didn't know he had two. Sorry about your dad, son. He was in my class. A Ranger."

"Yes, Sir."

"You planning to be a Ranger?"

"Like my dad, Sir," Rod answered.

"Your mother here? I'd like to pay my respects."

"I believe so Sir, in the bleachers. Somewhere."

"All right Private 1st Class Ramrod Strong, I'll find her after the ceremony. Perhaps you'd reintroduce us?"

"Yes Sir, proud to do that. Thank you."

Rod couldn't believe the commandant knew his father. When the officer walked on, Rod scanned the civilians again. Still no Beth. No Mom.

Once the drill sergeant dismissed the platoon, Rod rushed to the bleachers, anxiously searching the crowd. He faced a mass of Army camouflage, Class A green, and bright color as the new graduates milled among the guests shouting and yelling, seeking family and friends. In the pandemonium he almost didn't feel the tap on his shoulder. Rod whirled around, Beth's name on his lips.

"Private Strong, a word," Sergeant Badger said, pulling him away.

Rod snapped to attention.

"At ease Private," Badger said, a look of concern softening his expression. The major general stood beside him.

"There's been an accident, Strong. The taxi bringing your mother and girlfriend to graduation rear-ended a semi. Your family's in the Columbus Doctor's Hospital."

Rod stepped back, dizzy, feeling a rush of blood leave his head. His mouth went dry.

"Are they...?" he stammered, afraid to continue.

The sergeant grabbed Rod's shoulder to steady him.

"Your girlfriend's okay, a few cuts and bruises. They admitted your mom. You gotta a twenty-four hour leave to go to them."

"I'll take you, Private Strong," Shafter said.

Donna's face looked ashen. An IV dripped into her left arm while a cast wrapped her right. Bandages swathed her head above eyes swollen shut. Her chest moved up and down in quiet sleep. Beth sat in a chair beside the bed holding Donna's hand.

"What happened?" Rod asked as Beth rose to throw her arms around him and bury her head against his neck. He felt her trembling and hugged her close.

"Your mom told the cab driver to hurry, 'cause our plane was late", Beth started. "He did, weaving in and out of traffic, when all of a sudden a big truck stopped in front of us, just stopped. No warning. Our driver tried to swerve, but hit the back end of the truck anyway. Your mom was sitting on the side that hit the truck's bumper. Her head smacked the window."

"She was lucky, young man," said a nurse standing nearby. "No concussion. That's good."

Rod stepped back to look into Beth's face with a worried expression. "How 'bout you?" he asked.

She had a small bandage on her upper arm and her hands bore stains of iodine.

"I'm okay. So's the cab driver. His car's a mess though."

"You two can go," the nurse told them. "Mrs. Strong will be sleeping for a long while. We'll be keeping an eye on her. If anything changes, I'll call you."

Rod nodded and bent to kiss Donna's hand then pulled Beth from the room.

———

The next day, Rod and Beth returned to Donna's bedside to find her awake. No IV in sight and she was sitting up. An enormous bouquet of red roses dominated the room. She held a small white card in her hand and smiled when Rod came in.

Her eyes filled with tears when she saw him.

"Sorry I messed up your graduation, honey," she said.

Rod sat on the edge of her bed and squeezed her hand.

"Never mind that, Mom, I'm just glad you're okay." He looked into her eyes. "You are? Right?"

Donna laughed and nodded, then winced. The swelling around her eyes appeared less, and she seemed more like her old self. She held out the card.

"Rod! You didn't tell me that Longworth Shafter was the commandant of this post!" his mother said, turning to look at the roses. "I knew him when your dad went to Ranger School."

"He drove me here yesterday. Said he'd like to stop in tonight if you're up to it," Rod told her.

"Maybe tomorrow," his mother said. She seemed flustered and nervously patted at her hair.

The end of Rod's 24-hour leave was close. When he arrived the next day with Beth and Garcia in tow, peals of laughter greeted them. Shafter sat bedside in animated conversation. Donna's cheeks glowed. She looked prettier than Rod remembered, especially considering the accident and its traumatic aftermath. Yet another bouquet fought for space with the roses.

The major general smiled down at Donna, an expression of pure delight on his face. Rod looked back and forth between the two of them, noticing a spark he hadn't seen in a long time in his mother's presence. An awkward silence filled the room when Donna spotted Rod in the doorway, then she smiled.

"Roddie!" his mom called out.

"Hey, Mom," Rod said, bending to kiss her cheek.

"Evening, Sir," he said to Shafter, then introduced Beth and Garcia who stood in the hallway just outside the room.

Conversation grew loud as Donna and Beth related the details of the delayed flight from San Diego, the perilous taxi ride and frightening accident.

Garcia and the major general interrupted now and then to ask questions and explain how graduation had gone.

Rod paced in the back of the room, until his mother finally noticed his anxiety.

"Rod! What's the matter," she asked, the concern in her voice breaking through the din.

The room grew quiet.

"Okay," Rod blurted. "There's nothing wrong with me, it's just I have to do something right now."

"Beth?" he said, grabbing her hand then kneeling, looking up at her puzzled expression. "I'd planned to do this in some kind of romantic way, but...well, Beth? I don't have a ring yet, or anything but, will you marry me?"

CHAPTER THIRTEEN

Rod tossed restlessly on his bunk the night after he put Beth and his mom on a flight back to San Diego. Asleep across the aisle, Garcia snored noisily. Rod thought about the decisions he'd been making. Some of them planned well in advance, others dictated by events over which he had no control. Each one a step forward, like the 21-step march in front of the tomb he realized. The random thoughts gained importance as he considered them. One, enlist...two, training. Three, propose to Beth. He smiled as he remembered the delighted expression on her face when she'd said *yes*. Four, Airborne School...more training, and more training, and more...he sighed, then turned over, punched his pillow and fell asleep.

———

Although Rod's decision to continue through Ranger school after Airborne had been planned, he hadn't expected the deep bond with Garcia. His battle buddy's goodbyes hit him hard when he faced the inevitable loss of the man who'd been at his side since they enlisted. When he learned Garcia would ship out to Iraq with his platoon within a month, Rod's dark mood deepened. Going it alone would make both of them tougher, he figured. But what if it didn't? They'd supported each other this far, could they make it alone?

The day before Garcia's departure date, Rod sat on his bunk supervising his packing. They'd been through so much together, he wondered what it would be like not to have this man watching his back. The two men who'd become fast friends during the past thirteen weeks vowed to keep in touch. Though the time had come to part company genuine sorrow tainted the moment.

"You're not taking that hot sauce, it's almost empty. Give it here," Rod said, deftly catching the small bottle Garcia tossed at him.

"You want this Playboy? I can't take it anyway," Garcia said, handing the tattered magazine to Rod. "No porno, no pork, no booze," he added and rolled his eyes.

Rod picked up the magazine, ruffled through the pages, then placed it beside him. His thoughts went back to the farewell party when he learned Garcia would be going with him to Benning. His friend had changed a lot since then. *Had he too?*

"Keep the faith, dude, you hear?" Garcia said, turning his back on Rod to stuff the contents of his footlocker even tighter into his duffel bag.

Rod heard a break in his voice.

"Yeah, amigo, you too," Rod said. "Here, I got you something," he added, handing the soldier a small packet wrapped in brown paper.

Garcia tore open the taped ends to reveal a St. Christopher medal on a silver chain.

"Oh, just what I need to add to the rosary my mother gave me...another chain around my neck," he said with a laugh, and then clapped his friend on the back in a big bear hug. "I'll miss you, too."

CHAPTER FOURTEEN

When Rod reached the Airborne quarters of the 1st Battalion, 507th Infantry Regiment, a brawny jump school instructor stood at the door, his black ball cap pulled down to hood his eyes.

He couldn't see the man's rank and didn't know if he should salute or not, so he did out of respect.

"Get in there," the man growled. "Don't be saluting no Sarn'ts. Didn't you learn that yet? Where's your brains, troop?"

"Sorry, Sarn't, I, I..." his voice trailed off as he ducked into the open door and got in line behind other men hustling into the barracks.

He'd barely had time to stow his gear, when the barracks door banged open.

A shout of *Attention!* echoed through the barracks.

Rod slid around the foot of his cot and stood motionless, his arms at his sides.

"'Morning. I'm Capt'n Childers. I've been with the Airborne longer than most of you grunts have been alive, so when I say *listen up* I mean it. Got that?"

"Yes, Sir!" the troops shouted.

The captain began to walk the barracks aisles stopping now and then to look closely into the face of one person then another.

When he got near enough, Rod noticed the captain's name tag slightly askew as if missing some of its Velcro.

"You will be here the hardest two weeks of your training. And to make sure you don't die when you hit the ground, there's lots of work going into those two weeks, so you'll be running all the time. Got that?"

"Yes, Sir!" they said.

Captain Childers paused, then turned on his heel.

"There're females here. Air Force pilots. I don't want any disrespecting 'em. Understand?"

"Yes, Sir!" the troops roared again.

From then on, the days passed in a blur, with different Black Hats at each training station. Jump and roll onto gravel, then the yank of the harness as the tower winch caught it. What looked easy, wasn't, and Rod fell into bed at night his shoulders sore and bruised, his hips aching. Somehow he'd thought Airborne would be a snap; a mere fourth step towards his goal. He was wrong.

Several days later Rod stood in line on a landing strip watching a bulky C-17 aircraft warm up on the tarmac. Behind him soldiers fiddled with their chutes and gear. He gulped down a rising feeling of nervous anticipation as he eyed the open cargo bay door and the ramp. In his mind, Rod replayed the preparation steps he'd learned on the ground, hoping he wouldn't forget something once he plummeted out of that gaping hole.

"How many times you check your main?" a voice asked.

Rod turned to look at the diminutive woman in Air Force fatigues standing in the line behind him.

"Three or four, how 'bout you?"

He'd folded the silk six times, examined the folds six times, each time pulling it out of its deployment bag. He'd done the same with the reserve chute.

"At least that many," the woman said. She had a determined look on her face.

Now Rod sat on a bench along the cabin wall of the aircraft, gripping his weapon. The massive plane shuddered down the runway, pulled up and gained altitude. As it turned to maneuver for the drop, Rod imagined the troops waiting below growing smaller. He felt a hand on his shoulder and looked up to see the jumpmaster motioning the troops onto their feet. Rod got in line and hooked his harness onto the cable that ran the length of the cabin above his head. The deafening noise of the C-17's engines filled the packed plane. His mouth went dry. Frantically, he ran through the training steps in his head, trying hard to push down the growing panic he felt and ignoring the sour burp that feared to roil into his mouth. *Oh, don't puke now!*

The Air Force pilot stood directly in front of him. For a second he wondered if her lightweight body would tumble like a rag doll or float down delicately. A bump at his back pushed him forward as she walked onto the threshold of the open doorway. She turned to look once at the jumpmaster's hand signals, and then vanished through the door.

Rod stepped into her place, released his hand from the overhead cable to grab his static line and watched for the signal to jump. Peering down from 1,250 feet in the air, Fort Benning now appeared more like a topographical map, with its dense forest and waterways snaking through the landscape. The drop zone area resembled a pale green handkerchief, tiny and far away. The draft of air pouring through the doorway seemed to hold him in place, hovering, as if demanding a decision of him to jump or stay. The jumpmaster slapped him on the shoulder, shouted *GO*, and Rod fell into nothingness.

"One, two, three..." he yelled out loud, "...four," then yanked the cord on the main chute and felt a sudden jerk upward. At once a floating sensation and relief replaced the panic of free fall. All around him paratroopers in various stages of descent like so many tan mushrooms against the cloudless blue sky, slowly began to hit the ground.

"Pull, pull," he told his left hand, then his right, as he guided his chute, watching the long grass come up to meet him. The jolt of his boots hitting the ground flipped him into the air. Surprised, he let the chute fill once again and begin to drag him in a tangle of lines across the field. Rod struggled to release the harness then began to laugh.

"You getting up or what?" The Air Force pilot stood looking down at him, a big grin on her face.

Rod rolled over, came to his knees and began to drag in the lines and the chute.

"That was definitely fun," he said.

Adrenaline rushed through him, his panic and fear forgotten. He smiled back at her. "I can hardly wait to do it again."

"Fun this time, maybe, and every time we do it here, but for my job, it means I'm ejecting from an F-15 over the ocean. Not looking forward to that," she said.

As they walked to the truck waiting to take them back to the barracks, conversation flowed between the two.

"How'd you pick Air Force, Ma'am?" Rod asked.

"My dad. My uncle. Both Air Force. My uncle's still in. He's at the academy in Colorado Springs. I always liked to fly. Got my pilot's license when I was sixteen."

She looked at Rod. "You?"

"Sort of the same thing," Rod replied. "I go to Ranger School next," he added, but wasn't quite sure why he'd told her. Maybe to reassure himself. Because for those few minutes he felt his body hurtling through space, he forgot to count to quell his fears.

The rest of Airborne school flew by in a confusion of running. No matter how much Rod told himself to expect it, each time he completed one of the five jumps required, the moment his feet hit the ground, the impact always surprised him.

By the time he was Airborne qualified and a Silver Wing gleamed on his ACUs, Rod had his eye on his next hurdle: Ranger School.

CHAPTER FIFTEEN

All the men from Airborne piling into the white bus headed for the Ranger barracks seemed physically fit and motivated enough. Yet Rod knew from his dad's stories, many of them wouldn't make it. He was certain he would though.

As the bus rumbled along, he stared out a window, indifferent to the familiar post landscape. The men were quiet, some fidgeting anxiously, maybe worried. He pictured his dad taking this ride. He would have been calm and confident. The notion of the 21 steps popped into his mind. What would this one be? Five? Airborne...six, this will be six. He laughed aloud. Fifteen more to go?

Being in a Ranger battalion didn't interest Rod, but his dad earned his Ranger tab. *Dad would want me to do this*, he believed. Finally, the bus chugged to a stop in front of the nondescript barracks isolated near the outskirts of Fort Benning.

"Newbies! Get the fuck in line. Now!" A barrel-chested first sergeant standing at the barracks entrance roared at the soldiers tumbling out of the bus.

Rod shouldered his duffel and fell in line. As he passed the first sergeant, he took a hard look at the worked-up, red-faced man thundering instructions.

Ranger Instructor Cosmos turned his head to stare into Rod's face and caught him gaping.

"Whadda you lookin' at?" Cosmos said, glancing at the name patch on Rod's uniform, then down to a list on the clipboard he held.

"PFC Strong? That you?"

"Yes, First Sarn't," Rod stopped.

"You call me RI Cosmos, hear? Move on, you're holding up the line," the first sergeant said, gesturing for Rod to hustle along with the others.

Inside the door a Specialist 4 assigned bunks. Jostling and pushing, within minutes Rod found his, midway down the long line of beds. He threw his duffel on top just as the barracks front door slammed shut.

"Fall IN!" Cosmos said in a deep throaty growl that seemed to shake the windows of the barracks.

At once the thud of forty feet hitting the cement floor echoed throughout the room as the platoon jumped to attention.

"Newbie Strong!" he yelled.

"Yes, RI Cosmos," Rod shouted back.

"You friends of Major General Shafter?"

"Yes, RI," Rod said.

"Drop and give me thirty. Elevate your feet! A friend of a major general gets special treatment."

Rod fell to the floor and quickly pumped out thirty pushups, the toes of his boots resting on the nearest bunk rail. He yelled out the numbers as he moved up and down, and then jumped to his feet at attention.

"That it? Where'd you go to school? I counted twenty-nine, give me five more!"

"Yes, RI!" Rod dropped again, "One, two, three, four, five!"

The troops nearest Rod stepped back nervously as he once again rose to his feet.

"Humph. I see. Gotta keep an eye on you I think," the Ranger Instructor said before he strode out.

Rod sensed the rest of the men in the barracks were watching as Cosmos singled him out. Keeping quiet meant they might not be involved in the same treatment.

"Hey Strong, what's with you and the major general?" asked Private Goldman, Rod's Ranger Buddy. His bunk was the next one over.

Goldman had been the first person to talk to him after he arrived. Rod instantly liked the soft-spoken guy. A few years older than him, Goldman with his pleasant face, seemed open and honest.

"He served with my dad in the Gulf. Recognized me during graduation. He's an all right guy. I think he's keeping in touch with my mom." Rod answered.

He brushed his hand over the top of his head feeling the stubble that had grown in two days.

"I gotta see the barber," he said, heading out.

"Me too, I'll walk with you." Goldman said, falling in step. "By the way, if you want, you can call me "Ricky G"...like my friends down home do."

"And where's that?" Rod asked.

"Louisiana."

Goldman's broad shoulders reminded Rod of Garcia's. But this soldier's skin gleamed black. His demeanor puzzled Rod, that and the Star of David he wore. Goldman seemed better educated than most of the other troops, not quite as loud and aggressive. Rod would ask the private why he chose Rangers as soon as he felt he knew him better.

———

That night Rod lay awake, restless. The RIs had told the men their day would begin at 0600, and after that he'd heard training would be nonstop. Finally, he started to count, "One, two, three, four....," he whispered, continuing until his body relaxed. At somewhere near 2100 he drifted off.

An explosive sound of crashing metal broke the quiet of the barracks.

"Shit! What's that?" Goldman yelled.

Rod sat up, groggy and disoriented. Lights flashed repeatedly on and off. His watch read 0400.

Two RIs ran up and down the aisles between the bunks, yelling and slamming metal trash can lids together.

"Down, down! On your knees! On my command, you're gonna low crawl bare knuckled out of the building, down the stairs and outside. Go!"

Rod hit floor and started moving. He scrambled along behind another man, wincing as the rough cement beneath his knuckles rubbed them raw. His hands hit the coarse gravel outside, its sharp edges biting into his flesh, yet he struggled forward scraping his thighs and knees. It was pitch dark and all around him the RIs armed with flashlights continued yelling, screaming at the men to form up for PT. Rod had fallen asleep in a tee shirt and boxers with his socks on, but the thin cotton fabric did little to protect the tips of his toes and the soles of his feet. At the command to stand for jumping jacks, Rod looked down the line and saw one man, naked, gamely keeping up with the others.

Rod grimaced as a sharp rock sliced into his heel.

Dawn was breaking as the RIs finally double-timed the men back into their barracks to dress quickly, make up their bunks, and then run to the chow hall. As Rod filed out the door he noticed one unmade bunk and two RIs with their heads together talking in whispers.

"What's that all about," he said aloud.

"A guy ran off in the dark," a soldier said.

By the time Rod reached the chow hall, word had come down that each man was to eat in line as soon as he got his food.

"No knives and forks. Just grab a spoon and shovel it in," a guy yelled back. "You can't sit down!"

By the door, a tough looking RI scanned the men still waiting to enter.

"You got thirty seconds to eat and get the hell out of there! Back in formation with no food in your mouth. You hear me?" he hollered.

The scrambled eggs, potatoes, bacon and some kind of limp toasted bread all tasted pretty much the same as Rod stuffed it into his mouth and swallowed as fast as he could. He ripped open a carton of milk and downed it, gulping for air, then ran back out to the line of men forming up in front of Ranger Instructor Dickerson, the RI who'd been at the door. As he pulled up short into the line he stepped down hard on the heel he cut last night and his stomach churned.

Rod remembered Dickerson. The day he arrived, the giant of a man put on a hand-to-hand combat demonstration and decapitated a live chicken barehanded.

The first seven days weeded out men not prepared to become Rangers, so Rod wasn't surprised when RIs Dickerson and Cosmos began to walk up and down in front of the lines of troops.

"You can quit, you know. Anytime. Half of you want to quit right now. Don't you?" Cosmos asked, stopping to thump the chest of a skinny private, his voice barely audible.

"Naah, they'll wait till they're knee deep in mud and shit with chiggers crawling up their asses. Then they'll quit," Dickerson said.

No one moved. "No quitters this morning?" Cosmos asked.

"Then, let's get down to business, ladies," Dickerson shouted.

At once Rod fell to the ground with the other troops now stripped of rank and unit ID patches to sprawl in uneven lines with RIs bending over them shouting.

"Get them legs up there, you pussy", one yelled at a soft-looking solder with a red face.

"I said twenty pushups, not thirty, you fucking showoff!"

Rod averted his gaze, struggling to keep up with the changes in instruction. Sweat poured off his face and into his eyes.

What if he quit? He could still go on to The Old Guard. Who would care but him? Just because his dad did it, didn't mean he would have to be a Ranger too. Lots of guys couldn't cut it. Maybe he was one of them. Mike didn't even think about Ranger school. Mom loved him just as much. She'd love him too. Beth? No, Beth wouldn't care at all. Maybe *he* would care. Rod pushed the thoughts back into the black recesses of his brain and concentrated on the shouting RIs.

As the PT wore on, every so often a man would be yanked to his feet and told to leave. With Cosmos mere inches from his face, Rod managed the push-ups, flutter kicks and sit-ups, his muscles straining and burning. When he jogged out onto the five mile course, churning out the 8 minute miles required to ace it seemed impossible. Once again, thoughts of quitting surfaced. He felt the bandage on his heel slip, and his shoe grow wet inside. *Now, I'll just stop,* he thought, eyeing a group of trees shading the track up ahead. *Pull into that shade and just stop.* A hoarse yell made him look up and he saw RI Cosmos come along side, matching him step by step. *No way,* Rod figured, and sprinted to the end, his chest heaving. His heart raced as he ran into line behind two soldiers where a RI stood motioning them forward to a chin-up bar. One man made it, but the soldier ahead of him failed, dropped to the ground and stumbled off limping.

"Get up there," the RI yelled.

Rod jumped, grabbed the bar and pulled up six times, pausing each time with his chin above the bar. By the sixth pull, blisters on his hands had broken open oozing onto the raw metal. On the run back, he veered into the tree line bordering the road and heaved a stinking pool of breakfast into the weeds.

The next day, Rod faced the Combat Water Survival Test. Smoked for an hour of PT because one guy couldn't keep from running his mouth in formation, Rod hurriedly changed from athletic shoes to boots, pulled on his harness, added canteens and ammo pouches, grabbed his M-16 then ran to get in line. Other nervous Ranger wannabes shuffled their feet waiting for the plunge into the pool.

"I didn't think you had to know how to swim," a voice whispered from a soldier somewhere in the line.

Rod glanced over his shoulder to see Goldman behind him roll his eyes and shrug.

Rod shook his head.

"All right *Hotrod*," Cosmos yelled, tying a blindfold over Rod's eyes then gesturing for him to leap. Holding his M-16 at arm's length over his head, Rod fell backward, and at once the forty-five pounds of gear he wore carried him below the surface of the water. Struggling and fighting for air, he pulled off the leaden gear, surfaced once then fell back beneath the water gasping. With all the strength he had, he kicked hard to push up again, then swam the 15 meters required, coming up close enough to the exit ladder to reach it. Rod dragged himself out and as his raw palm grasped the top rail; Cosmos grabbed the weapon and looked down the barrel for water, then leaned over, snarling.

"You think you've mastered it huh? You wait, Strong. That's nothin'," he yelled.

"Right, RI Cosmos," Rod gasped, his chest burning, then wearily trudged back to join the other members of his RIP platoon waiting for orders to march back to the barracks.

"Twelve mile march tomorrow, newbies. 0400. Get some sleep. Dismissed," Cosmos yelled.

"You going to sleep?" Goldman asked after the troops returned.

"Shit no, I got studying to do," Rod replied.

He only needed seventy percent on the tests, but a score that low wouldn't cut it for him. Not good enough. Ranger history and standards interested him. Airborne Ops he knew. The physical tests of combatives, knots, fast ropes he could ace. He'd already qualified for driver training and gotten his combat lifesaving certificate. But the complexities of day and night land navigation coupled with map reading proved to be another matter. For some reason his brain rejected the notion of North and South, East and West. Even in Scouts he'd faked his way. Back on his bunk, he dragged out the study materials and read until the sentences began to blur on the page.

Exhausted after only four hours sleep, Rod stumbled into formation at dawn realizing his mission to run with a troop on a litter for 15 miles would take all the stamina he could muster. Time to *man up*. As Squad Leader, it meant leading the pack. Four men, each in full battle rattle stood poised beside the litters. Another soldier stretched out on each litter.

Cosmos and Dickerson walked over to a truck idling nearby to observe as Rod and his team bent to grasp the handles of a litter.

"You know you want to quit, don't you Ranger Strong?" RI Dickerson said.

He stood beside Rod, looking at the men forming up, glancing over now and then to watch Rod's reaction.

"You don't have to do this, you know," he said, softer this time.

The RI shifted his weight and moved in front of Rod, casting a shadow over him in the bitterly cold dawn. The big man stared hard, then wheeled and walked away.

"No, RI, not quitting," Rod said to Dickerson's retreating back.

But the dark specter of failure niggled his thoughts. Once again he considered the black and pitiful idea of dropping out. Who would care? Mike? No, he didn't even try for Rangers. His mom? No, she only wanted him home safe. His dad? He wouldn't even know.

A trembling voice broke into his thoughts.

"You guys don't drop me? Okay?" the man on the litter said. Cosmos had chosen the heaviest soldier for Rod's litter.

Rod looked down at him. "Just keep still, play dead," he said. "Don't thrash around and I'll give you the pound cake in my MRE when we eat."

The troop smiled up at him. "Right on Squad Leader."

On RI Dickerson's command, Rod moved his men out along the road. Other soldiers ran flat out, the litter they carried swaying precariously. In an instant, Rod made a decision.

"On my count, right, left, right, left," he called out and began to jog forward, feeling the rhythm of the men's feet hit the ground as he counted aloud, then broke into a familiar march cadence. He smiled. Getting the *injured* soldier through the fifteen-mile stretch safely was more important than speed, he figured.

As his men jogged along, other teams dropped by the wayside, needing help from the medics. Some stood with bowed heads, berated by the RIs for stopping to throw up or rest. Every so often, Rod had his team jog in place, their boots barely lifting, while the other team in his squad caught up and passed him, each time breaking the forward movement to give the men a moment's rest.

"You boys okay back there?" he hollered behind him, glancing back to make sure team two stayed moving.

"Hooah, Squad Leader," someone called.

At mile marker 14, Rod's energy began to fade. Muscles near exhaustion, his feet almost numb, Rod knew his men neared the brink of failure. Private Brown holding the litter handle on his right had begun to stumble, and the faces of the two privates holding up the rear end looked drawn and pale. They were struggling, too.

"No quitters on my squad, Rangers!" Rod shouted, slowing to jog in place to fall behind team two.

"Shout it out! No quitters," Rod yelled. "Brown, pull up beside team two." Rod directed, then jogging abreast of the second team, he looked over at the two men holding the handles of litter two. *Shit, no time to quit now*, he thought.

"Gentlemen, we're going to sprint the last quarter mile, show these RIs what we're made of. Ready guys?" he shouted.

Fatigue drew their faces into masks, but as he spoke, each man nodded and when Rod picked up the pace, they too began to run faster.

All the while, RIs Cosmos and Dickerson cruised along the road in a truck watching the soldiers in the platoon run, jog and fall; yelling at them to quit. To stop. To give up.

As Rod's men raced by the vehicle, now pulled over to the side watching for stranglers, Cosmos pointed and shook his head. And, Rod thought he saw the RI smile.

CHAPTER SIXTEEN

Half the guys in RIP washed out midway. By its conclusion sixty men out of the original 250 newbies remained.

Two were E-3s: Privates First Class Strong and Goldman.

As soon as the RIP cadre dismissed the graduates and shouted *Don your beret!* Rod got on his cell immediately to Beth. He walked along Ranger Road toward the Ranger Memorial as he waited for her to answer.

"Hey, babe," Rod said the minute Beth said "Hello?" In response, her laughter pealed so loudly he jerked the phone from his ear.

"You made it?" Beth asked.

"I did, and the only thing that spoiled it is you're not here to celebrate with me."

Rod had reached the monument marking the Memorial. As he talked, he looked up at the huge Fairburn-Sykes Fighting Knife centered between its two soaring marble pillars.

"I'm so proud. But I miss you, I do." Beth's tone slid from joyful to sad in seconds.

"I know, I miss you too," Rod said, turning to glance down at the stones set in the monument commemorating fallen Ranger members. For a second, his thoughts turned to the weeks ahead.

"How 'bout Rickie G?" Beth asked, drawing him back to the present.

"Him, too, we're going to go eat and pig out on steak and pie, we're so hungry."

Beth laughed again, and the sound filled an empty hole in Rod.

"The hard part starts next, Beth. Wish me luck."

"Of course. And I love you too. Keep that in mind, okay?" Once again she turned sorrowful, but Rod knew she had his back no matter what.

"I will. And, I'll be home on leave after the school. It'll be a while, so if you don't hear from me, don't worry, okay?"

"Okay," she said, her voice, tiny and soft.

———

Now assigned to the Ranger 3rd Battalion, Rod faced three months Infantry duty waiting for the next Ranger School class to begin. Time never passed more slowly. Every spare hour he had he spent doing PT. He pushed himself till his muscles were exhausted. RIP didn't compare to Ranger School he'd been told, so he reached deep inside himself to better each pushup rep and each weight he lifted. Except for activities with Goldman and a few other RIP grads who stuck around with him, as the weeks passed, the day-to-day repetitive training routine at Fort Benning grew boring. When he let it get that way, thoughts of Mike and Garcia obsessed him. Mom hadn't heard from Mike in a long time and Garcia? Well, who knew where he was?

Finally, the rest of the men in 3rd BN who'd survived RIP sat in a straggly cluster of folding chairs, each rising to stand in front of an RI for final assignment. In-processing took hours of tedious waiting.

"Son of a gun, here you are PFC *friend of a major general*", RI Cosmos said, looking down at the paperwork before him. The RI sat at a long table in the Ranger barracks with Rod's RIP file open. Rod stood before him at parade rest, staring straight ahead.

"You think you're getting through because someone pulled strings for you? That it Strong?" Cosmos asked.

"No RI Cosmos, no strings," Rod replied loudly.

Cosmos handed Rod his file.

"Report to Ranger HQ immediately for assignment," he said, then, "Next?"

Later, two British officers, three Marines and a Navy Petty Officer milled around the small reception room with Rod and the Army Ranger hopefuls at Ranger Headquarters.

The door banged open and a soldier wearing captain's insignia walked briskly to the front of the room.

"Attention," a voice shouted.

"As you were, gentlemen. I'm Captain Milton. You are standing in the 75th Ranger Battalion headquarters presided over by Lieutenant Colonel Francis who will be here in a moment. You may not see him again during your training, but be assured...," Milton paused for effect, "...he will see *you*."

At that moment, a tall officer entered the room and made his way to the front.

"Attention!" Captain Milton called out.

"Welcome to Ranger School," the man said. "I'm Lieutenant Colonel Francis." Rod stared at the Commanding Officer whose close-cropped white hair lay in a narrow strip above his ears. His tailored uniform fit his trim frame perfectly. Brown eyes twinkled behind wire-rimmed glasses, yet when he began to speak the color of his eyes turned dark as he squinted to peer at the troops.

Dad might have looked like that, Rod thought, pushing back a sudden wave of sadness.

"You are beginning the Ranger Assessment Phase. It's the first five days of the sixty-one-day Ranger School. We call it *RAP*. During the five-day RAP course, we will determine your readiness to become a Ranger. Troops who successfully complete this course will remain in training. Those of you who do not will be released and immediately returned to your units. There are no exceptions."

The men gathered in the room stood in silence.

"Good luck," the lieutenant colonel said.

"Attention!" rang out again, then as abruptly as he had arrived, the CO left the room.

The sound of feet shuffling as men moved uneasily roared around Rod's ears.

Captain Milton resumed speaking.

"At ease. Listen up, if you make it through RAP, Ranger training is in three phases. Each takes place in a different locale, starting here. In each situation you will be exposed to four missions: Ambush, Raid, Movement to contact, and Reconnaissance." Milton held up four fingers, as if to emphasize the situations.

He looked around the room and his voice took on a menacing tone.

"Every time you move, every decision you make will be graded. Screw up and it can mean a life lost. One of your buddies. Maybe yours."

A rumble pulsed through the room.

"In Ranger School you are all equals. No matter what your rank is, the rules are the same." Captain Milton turned his gaze to the two British Lieutenant Colonels sitting together in the back of the room then looked in Rod's direction.

Is he staring at me? Rod felt his stomach knot up.

"The men of the Ranger battalions are the toughest, hardest fighting, and most dedicated soldiers in the Army. Never forget that," the captain added.

"Hooah!" Ranger Instructor Cosmos said from the corner of the room as if on cue.

The next day training started in earnest at Camp Rogers. During AIT Rod had marched through the Harmony Church area where the Ranger Assessment Phase would begin so he knew the layout. Ready for the mostly physical missions, he cranked out forty-nine push-ups, fifty-nine sit-ups, and a five-mile run at eight-minute miles in forty minutes or less, concluding with six chin-ups. Completed to the point of exhaustion, he finished nevertheless.

Later that week though, he faced a water survival test more difficult than the one in RIP. Coming straight from an hour of PT Rod got in line behind other nervous Ranger candidates shuffling their feet waiting for the plunge into Victory Pond. The man-made water site encircled by grass bore the ragged signs of continual use. The previous week Rod and Goldman watched Bradley armored fighting vehicles move through it for amphibious training.

Rod handed off his weapon to the cadre standing by, then looked up. From the fifth rung of the ladder that stretched to the top of a telephone pole he saw a long narrow log bridge affixed at its apex. He began to climb. Poised at the top, he looked down the bridge to the three yellow-painted steps in the center emblazoned with the Ranger insignia. A wave of vertigo caught him by surprise. Rod shook his head to clear it then started down the log.

Thirty feet below him the RIs shouted, urging him on, their voices loud then fading as he shut them out and tried to concentrate. Unexpectedly, his mouth grew dry and his chest began to hurt.

"Breathe," he said aloud, then slowly started to walk across the narrow log, counting his steps. When he reached the yellow steps dead center, he cautiously placed one boot, then the other on each tread, up one side, down the other. The weight of his ruck and gear pulled against his shoulder muscles and shifted dangerously.

Finally, he eased onto his knees at the end of the log and quickly rappelled down the rope attached, hand over hand, fighting the pull of his weight and pack, until he reached the wooden Ranger Tab suspended in the middle. His fingertips touched it then, as instructed, he dropped thirty-five feet into the frigid lake. Pumping his legs to stay afloat, he struggled against his gear rapidly filling with water and swam to the ladder on the sixty–foot tower nearby, lifting his leaden arms as fast as possible. With his clothes and gear soaked and his boots full of water, he dragged himself to the top then grabbed the zip line that propelled him along a two hundred foot cable back into the pond. Goldman waited on the bank, his hand outstretched to pull him out.

"Son of a bitch, huh?" Ricky G said, his grin wide.

Rod bent over to catch his breath. "Shit!"

By day seventeen, Rod had survived, as did Goldman, yet both men still waited assignment to lead a patrol. Rod didn't have to wait long.

A few hours after nightfall, Rod's platoon dug into a dense swale of trees. Led there by another Ranger in training, the platoon had stopped to eat their MREs and sleep for an hour. Now, instructed to stay alert and focus on their surroundings, the soldiers knelt, staring into the wooded area. Rod fought sleep, trying to avoid toppling over in the blackness. The noises of the forest grew quiet adding to the eerie surroundings, as animals and insects seemed to hunker in too.

"Ranger Strong! Front and center," RI Dickerson yelled.

Rod startled.

"Yes, RI?" he said, moving up to peer at the grid map Dickerson held under the beam of a small flashlight.

"Word's come down, OPFOR's sighted here," he said, pointing to a small valley. At its center, three red dots marked an enemy platoon location.

"Approx two klicks from here," Rod commented.

"Looks like. Grab your buddy and Donaldson, Kimball, Hooker, Brown, Martinez, Lee and Robinson. Take a look down there, come back and report."

"Roger that, RI," Rod said.

Fumbling for his compass, he examined the map more closely. In the murky light, the blue color marking the streams nearby, and red indicating roads, seemed to fuse. He shook his head to clear it, desperately trying to recall the navigation pages he'd studied. His hands trembled when he finally located their position and shot an azimuth to determine a path to follow.

"All right guys listen up," Rod said after waving the men in close, on their knees near the map.

He began to brief the squad and realized there could be as few as fourteen or as many as forty bad guys waiting there, then he traced the line of march, assigning tasks to the men as he went.

"There's a building or water tank of some kind here," he said pointing to a black square to the left of their route. "I'm thinking that's about half way."

Robinson, the British officer Dickerson pulled into the squad, sat down. The man had been trouble ever since he entered the school. He seemed to have forgotten rank meant nothing here.

Rod heard the rustle of movement and looked up sharply.

"Robinson! Get up. Take a knee," Rod said.

"No."

At the officer's defiant response, the voices of the other men crowded around the map grew still.

"Get up, or I'll get you up," Rod said, starting to rise.

Robinson shook his head and turned his face away.

Rod felt the fury of fatigue and his empty stomach rile up.

He leaned in close to the officer and an animal-like tone of voice he didn't recognize erupted from his throat.

"Do *not* fuck with me. I'm in charge. You screw with my men, or my mission, and..."

He pushed closer then yanked the man to his knees.

"I *said*, 'take a knee'."

Rod knew the RIs were everywhere, watching, judging and grading his moves. With the uncertainty of his navigation skills to contend with, he thought, *no way this arrogant bastard's gonna ruin my marks.*

As the squad moved through the dark forest following the route Rod planned, they listened for the sound of water traversing the landscape on their left. A small stream, swollen from a recent rainfall, roared at places blocking out the noises of nocturnal animals and insects. Rod kept his map oriented North and called to the troops every so often to make sure they were in place. At one kilometer, he raised his hand to stop the men behind him. Off to his right, something large crashed through the brush.

"Squad Leader! That a bear?" Hooker called from his position nearest the sound.

The crashing stopped and then abruptly commenced again.

"Not a bear, Hooker," Rod replied.

He heard a man laugh.

"Shhh," Rod whispered, his voice too loud in the now quiet woods.

To his right, and much closer, twigs snapped sounding like a sniper's shot as a white tailed deer bounded inches from Rod's position, crossed the path and disappeared into the brush beyond.

Rod looked at his watch then checked the map. They had less than an hour to reach the valley. It meant moving quickly now and hurrying back at double time.

"Move out," he said, beckoning the men forward as he took point stepping in front of Robinson.

Rod pushed the men as fast as he could. *Droners, all of them. Except Goldman,* he mused, watching one then the other stumble and sway from side to side when they stopped. They were all tired and hungry. At the midpoint, he doled out packets of instant coffee and powdered cream and sugar he'd saved for himself. When they reached the valley and could see the OPFOR encampment, Rod heard a radio playing and voices laughing. Six or seven RIs sat around a small campfire.

"Not a platoon, Squad Leader," Kimball whispered, lowering his binoculars.

The men had moved into place. Rod checked his watch again. If he didn't get back on time with the correct size of the enemy, he'd be screwed. Quickly he counted heads.

He thumbed his ICOM. "Donaldson?"

"Here," Donaldson replied.

"Hooker, Brown, Martinez?"

"Here," each man responded.

"Lee and Robinson?" A radio crackled to his left, deep in the blackness.

"Lee, here."

"Fuck! Where's Robinson?"

"Lost 'im. He dropped back," Lee said.

"You see Robinson fall behind"? Rod asked Goldman who'd stopped and knelt beside him.

"Nope. I was watching those RIs near that fire, ami."

Rod found Robinson standing by a pine tree beside the path, mumbling and trying to force a coin into the tree's bark.

"Robinson! What'cha doin'?" Rod asked.

"Bloody Coke machine mate, fancy one?"

All the defiance had left Robinson's face, replaced by glazed bewilderment.

"Goldman, watch the men, I'm going to tie Robinson to my belt and make sure he doesn't wander again," Rod said.

When Rod led the squad back to where Dickerson and Cosmos waited by the truck, all eight squad members marched in.

At the After Action Review, RI Cosmos told Rod to stay behind.

"I don't know if you'll make it through or not Ranger, but it took guts to do what you did back there."

"Thank you, RI" Rod said.

"Robinson's out," Cosmos added. "He's going back to have tea with the queen."

By the time Rod's group moved on to Camp Merrill and the mountain training phase, Rod and Goldman had become a tight team and Rod realized what having a Ranger buddy meant to surviving.

As the days wore on, little sleep and food deprivation weakened Rod's body and fogged his thinking. His uniform hung from his shoulders, loose and grimy. Blisters opened raw on the bottoms of his feet and the smell of his muscle burning, an odd aroma of ammonia, permeated his lungs.

When the RIs called a halt to let the men eat and sleep, Rod's dreams were dark and curious. He'd wake up sweating, sure his dad sat right behind him, or that Beth's warm hand lay against his cheek. Yet he knew he was getting tougher, as always, counting silently to quell his fears or fight the seduction of sleep. He'd made it through two more patrols and didn't think he'd screwed up. Yet.

———

In Florida however, during the last training phase, something happened.

Why Rod's detail found itself slogging through a swamp in Camp Rudder, none of the five men could understand. Iraq. Afghanistan. No such terrain existed, and they all knew their final deployments would likely be there, not shoulder deep in putrid stagnate water.

"Hey, Hotrod, you got the fucking bearing right?" Martinez called.

They were slowly making their way through a stand of Mangrove trees with roots that rose in spidery platforms overlapping their heads. The waning October sun beat down on the treetops raising the humidity to hellish levels. Dead brush and decaying tree limbs cast dense murky shadows. With each ripple of water, Rod grew more fearful of their path.

He led the way with his M-16 held over his head shoving aside the dense shrouds of moss that hung to the surface of the water obliterating the sunlight. To get the squad back to camp by 1600 would be difficult he worried. It was already 1530. The only way he'd succeed would mean keeping the compass bearings sighted.

"Keep formed up, follow me," Rod hollered.

His eyes anxiously darted from the compass to the sun slowing sinking behind the thick Mangroves. He could feel the dank water oozing into his boots. Worse, the sweat running down his forehead nearly blinded him. Out of the corner of his eye he saw a small diamond shaped image rise above the water, then just as quickly, disappear.

"Snake," Rod yelled.

Seconds later, he felt a sharp pain in his thigh and realized a water moccasin had imbedded its fangs into his leg. With one hand frantically beating at the water, he almost dropped his weapon. Dripping moss wrapped around his neck and he wrenched away abruptly.

"I got it, Rod, hold on, man!" Goldman shouted, coming at him from behind and grabbing him around the shoulders.

Rod felt his buddy's strong arm yank him back then reach down to wrestle the moccasin's grip out of his leg and snap its neck spewing the snake's blood into the air.

"Come on Rod, I gotcha," he said, dragging Rod along behind him in a lifeguard's dead man hold.

A searing pain crawled up Rod's leg into his groin. His vision began to blur and his throat close. His tongue felt thick, and an odd minty metallic taste flowed into his mouth.

"I can't breathe," he gasped, suddenly going limp– desperately trying to focus–as what seemed like a fog descending blurred his vision.

Goldman towed Rod to the edge of the swamp and dragged him out of the water. A moment later the other three men in the squad emerged from the dense swampy underbrush.

"What the fuck happened?" Martinez asked, his voice fading in and out.

"Get the medic, then Sarn't Cosmos, fast," Goldman shouted, "Shit! Moccasin got Rod! Hurry man!"

"S' okay man, I'm all right," Rod mumbled, trying to stand then slumping to the ground.

Martinez frantically barked instructions into his radio rousing the medic then sprinted toward Cosmos who was supervising the platoon from a vantage point 250 yards up river of the swamp.

Rod's rapid breathing began to slow while Goldman struggled with the snakebite kit stored in his backpack. As his fingers fumbled to open it, Rod moaned and stared hard at the man bending over him.

"Goldman?"

"You're all right, Rod, man, stay with me," Goldman yelled.

He ripped Rod's camo pants leg away to reveal the fang marks oozing blood. The flesh around the bite had begun to swell and from it, slowly spreading, the poison pulsed in a web of red lines. With a steady hand Goldman found the CroFab antivenin syringe and plunged the needle into Rod's leg. At that, Rod's muscles started twitching. He moaned again and began tossing his head from side to side, clutching at the dirt, trying to push up.

Just then, the medic assigned to their squad appeared at the side of the two men and pulled Goldman away from Rod.

"I'll take it from here, Private," Rod heard him say, "You did the right thing. Probably saved his life."

CHAPTER SEVENTEEN

Rod woke up to the vague image of a dark face near his and he slowly started to process the setting. A green room, bathed in light. A crisp sheet and a soft blanket.

"Ah, you're awake," a soothing female voice said.

"Snake."

"Yep, snake bite, my friend. Bad critters, those water moccasins. You were lucky. You could have died out there."

Rod tried to focus his eyes, but the face kept moving in and out of his vision.

"Infirmary?" he asked.

"Yep. You've been here since yesterday."

"What?" Rod cried.

He clutched at the cotton blanket covering him, trying to rise up on his elbows.

"Hey, there," the voice said, and Rod felt a gentle hand push him back. "Look, Soldier, you'll get me in trouble if you do that. I don't need my nursing supervisor on my case," the voice said.

"What's your name, Ma'am?" Rod asked, his vision now beginning to focus clearly.

He saw the shining black face of a nurse wearing glasses and a plastic badge on the pocket of her green scrubs.

"Lieutenant Spencer. Call me Janine," the woman's voice said.

Then Rod heard a throaty chuckle that reminded him of Garcia's low-voiced laugh.

"When am I getting out of here?"

"It takes about twelve hours for the venom to clear your system. So, maybe tonight."

"Oh, God, no! I gotta go now...my platoon will be ahead of me," Rod replied, feeling his throat tighten. "That can't happen!"

"Well, it did. You didn't ask for that moccasin to strike your leg. The Army will still be there, don't worry."

Janine bustled around his bed, fluffing his pillow, pulling a bedside table near, and filling a glass with water and cracked ice.

"Here, drink this," she said. "That's an order."

Rod took the glass, sipped the cold liquid, but his mind tracked back to the swamp.

"Where's Goldman, Ma'am?" he asked suddenly.

"He's been around checking up on you. He'll be back at visiting hours, I'm sure. Maybe he can take you back," the lieutenant said.

She flipped through the chart at the foot of his bed, then stepped back, her chubby arms crossed against her chest.

"The best way for you to get back to your squad, quick, is to get better. You do what I say and you will. Understand?" She cocked her head to one side and narrowed her eyes.

"Yes, Ma'am," Rod said meekly.

But her assurances didn't resolve the unease he felt. If he fell behind, he reasoned, he'd be recycled. For the first time, Rod was unsure of his ability to make the grade. *Does this mean a step backward? This should be number five.* Not going to let it happen, he promised himself.

———

That night when a nurse's aide pushed a cart loaded with dinner trays passed Rod's door, Goldman trailed behind her.

He looked surprised to see Rod dressed and sitting on the edge of his bed.

"Shit man, you *are* alive. I had to see it for myself," Goldman said.

"Get me out of here, okay?" Rod asked, jumping to his feet.

Goldman waved him back. "Take it easy," he said. "I brought you something."

He reached into his pants pocket and held out a Hershey bar.

"Kinda warm, where you been carrying this?" Rod asked, holding up the candy, which slowly folded over.

He laughed and relaxed, then ripped off the paper, pulled off a piece and handed it to Goldman.

"Shut up. Glad to see you're okay," Goldman said, then licked the melted chocolate off his fingers.

"You saved my fucking life, man, I owe you," Rod said.

"You'd have done the same, ami."

"Yeah, but you were so cool. How'd you know what to do?"

"Just first aid, we all learned."

"Uh, uh. There's more."

Goldman sat down in the metal chair beside the bed and looked at Rod carefully, as if he didn't want to answer.

"Okay...I'll tell you. I worked as an EMT in New Orleans for a year."

"So! You gonna be a medic?"

Goldman sighed. "I guess. I got sick of patching up Creole gang bangers in my Parish and decided there was something better. As sappy as that sounds, I'd rather be helping guys like us, than them." Goldman said. "Now can we forget about it, ami, and get out of here?"

————

Three days after the water moccasin struck his thigh Rod rejoined his squad. The bite still pained him, and the bruised area around the fang marks remained swollen and tender.

"Private Strong, I see you're back among us. That snake dead?" Sergeant Cosmos asked.

"Yes, Sarn't," Rod replied, standing at attention, eyes straight ahead.

"How is it this happened, Strong? You not memorize the looks of them damned cottonmouth snakes? Where the hell was your head? Huh?" Cosmos bellowed.

Rod's brain whirled seeking the right response.

"Looking at my compass, Sarn't!" he said.

"Looking at your compass...with your head up your butt! You go down, your men falter and you disrespect me. Shit! Did you get water in your weapon?" Cosmos' face reddened, and Rod saw the veins in his neck pulsating.

"No Sarn't, my weapon stayed dry."

"At ease, Private," Cosmos said stepping back one pace. "Your squad didn't leave you there, you know, it was Private Goldman, got you out of there. Called the medic. You got him to thank for that."

"I know, Sarn't." Rod said.

"You ready to be a Ranger?"

"Yes, Sarn't, ready."

"Drop and give me forty. Let's see how ready you are."

Rod began the pushups, counting each one in a rush of noise. The muscles of his arms started to burn. By the time he'd completed thirty-five, sweat dripped from his chin and wet stains blackened his gray tee shirt.

From behind him, in the crowd of troops watching, Rod heard Goldman's voice quietly urging him on.

"Hit the shower Strong," the sergeant said, "then get to chow. Your squad's got a twenty-five mile march tomorrow."

Martinez kept relating the details of the incident to anyone who would listen, until finally Goldman told him to shut up. Each time he told the story, the events became more vivid-and embarrassing. Rod didn't need any more reminders of his run in with a snake he'd been taught to identify and avoid. Within a week, his stamina returned and he felt as though the moccasin never bit him. Still, his caution around the swampy Florida marshes heightened each time the platoon practiced maneuvers there. *Step five accomplished,* he told himself. *But just.* Before this, he thought if he made it through Rangers, he'd be okay. But now he wondered.

CHAPTER EIGHTEEN

A warm June rain threatened Ranger School on graduation day. Coming off a raucous weekend celebration, many of the troops still suffered the effects, but Rod felt only fatigue. That, and sunburn from passing out on a lounge at a Columbus motel's swimming pool. As he ran to form up with his squad to get his Ranger tab, he considered swearing off beer for life.

He saluted the officer passing muster then caught sight of a familiar face beneath a black umbrella held in place by an aide. The man in a sharply tailored uniform standing with a group of officers was clearly Major General Shafter.

When the drill sergeant dismissed the platoon, Shafter walked over. Rod jumped to attention.

Shafter returned his salute, then stood back and looked him over head to toe.

"At ease. Looks like you made it Private Strong," he said, then smiled, gesturing at Rod's Ranger tab.

"Yes, Sir, I did," Rod said, pumping the Major General's extended hand.

"Your mother come for Ranger graduation?"

"No, Sir, too many miles to travel on her salary. But tomorrow I'll see her, I'm going on leave for two weeks before I move on to Fort Myer. Thanks for asking," Rod said, noticing the officer's disappointment.

"Want to grab a bite? My schedule's clear tonight." The major general's eye brows raised in a question.

"Why yes, Sir, that would be fine, Sir," Rod said.

———

Later the two men sat over beer and burgers in the warm masculine atmosphere of Ben's Chophouse. Their conversation flowed easily as the major general quizzed Rod about his training thus far.

Rod had been hearing a lot about Major General Shafter from his mother. In fact, Shafter probably knew she wouldn't be at graduation. Her letters and e-mails were full of conversations about the two of them. It was *Longworth* this, and that, and it seemed they were getting more familiar with each other than Rod had imagined. Perhaps the flame of something else burned there, too. *Why not? She's beautiful.* At forty-five Donna's looks hadn't faded, even with the worry of Mike and him in the Army and the need to support them all.

"I've been writing to your mom," Shafter said, blushing a bit. Always appreciated the way your dad treated her. When he died? It must have been hard on you boys," he said.

The man's genuine emotion touched Rod.

"Is there something more you want to say, Sir?" he asked.

"Hmmm, I must be pretty transparent," Shafter said, then laughed. "She told me you were a shrewd son-of-a-gun."

"Well, I know you were a friend of my dad but Rangers graduate all the time, that isn't anything special to you."

"I did have a purpose coming. Actually, more than one."

"Sir?"

"First I want to tell you I'm seeing your mom. We seem to have hit it off, and I like her company. She appears to like mine, too. I fly to Oceanside about once a month. Have since your graduation from Basic. I hope that's okay with you?"

Rod nodded. "That's nice, Sir, she's been lonely."

"The other reason I wanted to see you is about your Army career."

"I've been doing okay." For a moment, a tingle of panic stirred his gut.

"Well, that's exactly the point. Maybe you want to consider something else beside The Old Guard."

"Such as what? That's all I ever wanted."

"West Point." Shafter let his words drop like a bomb.

"West Point," Rod repeated, hearing the name echo in his head.

"But I don't have the money to go; I'd never be able to do it."

"That can be arranged if you're interested. I can arrange it," Shafter said, then leaned back in his chair as if to observe the weight of his words.

Rod was speechless, and a little more than uncomfortable. Just then their waitress arrived to take their dessert order and the major general quickly changed the subject. Soon the topic of football had them both gesturing wildly and defending their favorite teams.

After dinner, the two men walked out into the soft spring night. The rain had stopped and the sounds of crickets and frogs merged with the noise of traffic passing by the restaurant.

Rod pulled his cap down over his eyes and turned to salute Shafter, then on impulse put out his hand.

"Sir, I'm honored that you'd consider me for West Point, and sometime in the future I'd like to think about it, discuss it with Beth, but after leave I'm heading for Fort Myer. I hope you understand."

Shafter shook Rod's hand then raised both hands to grip his shoulders. He looked into his eyes.

"You're already a good soldier, Rod; you make your mother proud. I suspect there's more coming for you. 'Night, Private."

Rod saluted then watched from the steps of the restaurant as the major general's driver pulled his car to the curb, ran around to open the door and Shafter got in. *My mom sure can pick 'em,* he thought.

CHAPTER NINETEEN

Twenty-four hours later Rod drove to the small one-story bungalow on Ocean Boulevard Beth shared with her parents. He could see her through the living room window, sitting on the sofa reading. Her cat lay curled up beside her. It was a scene he'd thought about often during Basic Training and Ranger school. At his knock on the door, she raised her head, grinned and ran to the door.

"I missed you!" she said, throwing her arms around his neck.

Her lips were soft as their kiss lingered a few moments too long. The warmth and scent of Beth's body stirred feelings in Rod he'd steeled himself to ignore. He wanted to feel her bare skin next to his, but they'd taken that vow to wait. Gently, he disengaged her embrace and forced his mind to think of something else.

"Look!" Beth pointed to a glossy magazine on the sofa, "I've been looking at wedding dresses."

Ever since he proposed, her e-mails and IMs were full of questions about wedding plans. Her bright smile made him wonder if the timing was right for this conversation.

"Nice, Beth...I didn't know there were magazines for that sort of thing."

He paused, then pulled her back down onto the sofa and sat down beside her.

"I want to talk to you about something," he said, desperately trying to formulate the words in his head.

"What? You're scaring me", she said, looking at him carefully.

"When I had dinner after Ranger school graduation with Major General Shafter he made me an interesting proposition. I need to talk it over with you."

"What? He wants to send you to Iraq? He didn't want you to go into The Old Guard? What?" Beth leaned forward, an expression of anxiety crumpling her brow.

"No, it's nothing like that, in fact, he had a suggestion for a career change I hadn't thought about...but I'd like to consider it. I mean *we* should consider it." Rod reached out and took her hands.

"Well, what then?"

"He wants me to go to West Point," Rod said, trying to keep the emotion from his voice.

"West Point? But what about the Sentinel Platoon? What about your plans to guard like your dad?" she asked.

"I can do all of it, Beth, and with West Point, I could become an officer and our future with the Army would be better, even more than I ever expected."

As the words tumbled out, Rod's palms began to sweat.

"Sounds like you're considering it."

"Sort of, I guess. His offer is flattering, don't you think? An officer at The Old Guard?"

He wiped his hands on his pants as he started to warm to the idea, growing enthusiastic with each word. His eyes glowed.

Beth jumped up.

"How can you be so determined to do one thing one minute, then change your mind? Do you know how immature that is?"

"I...a...guess it does sound like that, huh?"

"Yeaaah..." Beth threw the magazine on the floor.

"Why'd you do that?" Rod asked, alarmed.

"I thought I knew you, but since you've been in, you're different. I'm not sure I like it...or you."

She strode across the room and then turned to glare at him, her arms crossed against her chest.

"What? You can't mean that," Rod said, starting to feel off balance.

The excitement of five minutes before had withered into an ugly scene.

"Beth...please!" Rod said.

"Forget it. I love you, but you don't know what you want", Beth said.

"You don't understand," Rod pleaded. "We can still get married, just not right away."

"Why?" Beth asked.

He didn't like the look in her eyes.

"Cadets at West Point can't be married. It's against the rules," he said weakly, watching her face.

"So, how long does it take?"

She pulled out a chair across the room and plopped down with her hands clasped tightly on her lap.

Rod slumped back onto the sofa.

"Four years. It would mean we'd be engaged for four years. Plus I still have to serve some of my enlistment before I go. And, there's the paperwork and even though Major General Shafter says he can get me in, I have no idea how long it will take." He rattled on wanting to get it all out for her.

"Four years?" The pitch of Beth's voice rose to a screech.

Rod watched her expression change as she thought about the circumstances, the enormity of the situation. The sound of the kitchen clock ticking grew louder and someone started up a lawnmower outside breaking the quiet.

"No, that's too much," she said finally. "You left here with a plan, and I respected that. Now you come back with a different plan. What's next?" Beth rose to face him, her expression sober.

"Beth...I love you," Rod said, standing up to reach out to her, but something had gone off kilter.

She touched the side of his face, then leaned forward and kissed him.

Rod felt like his heart would explode with such warmth he could barely stand it and tried to gather her into his arms.

"Go home," she said, pushing him away. "When you figure out what you want, let me know. Just don't wait too long," she shot at him, her voice trembling with anger.

Bewildered and worried, Rod stumbled down the walk. Back in the car, the ringing cell phone in his pocket jolted his thoughts. Maybe Beth had reconsidered.

"Hello?" he asked tentatively.

"Hey man, wanna go up to Julian?" Rascal's voice boomed. "I'll loan you my old Harley."

Rod had planned to spend the last of his leave with Beth. But, now? A ride with his long time buddy from high school on the winding road to the mountain town sounded reckless–just what he needed.

"Sure...why not?" he said feeling a sense of wild abandon take hold.

"Get your leathers and meet me at my house."

"Give me fifteen minutes."

———

An hour later the two men sped full throttle up the curving highway toward the little mountain town of Julian past the sign to Palomar Mountain.

Spring rains drew lush wildflowers through the soil alongside the road, bringing with them swarms of insects that splattered on Rod's helmet.

Riding abreast of Rascal, he grinned then gunned the bike to surge ahead just as an enormous grasshopper struck his visor in a yellow smear across his eyes.

He lifted his hand to wipe away the sticky mess, and felt the Harley swerve, then tilt as he hit a patch of loose gravel. The next moment the ground looked upside down as Rod catapulted into the air.

———

"Well, crap, you ruined my bike, man," Rascal said.

Rod looked up at his friend, then around the brightly lit green Tri-City Hospital room that smelled of alcohol and disinfectant.

"Awwww, I hurt." A pain shot through Rod's shoulder as he tried to move.

"You more than hurt, you broke your fuckin' leg!"

"What'd I break? I don't feel it," Rod said, trying to raise his head to look.

His bandaged right leg looked like a bedroll.

"That's cause the doctor shot it full of painkiller. You broke the tibia bone. A clean break, but they can't put a cast on till the swelling goes down."

"I gotta report in ten days, what the fuck am I gonna do now?" After everything he'd been through, this was far worse than the snake. "You call anyone? Mom? Beth?"

"I called your house. Your mom's on her way. I don't have Beth's number."

Rascal loomed beside the bed, still dressed in his black leathers, a worried look on his face.

"Beth and I had a fight. Don't call her," Rod replied wincing as he moved his shoulder again.

The back of his hands were bandaged and felt hot and sore.

"Oh, my God," he muttered. "Give me my cell phone, I gotta call my NCO."

CHAPTER TWENTY

Beth refused to talk to him at all right after the accident. She hung up on him so many times he resorted to whining that her anger was making him worse.

His persistent attempts to make amends finally paid off a few days later when Beth called and offered to drive him to the Naval Hospital at Camp Pendleton for the treatment of his leg. Later he learned Donna had interceded on his behalf. Still it took several conversations over the duration and his earnest promise to not act like a fool again for her to forgive him.

No sooner had the plane left San Diego did Rod begin to replay the events of the previous weeks. Shafter's offer? And what of Beth? How could she have turned away from him in such anger? He loved Beth and wanted to marry her. That's a certainty. Arriving at The Old Guard with a broken leg? What was he thinking? Stupid to take that risk. Told to report anyway, he knew he faced some God-awful desk job till he could march. He considered the optimistic plan he'd conceived to become a Sentinel in 21 steps. So juvenile, he realized, but then even if steps six and seven were backward, they still counted, right? Feeling better, he let the drone of the aircraft lull him to sleep.

By the time the aircraft's wheels touched down at Reagan National Airport, Rod had compartmentalized all his worries and pushed them far back into his mind.

When the cab dropped him at the Hatfield Gate entrance to Fort Myer, he balanced on his crutches and stood for a moment taking in the view. Flanked by brick pilasters and huge trees spreading their limbs over a vast green lawn, the entrance opened to a campus of tidy Federal-style red brick structures built in the 1800s. Set amidst impeccable leafy landscaping, the 3rd U.S. Infantry Regiment housed here abutted Arlington Cemetery. *At last!* He shivered as he felt the mantle of history settle on his shoulders drawing him into the elite group that has served every President since Washington's time.

"Hey! You Private Strong?" a loud voice called.

"Yeah?" Rod turned to see a soldier opening a car door, preparing to get out.

"I'm here to pick you up," the man said.

"Thanks!" Rod said.

Later as the Army vehicle pulled away from the sidewalk outside the 1st Battalion Headquarters, Rod looked up in awe at the entrance. The two story building with its wide porch and wooden overhang spanning the width of the building cast shade over tall windows and double doors. The Regimental flag and the stars and stripes flanked the top step. He remembered reading on the Internet that the Army Chief of Staff lived with his family on General's Row somewhere nearby.

The scene felt familiar. Then he remembered a photo of his dad in front of this very building in one of their family albums. Rod smiled, grabbed his duffel and labored up the worn steps, absently wondering how many coats of white paint had been brushed on the building's old wooden trim.

"PFC Ramrod Strong reporting for duty," he said, presenting his packet to the Specialist behind a high counter.

The man flipped open a folder and quickly scanned a sheet of paper inside. "Sit over there," the soldier said nodding at two banquet chairs against the wall of the small anteroom.

Rod eased down onto one of the chairs, balanced his crutches against the wall stretched out his broken leg. In a glass case nearby photographs of the Army chain of command were displayed with a picture of President Bush at the top. One hung askew, he noticed. He counted the photos and began to memorize who they were when he heard his name called.

"Strong, PFC Ramrod Strong?" a deep voice said.

"Yes, Sir." Rod stood to salute then followed a tall captain into an office.

He dropped his duffel to the floor then stood at attention, pushing up as tall as he could on his crutches.

"At ease, Soldier," the captain said, pointing to a chair in front of his desk. "Sit."

Rod quickly scanned the interior of the office. The man's desk was bare except for a pen, a folder and his nameplate: *Captain Moreno.* Along with an American flag, flags of The Old Guard and the 75th Ranger Regiment hung against the wall. On the top shelf of a bookcase behind the desk lay a battered helmet with its cover ripped. Beside it, a US Army Ranger Association Ek Commando Knife in a display leaned against the wall. The engraving on the display base stated *Best Soldier*, an achievement that took more effort and stamina than Rod ever had in Ranger school. On the captain's hand a heavy gold ring with a blue stone caught the light from a window over his shoulder.

"Rangers lead the way," Sir," Rod said.

"What's that?" Captain Moreno asked looking up from Rod's file.

"75th Rangers, Sir. That's where I'm transferring in from."

"Well, I'll be damned, so you are."

122

The captain traced a line of type in the file with his finger then smiled.

"Hooah."

"Hooah," Rod replied.

"You're acquainted with Major General Shafter at Benning?" he asked, leaning back in his chair.

Rod looked into the man's questioning blue eyes then briefly explained, mentally preparing for his questions. To his relief the captain dropped the subject.

Moreno tapped the folder with his finger. "You know only a few who attempt Sentinel Platoon make it, don't you?"

"Yes, Sir," Rod said.

He sat straight, eyes front, trying to read the captain's face. This man could make his life easy or hard depending on his answers.

"Your paperwork looks fine. In fact, exemplary. PT score 362?"

"Motivation and diligence, Sir." Rod blurted, inching forward on the chair, then cringed, instantly regretting the arrogant remark.

The captain stared at him hard then spoke.

"What happened to the leg?"

"Bike accident on leave."

"Uh, huh. And?"

"That's it, Sir."

"You know what you're going to be doing until it heals, right?"

"My orders say *Training Room.*"

"That's right. No slip-up there, either."

"Yes, Sir."

Captain Moreno looked back at Rod's file. "What else have you done to prepare for Old Guard duty, Strong?"

"Learned about their history, and Arlington, Sir. Did it while I was in Basic. And I knew most of it from my dad. Been practicing."

"Your dad?"

"The Old Guard, 1990," Rod explained.

Captain Moreno turned to his computer keyboard and tapped, then peered at the monitor.

"Sergeant John Strong. Oh...killed in action, 1991?"

"Yes, Sir."

"Sorry for your loss, Private."

The captain stood and went to the window, looked out then turned to him.

"I'm a combat Ranger," he said. "But I have a high regard for the Sentinel's job, Strong. I don't mean to let anyone under my command achieve it if the soldier isn't one hundred percent. I expect you to know that."

"Yes, Sir," Rod said.

The implication that Rod wouldn't give his all surprised him. Yet he began to feel the glimmer of kinship with the commanding officer. He glanced again at the captain's damaged helmet. *Not like that, though.*

Captain Moreno picked up the phone and quickly punched in a number.

"Staff Sergeant? Captain Moreno. Got an E-3 here for 1st Platoon, Charlie Company. Send somebody over here to get him."

"Good luck, Strong," Moreno said, then, "Wait in the lobby."

Five minutes later, a soldier ran up the steps.

"Sarn't Owen. I'm your new team leader," the man said as he glanced at Rod's crutches and leg then grabbed his duffel bag. "Let's go!"

With his orders still clutched in his hand, Rod swung behind the sergeant and pushed his crutches as fast as he could to the 1st Battalion barracks.

"This here's PFC Strong," Owen said to the soldier behind the counter inside Charlie Company's two-story red brick building. "Stay put," he instructed Rod, then disappeared.

———

Soldiers in ACUs wearing black berets ran up and down the stairs, seemingly on urgent errands. Another two dressed in blue tee shirts, gray shorts and running shoes pushed open the double doors and walked outside.

Rod looked around the small lobby. On one wall of the long narrow room, a glass case displayed trophies. Alongside the front windows well-used free weights and lifting equipment sat idle. A mural depicting the Charlie Company insignia caught his attention. The painting of a waving American flag emblazoned with the letter C and the words *3rd Infantry 1784, Charlie Guard* looked like it had been there a long time.

"I don't know who painted the mural," a voice said startling Rod. "I'm PFC Mathews. I gotta take you to inprocessing, follow me," he said. "Look, Strong, you're going to be attached to me for awhile till you know the ropes. Stay alert."

Rod stared into the man's brown eyes, taking in his earnest expression and the high color on his round cheeks.

"No problem," Rod said.

A soldier sat typing rapidly into a computer when Mathews opened the door and ushered Rod in.

"PFC Ramrod Strong, reporting."

"Been expecting you, Strong," the man said.

The processing paperwork seemed to take forever. When at last Mathews stuck his head in the door, Rod brightened.

"Your room is 272, upstairs," Mathews said, jerking his thumb toward the stairs at the front of the barracks.

Rod bumped down the gray painted hallway behind Mathews, peering at numbered signs posted on the walls beside the doors. Number 272 contained a single unmade bed, a small dresser, bed stand, lamp, bookshelves, desk and a wooden chair. A tall window with mini blinds and blackout drapes dominated one wall drawing his eye to the high ceiling.

Rod dropped his duffel and stood at the edge of the bed.

"Put your uniforms and gear there," Mathews said, pointing to the small closet. He beckoned Rod back into the hallway. "The four of us in this area use this kitchenette and fridge. Keep it clean," he warned. "Get your stuff stowed and come over when you're done. I'm next door."

Just as he'd finished unpacking, the barracks doors below banged open. A flood of men in ACUs rushed into the stairwell, pounding upstairs, their voices loud and echoing in the small space.

"Hey, guys! Looks like Number 272 is here!" said a man with cropped black hair and a deeply tanned face who pushed to the front of the group. "Name's, Ortiz," he said.

"Strong," Rod said, gripping his hand.

"That your name?" Ortiz asked, his eyebrows rising.

"Yeah, last name. First name's Ramrod, but I go by Rod."

"Yeah, I bet you do. What kind of person names their kid *Ramrod*? Your parents watchin' porno or something?"

Rod looked at Ortiz closely before he answered.

"My dad loved war history. I got that name from General Winfield Scott's book *Militia Tactics.* Scott fought in the War of 1812 and the Mexican War against Santa Ana. *Ramrod* refers to the way he expected his troops to behave. I've had to explain it a hundred times."

Ortiz nodded, then rambled on. "What happened to your leg?"

"Accident, being stupid. Flipped a Harley."

"Ortiz, shut the fuck up" an annoyed voice yelled from the hallway.

Ortiz looked over his shoulder, "Shut up yourself Barton," he said, then made a face. "Don't mind him. Can't stand that I talk so much. It's a kind of nervous habit, I think. I just can't stop myself." Ortiz said, then laughed.

"S'okay with me," Rod said then asked when the sergeant would be back.

"Don't know for sure, we're on our own until chow. He usually comes by to *tuck us in* though," Ortiz said and laughed again.

Mathews stood in the doorway to his room. "You'll like Sarn't Owen, he's fair," he said.

"Right, if you do what you're supposed to, he's okay, but if you don't, well let's just say he don't take no bullshit." Ortiz pointed to the open door to his room. "I'm in 270," Ortiz rushed on.

"Let me know if you need anything," Mathews said, sitting down hard on the side of his bed. He pulled a book from beneath his pillow and flipped it open. "Gotta study, sorry," he said gesturing at the page.

Mathews slight build and posture gave him the perfect appearance of a Sentinel, yet Rod knew not all the men in The Old Guard served that duty. For some, they'd already done a tour in Iraq or Afghanistan. Maybe at this time in his training they all lived together. Maybe Mathews and Ortiz served on the President's detail or for funerals at Arlington. He hadn't sorted this out yet, and no one had explained.

"Gotta get your name on it," a gruff voice said, the same one that had warned Ortiz earlier.

"Hey you guys, gimme a break here," Mathews said, getting up to close his door.

"On what?" Rod turned to face a soldier whose square jaw and cropped hair gave him the look of the perfect soldier; the one the Army liked to show off as their *regular* guy.

"Name plate," he said, pointing to the small plaque beside the door to Mathews' room. "Like that."

"How?" Rod asked.

"I'll show you tomorrow," the man said thrusting out his hand. "Name's Barton. Glad to see you."

"What about the rest of the guys? Anyone else new?"

"Just you, but I expect you'll find out soon enough how to fit in. Word is you come from Rangers, that true?"

When Rod nodded, Barton went on, "You know the captain's a Ranger?"

"Why'd you want this duty? I mean Ranger school is a big deal," Ortiz said. "Seems to me you'd want to deploy right away."

Rod ignored him. "What's up with the rip in the captain's damaged helmet?" he asked.

He glanced from man to man and noticed a mischievous look pass between them.

"Republican Guard nearly took his head off in 2003 when the 3rd Battalion Rangers led that air assault in Iraq to get Objective Serpent. You know, *Baghdad*?" Barton said.

"Tough son-of-a-bitch," Ortiz said. "Word is, he came here to decompress."

"Didn't make Guard training any easier, though," Mathews commented. The men groaned.

"He's out running with us almost every day. Like he's trying to prove something," Ortiz said.

Mathews glanced at Rod's cast and crutches. "Tomorrow you normally would start ROP–the Regimental Orientation Program. Shouldn't be any problem for a Ranger."

Odd sound to his voice, Rod mused. Was he envious or did he hear a veiled dare there?

"Nope, won't be there. Going to the *Training Room.* Look Ortiz, to set the record straight, I've *always* wanted Old Guard. Rangers was a step. That's all."

Rod had read the short description of the Training Room duties in his packet. Until his leg fully healed, checking all the company's paperwork to make sure it got signed by the commander and filed in the right places would be his mission. Not the job he expected, but for as long as he worked there, he'd know about every rumor that circulated–true or false.

Ortiz rolled his eyes.

"It's not so bad." Rod laughed. "I'll get through it."

Just then an electrified bugle tattoo signal blasted through the barracks and as if they were one, the men surged for the door to begin the walk to the chow hall.

"Walk with me," Mathews said, nodding at Rod, "I'll give you the down low on everyone and introduce you to the rest of the guys."

CHAPTER TWENTY-ONE

Six months later Rod bought an airline ticket to San Diego. When he arrived home in Oceanside, Christmas decorations hung from lampposts and vacant lots bristled with live trees for sale. Like always, the beach was crowded with tourists escaping Eastern snowstorms, and Marines awaiting deployment to Iraq lounged on Hill Street, jammed restaurants or pushed into shops in the mall where cell phone kiosks hawked the latest electronics.

Finding a ring for Beth was Rod's main objective. He also planned to stop by the Walgreen's warehouse to see Big Ed, and catch up with Rascal at the motorcycle shop. He'd promised Eric he'd visit his mother, too, so the ten days allotted for his time at home bulged with duties. First up though, call Beth.

The phone rang twice before she answered.

"Hi, babe," he said when he heard her sweet "Hello?"

"Oh, Rod, you're here," she squealed. "Where are you? At home? At the airport? Come see me!" Beth's tone of voice escalated with each question.

"I will, I will...are you dressed? I'm home. I'll come over now."

"By the time you get here I'll be ready to give you the biggest hug, ever. Hurry!"

"Be right there...and I want to go shopping, okay?"

"Yeah...sure...shopping? For Christmas?"

"Well, something like that," Rod answered.

When Beth answered the door dressed in a pink sweater and tight blue jeans, Rod's heart began to beat faster. He had forgotten her real beauty after weeks of only a photograph to stare at. Her blonde hair hung loose around her shoulders and glowed in the light of the early morning. He looked into her shining blue eyes and knew right then and there he'd made the right decision to go buy the ring. He gathered her into his arms and reveled in the soft suppleness of her body, the familiar lemon scent of shampoo in her hair. Yet the experience felt awkward.

"I missed you," he murmured, suddenly aware of an urgency he'd suppressed for too long.

"Me, too...Rod...I missed you so much."

Beth stepped back to look at him.

"You look older or something," she said, cocking her head to inspect him. "I'm not sure what it is but...well, this time I like it," she said then smiled. "Yes, I like it."

Rod knew he'd put on weight, he could feel it in his civilian clothes. His tee shirt fit him like a second skin. He'd worked hard to keep his weight under control to make sure his physique stayed within Sentinel guidelines and his body felt taut like a metal spring; ready for standing guard.

"Before we go, your mom telephoned. Said to call her back right away," Beth said edging away from him as if she too felt unsettled by their reunion. "Here, use my cell," she added, tossing the phone to him.

"What, Mom?" Rod asked, when Donna answered.

"Come home before you go to the mall, and don't bring Beth in with you."

"Yeah. Right, okay." Rod said with a sigh.

He'd told his mom why he planned to take Beth to the mall. Was she planning to talk him out of it?

When he got home, he left Beth in the car listening to music and bolted up the steps, banging the front screen behind him. At the sound, Tango bounded in from the kitchen, his tail wagging furiously. Rod grinned and ruffled the dog's ears.

"Hey, boy," he said as the dog danced around his feet.

"Mom?" He heard his mother slamming drawers in her bedroom.

"Be right there!"

Rod plopped down on the sofa and nervously flipped through channels on the TV. He glanced at his watch as Tango settled on the floor at his feet. If he didn't leave soon, Beth would come looking for him.

"I have something for you," his mother said as she appeared in the hallway then sat down facing him.

"What's up?" he said, looking at her curiously, "I gotta go."

Donna pulled a small leather box from behind her back and held it out to him then thumbed open the clasp to reveal a ring with a Tiffany cut yellow diamond mounted at its center.

"Where'd you get this?" he said, staring down at the small gold ring.

"It was Grandma's," Donna said, then smiled. "It's for Beth...I always planned to give it to you when you decided to get married. Now's the time."

"Oh, Mom, Beth's going to be stunned. This is beautiful. Thanks," Rod said, throwing his arms around his mom in a tight hug.

Now, instead of browsing jewelry stores as he'd planned, Rod asked Beth to help him with his Christmas shopping. It took an hour.

"You hungry?" Rod asked.

"Oh my gosh yes," Beth said. "How 'bout that Starbucks?" She pointed to the cafe with its tables outside.

He'd hoped for a more romantic moment to present the ring, but it just seemed like the right time. With the mall decorations twinkling and the Christmas music playing, he couldn't wait any longer.

She was sipping the last of her coffee when he pulled the box from the pocket of his jacket and placed it on the table, covering it with his hand.

Beth looked down. "What's that?" she asked then looked back at him.

"You know we don't have a ring yet and I want you to wear one. I planned to buy one for you...but my mom had another idea," Rod started, all the time watching her face.

Her expression started to change.

"When I told her what I was going to do, she gave me my grandma's. So, here it is, from me to you...forever."

He opened the box and turned it so she could see the ring against its blue velvet bed.

At Beth's yelp of excitement, people sitting at the tables nearby looked in their direction.

"Can I wear it now?" she whispered.

"Of course," Rod said, pulling the ring from its box and placing it on the ring finger of Beth's left hand.

Suddenly, she began to cry and dabbed at her eyes with her napkin.

"Beth...what's wrong?" Rod said, leaning across the table to grasp her hand.

"It's just...just...oh, Rod, I'm so happy, but, but...I'm sad, too. You're leaving again...and we have so little time." She sniffed and wiped her nose.

"I'll be here 'til after New Year's, and I promise, we'll spend every minute together, okay?" Rod said. "Let's go show Mom how pretty the ring looks on your hand."

CHAPTER TWENTY-TWO

Even with the wall furnaces blasting full on, Rod felt the cold concrete of Charlie Company's balcony floor through his *spits*. The heavy soled black shoes meant for walking served Guards fine as long as they kept moving, but not standing immobile for twenty-five minutes while snow flurries wrapped the building. The excitement of Christmas and New Year's Eve at home seemed too long ago. He thought about the sad look on Beth's face when he'd left her at San Diego Airport, and felt a pang of loneliness that made him frown; a forbidden gesture.

"That's one gig, Strong!" yelled Staff Sergeant B.J. Hawkins, descending on him like the predator bird she unfortunately resembled. "Don't let me see five more!"

The tall NCO walked up and down in front of the new class of Old Guard Soldiers, black eyes darting back and forth watching every soldier for mistakes. Rod heard about Hawkins when he arrived. Of the two noncoms assigned to week one of ROP, she had the rep for being the toughest in the bunch.

Instantly, Rod pulled his face into an emotionless mask and began to count the minutes, seeing them fall from a clock, rather than speaking them aloud. Inwardly, he cursed his failure to sustain the ceremonial composure he desperately strove to learn. For all the rigors of PT and the stamina he'd developed, standing absolutely still became an almost insurmountable obstacle. *I'd better figure this out,* he thought. *I got 50 minutes to stand next week and 75 week three. Shit.*

An image pricked his memory. His boot lodged against a Mangrove tree trunk, his knee braced alongside, eyelids heavy, weapon up and pointed at the humid darkness. Camo paint streaked with dirt on his face. The fetid smell of rotten fish and Florida mud. He'd stood there for hours, or was it minutes? His memory failed to recall exactly.

He came into The Old Guard training, in his mind, the hotshot Ranger, thinking he knew what to expect, but it proved to be nothing at all like he anticipated. After his broken leg mended, he felt like he had something to prove. He still did.

Three days into week one and he'd already faced six uniform inspections; one each morning and one after lunch, and failed three. Measuring the precise location of a pin on his uniform with fingers stiff with cold seemed impossible.

If he wasn't standing or working on his uniform making sure no wrinkles, stray threads, nor lint existed, memorization filled his brain. Rules and regulations became the drill of the evening with fellow trainees. All of them were tired, even Rod whose obsession pulled him forward.

On Tuesday night in the second week, Rod and two other trainees sat in the chow hall talking about ROP.

"You hear about Madison?" Private Cook asked.

"I know that guy, keeps to himself," Jackson drawled.

"He went ballistic and cussed out Sarn't Hawkins then up and tried to quit!" Cook said. "I heard he told someone he changed his mind about Old Guard. Just wanted to fight."

"I'll bet his team leader smoked that idea out of him," Jackson said.

The three men laughed, but Rod knew Madison's life in ROP wouldn't be the same for a long time, if ever.

At muster the next morning the two instructors assigned to week two made a speech about the importance of The Old Guard and why ROP is so important to them and the soldiers who've gone through it before them. The men stood at attention and looked as if they were listening intently, but Rod suspected otherwise. He remembered Captain Moreno's comment about not everyone making it then mentally listed his own shortcomings and began to devise methods to conquer them.

By the beginning of week three he'd sorted out a way to trick his mind into standing for 75 minutes with ease. Visualizing the manual of arms, he'd picture the steps like a movie, counting the movements in each routine. Later, he practiced the exacting steps physically under the tutelage of a sergeant. To strengthen his legs, his daily workouts on the roads within Fort Myer became positive highlights. Not content with the three-mile round trip *pussy run* to the Iwo Jima monument every day, on alternate days he took off for the Washington Monument, six miles. He'd finish the last leg up *Cardiac Hill* doing *Iron Mikes*. The punishing lunges strained his thigh muscles to the burning point. He never thought he'd be grateful for the Ranger School endurance ordeal he withstood, yet admitted it prepared him for this.

Manual of arms physical training took its own toll though. Accustomed to the rough treatment of war artillery, learning how to handle weapons The Old Guard way taxed muscles Rod didn't know he had.

One Tuesday, turned out in ACUs, Rod and Private Jackson stood with Sergeant Cleveland on a third floor Charlie Company balcony practicing *Eyes Right, Right Shoulder Arms*. The nearly twelve pound Army M-14 felt like a beast in his hands compared to the lightweight M-16 he'd left behind at

Ranger School. Rod and Jackson stood at parade rest waiting for instruction.

"You two are going to march until shit runs down your leg," Cleveland said, "So I don't want to see any mistakes when that happens. Half second off and we do it again and again. Got it?"

"Yes, Sarn't!" They responded

Rod and Jackson kept their eyes on the sergeant, watching his every move and adjusting their weapons. Each then stood at attention, eyes front, left hands clenched.

"All right," Sergeant Cleveland drawled. "And that left arm swings smoothly in unison. You are not puppets!"

"Okay, here's the drill. We're marching, just as our right feet hit the ground, I yell *Ready*. Next, right foot hits the ground I yell *Eyes*. Got that so far?"

"Yes, Sarn't!"

"Don't anticipate the command. Eyes are forward. Then I give the command *Right* and you snap your head forty-five degrees to the right. Everybody does it at the same time."

"And I want to see your heads snap on those chicken necks." The sergeant paused and looked at Rod. "Show me forty-five degrees, Strong!"

Rod jerked his jaw over his right shoulder.

"That's ninety degrees you idiot! Watch me."

At that, Cleveland snapped to eyes *right*, his chin pointed halfway to his right shoulder. Jackson, show him how."

Private Jackson executed the 45 degree head snap, glanced at Rod then turned his attention back to Sergeant Cleveland.

"Next step, now that Hotrod knows his geometry, is to bring the weapon down. And I don't want to see any jackrabbit or *slo mo* actions. It's *uniform*. Got that?"

"Yes, Sarn't," both men said.

Snow had begun to fall and blow onto the balcony, making the floor slick, yet still they drilled. Soon Rod's breath enveloped his face in moist bursts and the M-14 began to feel twice its weight. By 1700 when winter blackness closed in on Arlington and Sgt. Cleveland called a halt to that day's lesson, Rod's arms and legs felt like lead.

He passed week one and two of the Friday tests, even managing to get a little positive nod out of Sergeant Hawkins. When Friday rolled around on week three, he faced Cleveland for his test just before ROP graduation.

"Well, well, Strong, you got your math straight now?"

"Yes, Sarn't Cleveland."

"Let's see you execute *eyes right* while marching, call it out for me as you do it. I'll tell you when to stop."

Rod stepped off ten times, counting each motion and performing it as routinely as possible, until finally, Sgt. Cleveland called out.

"Stop. You got it. Stop," the sergeant ordered, throwing up his hand in exasperation. "At ease."

———

Twenty soldiers began ROP training, three weeks later fifteen graduated.

After the CO yelled *Fall Out*, Rod glanced around for Cook and Jackson and spotted them by the door.

"We gotta celebrate, brothers," he said, then smacked Cook on his shoulder and bumped fists with Jackson.

He pictured the small calendar in his desk drawer where he'd itemized the steps of his plan, mentally checked off number eight and returned his attention to the men.

"Okay by me, I got money burning a hole in my pocket," Jackson said.

"You can buy, then, I got debts," Cook said.

"How about that place by the Holiday Cleaners?" Rod asked. "We can walk."

"That gate closes at 1900," Cook complained.

"So we go around to the back gate," Jackson said, "You afraid of a little walk? Shit, man, you just graduated from fuckin' ROP!"

"Hey, Hotrod, you can sing there. They got karaoke," Cook said, pounding Rod on his back and laughing.

"Yeah, right," Rod said, then rolled his eyes and punched Cook on the arm good-naturedly. "No singing."

At this moment, the perils of Ranger School seemed so long ago.

By the time the three men pushed through the open door to the bar, crowds of soldiers packed the room two deep in front of the beer taps.

Rod bought a Coke and eased over against the wall to wait for Cook and Jackson. From the look on the bartender's face he recognized both men. They had come to The Old Guard the long route, and were way past 21.

"So who's going to transfer Echo Company with me?" he asked when Cook and Jackson returned.

"Not me," Jackson said. "I'm on to Caissons. I came here to be around horses. But shoot, we got six months to serve in C Company first."

Rod nodded. No matter what he wanted, the Army always made you wait.

"*Caskets* for me," Cook said, flexing his muscles.

The big man stood over six feet, but instead of resembling Rod's lean stature, with his beefy shoulders he could move boulders on a field.

The friendly conversation turned back to Old Guard gossip as they traded rumors with fellow graduates shooting pool and talking trash. Word was Company C, 1st Battalion might be deploying to Iraq sometime in the near future. Training hadn't begun, but the rumors were flying.

When the three men left the noisy chaos and headed into the winter night, snow had begun to fall again, piling deep along the road and settling on the bare twiggy forms of bushes snug against the fences. The snow cover hung low in the night sky blanking out the stars, seeming falsely intimate and protective.

Rod looked at his watch. "Shit, it's 1900, we gotta go the long way after all," he said, gesturing to Cook and Jackson to follow him.

Jittery from the Cokes and still high on celebrating graduation, Rod trudged through the snow, absent-mindedly counting the steps, heel to toe, thinking about wanting to share this with Beth. Even with e-mail and IM, they'd been missing each other because of Rod's schedule. He desperately wanted to hear the sound of her voice.

"Whatcha thinking about?" Cook asked. He'd slowed to wait for Rod to catch up, his breath quivering in the cold air above his head.

"Calling my girl," Rod replied.

The phone rang four times before Beth's sleepy voice answered "Hello?"

Rod was so cold at first he couldn't make his lips move.

"Hello? Look if this is some kind of dumb joke, it isn't funny," she said.

Rod heard anger seeping into her voice.

"It's me, babe," he said softly, "Rod".

CHAPTER TWENTY-THREE

Rod hefted the M-4 carbine to his shoulder, squinted into the scope and squeezed. Ten minutes on the firing range and he'd blasted round after round straight through the forehead of the black silhouette target. *Pretty good, considering all this time just carrying a weapon for show,* he mused.

His nineteenth birthday had come and gone in the past four months he'd been at Fort Myer. Cards from home and a call from Beth marked the homesick moment. So far his duty consisted of retirement ceremonies, funerals, and somber Dover missions. Paying his dues; theoretically marked as step nine on the same dog-eared calendar he'd started months before. It was a seemingly very long step. One more week and he could finally volunteer for Specialty training with the Tomb Guard Platoon. From the moment he arrived at Fort Myer, he'd been marking off the days.

Being part of the honor guard responsible for the fallen soldiers coming back from Operation Enduring Freedom brought the war to his doorstep. Each time he formed up to preside at funeral rights he got a knot in his stomach. Any day now it was inevitable that it would be someone he knew. He tried to focus on his daily missions but found he often worried about Mike and Garcia.

"Strong!" A voice barked.

Once again Rod fired, then felt a tap on his shoulder. When he turned, the Assistant Instructor motioned at his head.

Rod lowered the rifle and pulled out his ear plugs.

"Sarn't?"

"Capt'n wants you, *now,*" the man ordered. "Sent a vehicle."

Rod pushed the weapon's switch to *SAFE*, let the magazine drop and quickly scanned the barrels. He handed back a lone round and the half-fired magazine to the AI then came to Port Arms.

"Weapon safe, five unfired rounds, Sarn't."

"Clear. Proceed to the firing line to get rodded...and no running on my range!" the sergeant said.

As he hurried up to the Range Officer, concern knotted his thoughts. Re-qualifying with his M-4 had been scheduled for two weeks. What could be so important it would interrupt the routine?

"No brass, no ammo!" he said presenting the weapon for clearing.

The Range Officer snapped a rod through the barrel. "Clear! Close the dust cover on your ejection port! Keep your weapon at Port Arms until you're past the range hut."

"Hooah," Rod said and broke into a run toward the car idling in the parking lot.

"Hey, troop! No running!" the NCO yelled after him.

"Do you know what this is about?" Rod asked the driver.

"Uh, uh, but he don't send a vehicle for just any old reason," the driver said.

Rod sat in the back seat with his M-4 clamped between his knees, uncomfortably conscious of the sweat dripping down the back of his shirt and the dark blotches under his arms. The two-hour drive back from the firing range at Fort A.P. Hill gave him time to worry. As the lush green Virginia landscape slid by, his concern grew.

Finally the driver pulled the car up in front of HQ and stopped. "End of the line, Bro," he said.

Coming into the interior of the headquarters building, Rod felt a blast of cold air. The master sergeant shuffling papers looked up as Rod drew to attention in front of the mahogany counter.

"Specialist Ramrod Strong, reporting to the capt'n as ordered."

"Third door on your left, go on back."

He hadn't been in this building since the day he arrived from Fort Benning. He stopped in front of the door bearing Captain Moreno's name lettered in gold leaf, then knocked.

"Enter," Moreno called out.

"Strong, Rod, reporting as ordered." He stood at attention and saluted.

Along with Captain Moreno, the Fort Myer chaplain with the ruddy complexion and cropped curly hair stood in front of the windows overlooking the post. An older woman wearing a Red Cross jacket sat beside him, her hands folded in her lap.

Rod looked at the woman and blood rushed to his head. His legs felt rubbery and he grabbed the corner of Moreno's desk to steady himself.

"At ease, Strong. Sit down," Captain Moreno said, gesturing to one of the chairs facing his desk.

Rod looked at him expectantly and his mouth went dry.

Moreno picked up a folder and removed an official looking document, then glanced up at the chaplain.

"Strong, I have some unsettling news."

"Yes, Sir?" Rod leaned forward, his hands gripping the arms of the chair.

"I've just received intel from Division HQ. Your brother Mike's been reported Missing in Action. Doesn't say exactly where, some outpost near the Afghanistan border. There's been an earthquake in the area. Lots of damage. Seems your brother's squad was nearby." The expression on his face softened. "I'm sorry."

Rod felt his lungs contract and he gasped. For a moment he thought he'd pass out. A second later, he became acutely aware of sounds in the room, the wall clock ticking, and outside, the buzz of a lawnmower, then the sharp blare of a horn.

"You okay, son?" The chaplain asked, walking around the desk to place his hand on Rod's shoulder.

"Does my mom know?" Rod asked. "I need to call her. I need to call her now!"

"I can help you with that, Soldier," the Red Cross worker said, moving to his side.

"Two officers will be at her house in about five minutes," Captain Moreno said. "I'd wait a bit, then call her."

"But you don't understand, Sir, she didn't want us to join up but we did!"

The captain glanced up at the clock then back at Rod. "It's six in the morning there, she'll be up?"

"Yeah, she's nurse."

A familiar picture of Mom in her green scrubs popped into his head. She'd have her badge on a lanyard around her neck, and her glasses down on her nose as she read the newspaper.

"Someone will call when they've left her house," the chaplain said. "Go on back to your barracks. I'll let you know when I have news."

Rod stumbled down the headquarters' wooden steps and turned in the direction of the barracks buildings. The landscape blurred as he picked up his pace and began to run, feeling the weight of the M-4 in his hand and the salt-crusted shirt clinging to his back.

Rod saw the chaplain and the woman from the Red Cross follow him out, but when he broke into a sprint, they turned back. A half mile later, he stopped, clutching his gut, his chest heaving as he bent over, gasped for breath and sobbed.

By the time he got back, Sergeant Owen already had news for him.

"Chaplain says *Call your mom*, I suppose you know what that means?"

"Yeah," Rod replied, then pulled out his cell phone and hit speed dial.

"Mom?"

"Oh God, Roddie, what am I going to do?"

Rod could hear the pain in her voice; her words slurred as she talked. He pressed the phone to his ear. In the background he recognized the sound of the washing machine.

"Mom, I know. My chaplain told me," Rod said, all the while listening to her sobbing.

"They don't know where he is. Why is that? I thought this war was different. Everyone is supposed to be in a planned space, I thought...why don't they know where Mike is?" Donna asked, her voice breaking. "I telephoned Longworth," she said.

"And?"

"He wasn't there. His orderly said he'd call me. You think he can find out something?" Donna's voice sounded childlike.

Suddenly he rushed ahead, his emotions pulsing deliriously.

"Mom, I'll go find Mike. I promise," Rod said, certain his words were more sincere than his own conviction. A split second later he regretted his pledge to Donna. Did he make a promise he couldn't keep?

CHAPTER TWENTY-FOUR

"You think you can leave us?" Owen hollered, leaning across his desk. "Dishonor the badge? Uh, uh. No way. You do some screwy something and you'll get me in trouble. Hell, all of us. Ain't gonna happen." The veins on the sergeant's neck pulsated as his face grew red.

Any pretext of friendly conversation about changing his contract to leave The Old Guard temporarily, vanished.

———

At chow that night, Rod told Barton and Ortiz what happened. He poked at the pile of mashed potatoes on his plate noticing grease beginning to congeal in the pool of brown gravy on top.

"Oh, man, I am real sorry about your brother," Ortiz said, glancing at Barton. "How the hell did he get *lost?* I mean MIA is a tough call. Someone's gotta know where he is."

"I told my mom I'd go find him," Rod said, "Stupid. My contract won't let me. I talked to Sarn't about it and he went ballistic. But if I knew a way, I'd do it."

"You're not the first guy something like this has happened to," Ortiz said.

He looked up from the wad of bread he'd pushed around his plate then stuck in his mouth, shoved his tray away from him and drained his coffee cup.

"No medical damage. Your brother missing doesn't count," Barton commented.

"Nope. Can't see you leaving at all, my friend," Ortiz said, as if the matter was closed.

147

"This is just shit," Rod said, banging his fist on the table.

After lights out, he stretched out on his bed staring at the ceiling. The sounds of snoring and restless men talking in their sleep sounded like thunder through the thin walls. Even with the whine of the air conditioner blasting at full throttle, sweat drenched his shirt. Worry and fear spun his thoughts. *How's Mom doing? Did someone tell Beth? God, where's Mike? Oh, please don't let him be hurt. Oh, my God, what if he's dead? If I could get there, what could I do?* The weight of the dilemma pressed on his chest.

———

A week later, still no news of Mike even though Rod talked to his mom every day. He stayed glued to CNN whenever he wasn't on shift. On Friday, while he and Ortiz worked on their *spits,* they watched the news.

"Listen," Ortiz said, poking the blackened rag he held toward the TV set. Rod looked up from the shoe he'd just covered in polish.

"Wolf Blitzer," he said as the reporter began to talk over the footage of an earthquake scene.

Entire mountainsides have fallen away, burying villages and people. The Joint Chiefs have decided to deploy additional troops to Afghanistan to help civilians manage the catastrophe in the wake of the devastation. Images flashed showing the chaos as frantic villagers pulled remnants of homes and walls away from foundations and then the camera panned the face of a dirty child with frightened tear-filled eyes. *The International Red Cross has arrived, but a spokesman told this CNN reporter they need U.S. Army troops to aid their efforts as soon as possible.*

Rod dropped the shoe.

"He's not there, man," Ortiz quickly assured him. "Don't worry, he's not there."

His voice trailed off, but in its wake Rod felt a chill.

"Cold in here," he said, then turned off the TV.

———

Mike's whereabouts obsessed him as he prepared for the Twilight Tattoo with his platoon on Summerall Field a few days later, shouting out cadence as they practiced in the crisp Virginia morning. Rod's fingers cramped with cold on the butt of his M-4 and it took everything he could muster to concentrate.

"Specialist Strong!"

Sergeant Owen suddenly appeared at Rod's right shoulder and pulled him out of formation.

"Look, Strong, I'm not sure how this happened, your wanting to go to Afghanistan and all, but I got an order to send you in-country. Know anything about that?"

"No, Sarn't," Rod replied.

"You some kind of dog trainer? Huh?"

"Yes, Sarn't," Rod said, "Civilian certified." *Ah, shit. What's this all about?*

"Says you put it on your enlistment application. That true?"

"Uh, yes. I put a lot of things on the form. Just filled it out."

"Well, a computer glitch has pulled your name out of the Army's files and I'm pretty pissed off about it."

"Yes, Sarn't."

"I've got orders to send you to Afghanistan. Army dog handlers are leaving to help with that earthquake," Owen said, then turned on his heel and strode off.

CHAPTER TWENTY-FIVE

The next day Sergeant Owen sent Rod to The Old Guard's canine unit to brush up on his skills. When he showed up at the bunker-like building and kennels of the 947th MP Detachment, Specialist Brooks opened the gate and greeted him with a big smile.

"This is a first," the soldier said, punching in a code to open the security door. Rod followed him in.

"I didn't know we had any other dog handlers here."

"Yeah, well, I didn't ask for this duty," Rod commented as the door closed behind him.

Rod looked around at the neat hallway with its bulletin boards and duty roster. He pointed to a scrawled threat on a white board *Clean up your shit around the kennel or it's trashed by COB.* Rod laughed.

"When's *close of business*?" he asked.

"1700 and I mean it," Brooks said, "I'm the low man and I have to clean. I don't like it."

The two men walked the length of the corridor, Brooks pointing out training rooms and other areas Rod would use for two weeks. Then he put his hand on the knob of the back door.

"Wanna see the dogs?" he asked, then smiled.

Rod nodded.

When the door opened, a chorus of barking greeted them. Brooks headed out, walking briskly along a row of cages. The first ten enclosures held German Shepherds, then two Belgian Malinois, all big, bright-eyed and strong-looking animals. Their names and dog tag numbers were engraved on plaques mounted beside each cage door. Some had small signs indicating their specialty.

"These are all attack trained," Brooks said, stepping into a cage now and then to ruffle the ears of a dog or stroke its thick coat.

Brooks opened the door to a cage marked *Roja* and squatted down to play gently with the sleek shepherd inside. Roja's tail thumped the ground.

"We just got back from Iraq," he said quietly. "She's still a little bit shaken up. Not used to being separated from me."

The next cage appeared empty, yet the plaque indicated *Becky* lived there.

"Where's this one?" Rod asked pointing to the vacant area.

"Oh, she's in there; probably sleeping against the back wall. She just got back from Iraq, too. Stood a little too close to an explosion."

Brooks closed the door to Roja's cage then stepped into Becky's kennel. He peered into the dark interior of the doghouse in the back. "Becky, come girl," he called softly. At that, a shiny black muzzle poked out, followed by the wriggling and quivering body of a small Labrador Retriever that immediately jumped up on Brooks.

"You're gonna be working here with Becky," he said to Rod. "Come on in an meet her."

––––––––

Rod showed up at the kennels at 0600 the next day to practice with Becky on the adjacent training field. She obeyed his hand signs, moving easily through the field with its buried scents. Within a few days he felt a bond beginning to form between them as he took over her care, but knew she would stay behind to rest when he deployed. A new dog would be waiting in Afghanistan.

The pull to save Mike festered in Rod's mind while he trained with Becky, yet he felt conflict, too. What would happen to his dream now that he was leaving the Guard? At once shame threatened, and he felt he'd betrayed his father. But his dad would have tried to save Mike too, wouldn't he? Oblivious to his surroundings, as uncertainty began to knot his gut, he fell back on a familiar numbing routine. "One, two, three, four..." he counted, quieting the building stress.

———

"What're you thinking about, Strong?" Ortiz asked, "You worried about goin' to Afghanistan?"

Once again the two men were in the platoon room rubbing black shoe polish onto the leather of their shoes.

"I'm not afraid of deploying, but what's going to happen to my Old Guard training? I enlisted to be a Sentinel, not to work dogs. They're making me go."

Instantly, Rod recognized the pathetic sound of his words.

"Sorry, Ortiz, I'm just complaining. Sorry," he said and stood up. "I'm going to call home and tell my family."

Bundled in a long coat, Rod set out to walk through Arlington Cemetery. Patches of snow still on the ground had turned to ice, the result of an early spring thaw. The trees dotting the landscape were budding fresh green, and a gravesite crew dug into the damp soil nearby. Rod found an iron bench in a patch of weak sunlight, flicked off bits of ice clinging to its slats and sat down.

He used his teeth to pull off a glove and quickly punched in his mom's number on his cell, then wrapped his muffler tighter around his neck.

"Hey! Mom! It's me."

"Roddie! I didn't expect to hear from you until Sunday. Why are you calling early?"

"You know how I said I'd go help find Mike?"

"Yes. So?"

"The Army found out about that dog training I had. They're deploying me."

Donna didn't respond.

"Mom?"

"I'm here," she said quietly. "Tell me about it."

Rod explained the best he could, answering her questions quickly. The pitch of her voice rose and he pushed her concerns to the back of his mind. A cold wind had come up and he shivered.

"Look Mom, I gotta go, I need to call Beth."

"Okay, son. I love you," Donna said.

Her voice reflected a certain weariness he'd heard before.

"Love you too."

When Beth's cell phone rang, her cheery recorded voice informed him she was in class and to *leave a message*.

Rod turned up the collar of his coat and retraced his steps.

When he got to the walkway leading back, he abruptly headed into the cemetery, striding with purpose. Twenty-five steps exactly from the cement walkway he stopped in front of a white marble headstone. He traced the engraved lettering with his gloved hand. *What kind of stupid promise did I make?*

On the walk to the barracks he considered any possible scenario for finding his brother and came up with nothing.

CHAPTER TWENTY-SIX

Rod threw himself into daily physical training and working with Becky, even though he felt more and more lost each day. He tried not to dwell on his goal slipping away, but there it was, eluding him again.

His training with the dog came to an end just in time.

"Strong, get in here!" Sergeant Owen shouted up the barracks stairwell.

"Yes, Sarn't", Rod replied, then ran to Owens' office, taking the stairs two at a time.

The sergeant was busily rifling through a folder thick with paperwork. "Got your orders," he said.

"When do I leave?"

"Tomorrow," Owens replied, waving a sheaf of papers in the air. "I hope you're ready. Get your gear together. Chopper to Andrews. USAPAT aircraft to Bagram Air Base."

Word travels fast in the barracks. When he got back, Ortiz and Mathews were waiting outside his room. Mathews lounged in the doorway while Ortiz sat on the bed keeping up a running dialog while the two men watched Rod pack. He stuffed the photos of Beth and the one of Tango and his mom among his socks to protect them.

"I'm kind of jealous, man," Ortiz said. "You're going to see some action. Maybe I should have learned to train dogs."

Rod looked at Ortiz, then shook his head

"You know exactly where you're going?" Mathews asked.

"Kabul first, don't know more than that," Rod replied. He zipped his duffel and picked up his packet off the bed.

"Oh my God, I forgot to tell Beth I'm leaving!" Rod said, dropping the duffel on the floor and frantically searching his pockets for his cell phone.

"Use mine," Ortiz offered.

"Thanks," Rod said then quickly punched in Beth's number. When it finally clicked onto *messages* he sputtered, "Beth, it's me. I'm leaving for Afghanistan in about two seconds. I'll e-mail as quick as I get there. Don't worry. Love you."

He tossed the cell back to Ortiz and then grabbed his gear.

"I'm out of here, guys. See you soon–I hope," he said. He turned to Ortiz and stuck out his hand. Ortiz paused then grabbed Rod by the shoulders in a quick hug.

Mathews slapped him on the back.

"I gotta feeling you'll be back before we know it, man," he said, but his somber expression revealed his true thoughts.

Rod ducked under the back draft of the chopper, pulled himself into the doorway and slumped into a seat. At Andrews, a USAPAT C-37 sat on the tarmac. The incongruity of its civilian markings and the chirpy airline attendant heightened the surreal aspect of the mission catching him off guard and diminishing his confidence. Plunging into a disaster area where he didn't know anyone and couldn't speak to the victims worried him. Soon the lights of Arlington and the Washington Monument became small as the aircraft banked and headed out over black water.

Army personnel occupied all the seats in the cabin. Rod sat forward in the aircraft with his M-4 between his knees, trying to quiet his jumbled thoughts. Behind him four soldiers kept up a steady stream of chatter. All belonged to the same unit, returning to their battalion. They grumbled about their R&R cut short because of the earthquake, yet Rod detected eagerness in their voices he did not share. He closed his eyes and tried to tune them out.

"That weapon loaded, Soldier?" a soft female voice asked.

The flight attendant standing by his seat smiled. Her blue uniform, nipped in at her waist, outlined a trim figure. Shiny brown hair, tucked behind her ears fell loosely over her collar. A silver badge on her jacket identified her as *Sandy.*

"Yes Ma'am," Rod replied. "But don't worry about it," he said, turning his face toward the window wishing she'd move on.

"Heard some of you guys are specialists in something. Are you a doctor?" she asked.

"No," Rod answered.

"Well, good luck," she said, then moved on down the aisle. A minute or two later she was back with a Coke and a cup of ice.

"Thought you might need this. May be the last time you have one for a while," she said, then pulled out a tray and placed the can on it.

Rod looked up at her and nodded his thanks.

———

Seventeen hours later, a loud thump broke his sleep and he recognized the sound of landing gear locking in place. He peered out the window but saw nothing but a dense cloud of dust.

When he rose to grab his gear, he felt the stiffness that came from sitting in a cramped aircraft, knees touching the seat in front. He gladly grasped the handrail and started down the stairs.

"Take care Soldier," Sandy said, waving. Rod nodded.

"Thanks Ma'am."

As he stepped onto the tarmac into a howling wind blowing sand across the airfield, a soldier in battle dress approached.

"You Specialist Ramrod Strong?" he asked, pausing to cuff at the dust coating his goggles.

"That's me," Rod replied.

"Get in," the soldier ordered, gesturing to the idling cattle truck nearby. Two other soldiers already sat on the long benches in the bed of the truck. Rod pulled himself up and nodded to the men, covering his face against the thick dust swirling around the vehicle. As the driver barreled down a gravel road away from the landing strip, a convoy of Humvees closed in around the truck with gunners poised in their turrets. Through the murky beam of the truck's headlights Rod could see the Military Police sentries and concertina wire that protected Bagram Air Base. But the rubble of abandoned cars and walls destroyed by IEDs outside left him with the certain feeling he wasn't safe. Finally, the truck skidded to a stop in front of a large enclosure resembling a circus tent.

"This is it, guys," the driver called back over his shoulder. "FOB Miracle, your home away from home. Time to get good and dirty. No mama here to tell you to wash up."

Rod stumbled out into the cold dusty night with the other troops. They stood anxious and shaky, waiting for directions.

Rod looked around at the bleak landscape, barely able to discern shapes in the dust storm. Not a sign of green. What trees and brush that might have been here were scraped away to make room for the emergency shelters and temporary roads. Someone sneezed.

"You'll get used to the dust," a voice said. "Then it snows. It's worse." A man laughed.

Rod pulled the collar of his jacket up around his neck, and hoisted his gear.

"In there," the driver said to Rod, pointing to the tent. "Y'all report to Lieutenant King," he added, then hopped back into the truck and sped off.

Rod pushed the tent flap open and stepped inside. The burly lieutenant sitting at a long brown folding table looked up.

"Specialist Ramrod Strong reporting for duty Sir," Rod said, saluting then offering his packet.

The lieutenant opened the brown envelope and scanned the pages. "Ah, been waiting for you!" he said. "Dogs got here yesterday from Lackland, they're pacing back and forth; uneasy. You're my first handler to arrive," he said. "Let's get you billeted, then at 0600, report to the kennels and pick out your dog. You're going to search and rescue. It's the worst problem right now."

"Yes Sir, and where's the billet?" Rod asked.

"Sergeant Black, show this troop where we've set up the dog handlers," the lieutenant shouted.

A small, wiry soldier separated himself from the group of men clustered around a map nearby. He caught Rod's eye and motioned to him.

Rod followed the sergeant down a narrow dirt path to a large barracks tent. Two long rows of cots stretched its length.

"In here," Black said. "Take your pick. Chow's at 0500. If you're hungry now, there's a stack of MREs on that table there. Lights out in about an hour."

Rod looked at the empty rows of bunks, threw his gear on the ground and slumped down on a bunk near the doorway. His fingers stroked the weapon by his side. He never expected to use the M-4 for its dedicated purpose, yet it felt strangely comforting to him, like a best friend or as some of the guys called it, *the wife.* As he drifted off to sleep he heard a single bark. For a moment he thought he recognized Tango's voice and he was back in Oceanside beneath the soft goose down comforter on his bed. Then grinding gears outside the thin tent wall reminded him Afghanistan was far from home.

CHAPTER TWENTY-SEVEN

"Hey buddy," Rod said, slipping his hand under the muzzle of the big black dog.

The nameplate on the animal's kennel door read: *Bigger: Search/Rescue.*

"You and I are going to be partners."

Rod knelt down to stroke the dog's sleek coat. Inside the tan metal cage, the food bowl was empty and the water dish almost dry. The wind had calmed after depositing fine silt on the canvas protecting the kennels but a cold blue sky added little comfort.

"Let's get you something to drink Bigger," Rod said, his breath mushrooming in warm bursts in the near-freezing air.

He picked up the water dish and headed toward a large tank set up on a portable table nearby.

"Hey, where you goin' with that?" a deep voice asked.

Rod turned back to see a tall, rangy soldier dangling a leash alongside his M-4. His cheeks were red and chapped. Drops of mucus glistened in his nostrils.

Rod stopped. "Specialist Strong. Just arrived to work the dogs."

"Yeah, we'll I'm Specialist MacKenzie, them dogs are my responsibility," the soldier said, then pulled out a blue bandana and blew his nose.

"Damned cold."

"Sorry. That big Lab didn't have water. Sarn't Black told me to come out here this morning and choose my partner."

"So you want Bigger? He's a good dog. Worked him myself a couple of days ago. Good nose on him."

160

MacKenzie opened a large canister then hefted a 40-pound bag of kibble on his shoulder and poured it in.

"Reminds me of my own Lab at home," Rod said, then filled Bigger's food bowl.

"Well, he's all yours. Put that old water dish back in the boy's home there too, and grab a leash. Someone will be along to take you to the search area."

Rod clipped the food and water dishes onto a rail in Bigger's cage then busied himself checking his gear.

"You been at an earthquake before? You afraid?" MacKenzie asked. He seemed amused.

"I'm from California. I'm used to earthquakes," Rod said. "Nothing like this, though," he admitted.

"Stay alert out there. We got Infantry keeping track of the bad guys, but it don't mean bad guys aren't hanging around the site where you'll be."

Rod looked at MacKenzie for a long moment then opened the cage door, snapped the leash on Bigger and walked him out.

"You're gonna need emergency water for the boy there," the specialist said pointing at a large wooden crate of canteens. "Hang 'em on your harness." He pointed to his own chest rig which had four canteens clipped to the sides.

Bigger was straining at his leash.

"Sit, Bigger," Rod said.

The dog dutifully obeyed, alert brown eyes looking up at him. His long tail slowly wagged, brushing the cold dusty earth into the air.

"Okay, Strong, let's go," Specialist Mackenzie said, raising his weapon in the direction of a camouflaged flatbed truck behind an up-armored Humvee.

Three other men emerged through the early light, each leading a dog. These troops were all older than Rod, he knew that. When one of the soldiers spotted Rod's Ranger tab and nudged his companion, Rod looked away.

"Heel, Bigger," Rod commanded, pleased that the big dog trotted alongside without hesitating.

———

As the sun climbed higher, the entire Forward Operating Base rapidly began to spread out. Two battalions with medical teams and transport, logistical staff and National Guard engineers diverted from Iraq started to arrive and assist. Like Rod, for the fresh troops, the war in Iraq had become the focus, but the weary men on the ground who'd been in Afghanistan awhile knew Taliban insurgents hid in the hills there, also. As a result, Infantry troops were arriving to secure the rescue area.

Far from being alone now, Rod's new attachment to the 25th MP Company meant activity that diverted his attention. Regardless, the mystery of Mike's whereabouts lurked never far from his mind. He mused about what Ortiz and Mathews and the rest of men were doing, too. He pictured them marching, drilling. He should be there, carrying the California guidon like always watching it snap in the breeze, then standing quietly as a funeral procession passed by. The sky would be that color of blue which hurt his eyes, the green grass now a patchwork of autumn leaves. Then there was Beth. No time to call, and e-mail wasn't working yet. She'd be worried. Mom would tell her not to, but that wouldn't change a thing.

Dust began to roil into the back of the truck as it bounced along. Rod pulled his goggles down over his eyes, and quickly wrapped a handkerchief around his mouth to keep out the dust.

"Eye protection for the dogs?" he shouted to the soldier beside him, raising his voice above the din of the engine.

The man tossed him a camo bag.

"In there," he yelled back.

Rod fumbled with the zipper, bracing against the motion of the truck as it careened around piles of rubble and fallen trees.

"Here ya go, boy," he said as he fitted goggles onto the dog's head.

"Hey, there's paw booties in here too," he added, rummaging in the bag. He grabbed four and pushed them into the pocket of his jacket.

The big dog had lay down at Rod's feet as if he was ready to work.

Five miles in from the FOB, the massive rubble of the earthquake came into view. Spirals of dust still rose in the air beyond the main site indicating earth movement might be continuing along the unstable fault. Stunned by the magnitude of it, for seconds he stood speechless with Bigger panting at his side, poised for action. It looked like the entire side of the mountain had collapsed. Afghanistan Red Crescent aide workers crawled among the boulders and jagged pieces of walls and splintered trees, dislodging precarious mounds of debris. Afghani soldiers and a squad of Army Engineers manned earth movers and teetering backhoes. Two soldiers rushed by with a child on a litter, a tiny arm hanging over the side flopping with each step. The chaos of shouting, the grind of machinery and cries for help melted into a shrill pulsating sound. With sudden clarity Rod recognized the racket beating at his ears as the terrible anguish of loss.

"You, Soldier! Over here," shouted a worker in a Red Crescent vest waving his arms over his head.

The man pointed at a massive pile of stones, shattered glass and concrete.

Rod rushed Bigger to the site and gave him the command. Nothing in his Scouting training or even practicing with Becky prepared him for this scene. Bigger pulled him onto the pile of rubble, his nose working the ground. Suddenly he stopped and pawed at the remnants of a thatched roof, then sat watching Rod for instructions.

"Here! Here! There's someone right here," Rod shouted.

He dropped the leash as the big dog lay down and stretched to reach the scent. At once, Rod and the workers began to dig, tossing rocks, bits of wood and thatch to the side. Slowly they exposed a man's dirt covered body, and in his arms, a small child whose eyes opened wide in fear.

"Oh, Jesus Christ," Rod murmured.

Another Afghanistan worker shouted, and Rod ran to the Red Crescent volunteer who beckoned ignoring another area where dirt continued to slide.

"Be careful," a soldier shouted, drawing Rod's attention to the still-moving boulders.

Bigger scrambled atop the rock-strewn area, nose to the ground, Rod desperately trying to keep up. The dog pawed the rubble, climbed higher and then ran down the other side jerking Rod along in his wake. Out of breath now, Rod unsnapped Bigger's leash to rely on voice and hand signals.

"Back!" he called, throwing his hand up then watching Bigger run farther away and up the slope.

"Stop. Sit. Look at me!" The big dog turned into a sit and stared at Rod.

"Search!" Rod commanded, setting Bigger's nose to the debris once again.

When the dog stopped and lay down, stoically astride shards of a stone and mortar pillar, Rod yelled at the Red Crescent workers and Afghani police nearby. In a blur of movement, rescuers swarmed the site pulling at the broken concrete with bare hands.

A bearded man with dried blood on his face screamed, his words unintelligible. Rod turned to the interpreter nearby, a question on his face.

"Your dog found the school of the kindergarten children," he replied sadly.

———

Four hours later, Rod pulled Bigger under the protection of a temporary canopy flapping wildly in the cold wind. He poured water into his drinking cup for the dog then sat down on the ground to lift his canteen to his lips. The water tasted of chemicals but it washed away the dust that infiltrated his bandana. Rod flopped back on the tent floor, and tried to close his eyes and rest, but the din of soldiers shouting and Afghan civilians crying as they moved about in a daze, proved too much.

"How long you been layin' there?" Mackenzie asked.

His voice seemed to come from a long way above Rod's head. "That Bigger, there, he's rested up. I 'spect you'd better get goin'."

At hearing his name, Bigger jumped up.

"I'm ready" Rod said, standing up slowly.

He took a long drink from his canteen then pulled Bigger into a heel. Once again, he and the dog began to patrol his assigned area on the site now blocked off by emergency medical aide personnel and more Army MPs. Above the dust and haze that swirled around the debris and piles of rubble, Rod glimpsed the brilliant blue sky and massive snow capped mountain peaks in the distance. The cool and peaceful imagery failed to quell the noise and desperation on the ground as he slowly picked his way through the debris. The cries of the townspeople who vainly sought family members zipped into body bags and piled in the makeshift morgue refused to cease and by sunset, Bigger's tail drooped and Rod could barely put one foot in front of the other.

"You're done here, buddy," Mackenzie said, walking up behind Rod who squatted alongside the Red Crescent tent with Bigger laying on the ground beside him.

The dog's eyes were closed, and if Rod hadn't felt he'd fall off balance, he would have closed his too.

CHAPTER TWENTY-EIGHT

Rod stood unsteadily then swooped up Bigger's leash and glanced around for the transport truck and other troops waiting to go back to the FOB. As yet no vehicle appeared, nor had other soldiers emerged from the site.

Nearby, a child clutching a worn blanket held the hand of a woman whose long yellow *chaderi* robe was streaked with dirt. Rod started in their direction, hand on his canteen, watching the boy's eyes widen as he stared at Bigger.

Rod offered the open canteen to the boy who quickly dashed behind his mother. When she grabbed the water and knelt to place the bottle to her son's lips, the boy took a long drink then pulled away from his mother's grasp to lay one small dirty hand on top of Bigger's head. Rod smiled at the woman and she nodded as she lifted her son in her arms and turned away.

As night fell, the temperature dropped, adding its nasty contribution to the tragedy of the earthquake. A late snow, picked up by the wind into flurries settled the dust yet clung to Rod's clothes and stuck to Bigger's dirty coat. Muddy and exhausted, and barely aware of the riflemen riding point, Rod collapsed into the corner of the truck bed and dozed as the vehicle slowly bumped its way back to the forward operating base.

With only MREs midday, the smell of chow coming from the temporary mess tent drew Rod to its line of troops waiting outside. Now washed with as much of the grime off as possible, he stood with two other handlers, slowly shuffling closer to the food. His head ached, and the smell of the dust, blood and excrement from bodies lifted from the remains clung to his lungs. Someone passed him a baby wipe. He swabbed his face and hands then balled it up, stuffed it in his pocket and shivered as the temperature continued to fall.

"First time?" a female voice said. Rod turned.

Behind him stood the slight figure of a woman whose ACUs bore the patch and armband of the 25th MPs.

Rod looked at her warily, then his eyes fell to the name patch on her uniform and he spotted the chevron.

"Yes, Sarn't," he said. "Sorry, he stammered.

"At ease Specialist, I'm as tired as you. I'm First Sergeant Amy Morgan, kennel master for the 25th," she said.

Rod smiled and nodded. "Pleased to meet you," he said.

"Where you from?" Sergeant Morgan asked.

"The Old Guard," Rod said, gesturing to his sleeve patch. Morgan's eyes widened.

He'd reached the open doorway to the mess tent and pulled a paper tray from the rack. The duty cooks busily ladled out food from steaming Mermites. He felt his stomach rumble, then stepped aside, gesturing for Sergeant Morgan to precede him.

"That's okay," she said, shaking her head. "I'm no hungrier than you, go ahead." She grabbed a tray.

Rod nodded each time a cook offered a ladle of food and kept moving down the line. At the end, he picked up a handful of the catsup and PB&J packets and stuffed them in his pockets.

He made his way to an unoccupied table, sat down, drained his cup of orange juice then bit into a chicken leg.

"Can I sit?" Sergeant Morgan asked.

Rod looked up then nodded. "Of course, Sarn't," he said.

"Look, if I'm making you uncomfortable, I'll sit somewhere else," she said softly. "I just figured we dog people had to stick together."

"Sure," Rod said. He began to relax as Morgan dug into the huge pile of potatoes on her plate.

"You see my dog? She's the big Malinois, the brindle one. Love that girl," she continued.

"I'm working Bigger," Rod said. "He reminds me of my dog at home."

Sergeant Morgan laughed. "You seem kind of young to do this work. How old are you?"

"Almost twenty. Trained in search and rescue as an Eagle Scout," Rod said.

"I was a kennel tech for a mom and pop dog groomer in Texas before I joined up", Sergeant Morgan said.

"But this?" Rod asked.

"I took a class with a dog trainer in Austin. Couldn't find a job. I love dogs, and I love helping people, so I joined up to do both. Sounds noble, huh? I don't feel *noble*. Just tired. Way more tired than I expected."

"I hear you Sarn't," he said, getting up from the table. "Gonna check on Bigger, then hit the sack." Rod turned back to her. "Good luck tomorrow."

"You too, Soldier," Morgan replied.

———

With his wool cap pulled over his ears, Rod hunkered down into his sleeping bag that night thinking about the events of the day. He couldn't feel his toes and still wore his gloves. He hadn't bathed, e-mailed Beth or written to her since he'd arrived in Kabul.

CHAPTER TWENTY-NINE

A driving cold spring rain replaced the snow that fell during the night, rocking the FOB and tearing at the tarps draped over the kennels. Rod knelt sheltered under a large canopy to open the wire door to Bigger's space. He snapped on the dog's leash and ran him out to the waiting truck. Five men sat in the back of the vehicle, talking trash and laughing, their dogs at their sides.

"Good morning!" a bright female voice announced, and Rod turned to see Sergeant Morgan hurrying through the mud, the big Belgian Malinois running beside her. She hoisted herself into the truck bed as the dog leaped up beside her.

The squad started to their feet at attention.

"At ease men," she said then assigned each soldier to duty for the day.

"Specialist Strong, take your squad and keep track of the digging activities by the school," she said. "And all of you, watch that muck. I'll be working the slide area where the roadway collapsed. Check in at the command post by 0300."

With more rain predicted, Rod's soldiers now wore heavy gloves and ponchos under their helmets. As the truck rumbled along their conversation turned to home.

Rod closed his eyes and began to count the thumps of the tires bumping over the ruts.

———

The sky cleared by the time the truck finally geared down alongside the digging site. The men hopped down from the bed of the truck and immediately Bigger caught a scent and jerked Rod forward into a tangle of cables and shards of a roof.

Rod and Bigger entered the shadowy recesses of a villager's former home. The dog nosed over the ground snuffling away at debris while Rod scanned the area looking for signs of life. Bigger whined, pawed the muddy ground and stopped. Against the background of a bedroom wall, Rod saw a small foot half buried in loose gravel. Rod knelt to brush the debris away. When he touched the cold skin, a faint cry came from just beyond his reach.

"Medic! Medic! Over here," Rod yelled, then began to dig faster, pushing mud and rocks to the side.

He crawled into the narrow space. Small particles of wet plaster fell from above.

"*Salaam! Salaam!*" he called out, hoping the noise came from the owner of the feet.

Again, he heard a sound, this time distinctly a whimper. He pushed farther into the space, clawing at the dirt and debris. Deep in the shadow he spotted a boy whose face lay to the side protected by a rough curtain beneath a broken window. The child's chest moved faintly.

"Salaam," Rod repeated, inching the frame away from the child.

His lungs expanded with the effort as he worked his hands under the boy's shoulders and began to pull him out. He eased backward, listening for sounds of more falling plaster, aware the child's tear-filled eyes never left his face.

"*Baba, Baba,*" the boy cried, pointing back where he'd been trapped.

"I got one alive here," Rod shouted lifting the freezing child in his arms and rushing to the Army medic nearby who placed him on a gurney.

"*Baba! Baba!*" the boy wailed, fighting against the medic's attempts to quiet him.

Rod nodded, grabbed Bigger's leash and ran back to the cave-like hole. Once again, he scrambled into the opening, using his flashlight to scan the area inside but spotted nothing except broken crockery and scattered toys. Bigger scooted in past him, pushing his way with his strong back legs until all but his wagging tail disappeared. When his tail grew still, Rod knew Bigger had found the body of the boy's father–*Baba*.

———

On the trip back to their billet, the team slumped against the sides of the cattle truck. Their canine partners lay wet and muddy panting at their feet. Sergeant Morgan pulled herself into the open rear as the driver started the engine. Mud smeared and pale, she sat with her eyes closed leaning against the back of the truck.

Rod couldn't get the face of the boy he'd rescued from his mind. He pulled the handkerchief from his mouth and nose and stuffed it in a pocket, then took a long drink from the canteen clipped to his ruck. Not AIT nor Ranger School, and certainly not Fort Myer for all its duty, PT, and studying, nothing prepared him for this. This was the Army Mike knew, and his dad; it was nothing like Rod expected.

Night had fallen by the time the weary squad climbed out of the truck. Rod brought up the rear. Sergeant Morgan glanced at each man as he passed her then fell into step alongside Rod, walking in the direction of the kennels.

"Good save back there today, Strong," she said. "Maybe you want to stay with the 25th? I know this is temporary duty for you, but you're good at it. You care."

"Thanks," Rod said, letting her attempts to recruit him drop.

"Think about it," she added.

"Yes, Sarn't," he replied, too tired to think about anything now, or maybe never.

This mission gave him purpose, but over time fatigue and the ever-present sadness became a burden he didn't want to carry. Skirmishes with Taliban fighters were drawing more Infantry and Airborne units to the area adding danger to the earthquake search efforts and jitters plagued the 25th MP soldiers. No news of Mike surfaced, Beth's letters arrived farther apart and contained information of little importance to him, and memories of his life at The Old Guard began to fade. He thought about the little calendar that held his dreams. Now a bookmark with torn edges repaired with tape. He hadn't checked off another step in a long time. For all the good he did here, he wanted to go home.

The handlers were the last five in for chow, and for their trouble got larger scoops of meat and potatoes and a pile of green beans. Rod tossed two slices of bread on top of his plate of food, grabbed a cup of coffee then headed to a table to eat with the rest of the squad.

"You know Strong, I think I heard someone talking about you today over at HQ."

"Me? I don't think so, Tuck," Rod replied to the rangy Texan.

"Maybe someone with your last name, then, lot of guys not part of this outfit here," Tuck said, then fell silent as he methodically put away two mountains of fried potatoes.

"There were three Thompsons in my first outfit, beside me," Corporal Thompson said. "Sarn't assigned us all numbers."

Rod smiled at that, imagining the man with a big red *4* on his chin.

He liked Tuck and Thompson. Both soldiers were on their second tour and knew a lot about the dogs that other men didn't. They shared their experiences if asked.

Sergeant Morgan sat with other NCOs nearby. The four men stood up when she approached the table where they sat.

"As you were," she said. "Early call again tomorrow, men. Mac, let's you and I go check on the dogs before we turn in," she said to MacKenzie who threw his cardboard tray into a trash barrel then followed her out into the wet night.

———

Later Rod stood in line to email Beth, wearily responded to her chatty message about summer plans and looked at the photos she'd sent of her in her first set of scrubs. He cleaned his M-4 then wrote a letter to his mom. Now he lay wrapped in his sleeping bag wearing his wool socks and Tuck's extra pair of thermal underwear.

After lights out, conversation slowly quieted. While rain once again pounded the tent, saturating the canvas and dripping onto the men inside, Rod huddled in his bunk. He wondered if his feet would ever be warm again. When his thoughts took a darker turn, he heard a plaintive voice call out *Baba*.

———

By early June, wind-whipped sand blurred the sky once again in a ruddy hue adding to the stress Rod fought each day. He and Bigger were now digging into the rubble to remove the remains of humans and animals that died in the earthquake. The parade of Afghanis seeking relatives snaked around the morgue tents as bodies by the hundreds stacked up. Rod's hasty search and recovery training didn't prepare him for the numbing chaos of people suffering such tremendous losses. Even using the interpreters, he found it difficult to express what he felt to the distraught people he encountered. They were wary of Army uniforms regardless of the helping hand he offered.

With a rare day off now and then to let the dogs rest, the tension was unbearable. At night, Rod would fall onto his cot without washing up, numb to the sand caked between his toes and layering his scalp. He slept without moving, leaden, and too dull with fatigue to remember where he was or why. Mike was still missing. That much he did remember.

CHAPTER THIRTY

Hindu Kush Valley, Afghanistan 2008

The chatter whine sound of a Black Hawk medevac from the 50th Medical Company kicked up clouds of dust as it lifted from the terrain where the patrol rescued Mike. Inside, two medics leaned over Rod, one running a line into his right arm, another pressing something cold to his left knee. A pain so intense it addled his thoughts tore into him. He smelled the grease pencil one of the medics used to write on his bare chest.

"Gotta get Mike," he whispered. His eyelids grew heavy and his tongue seemed to have a will of its own. He lifted a hand to feel for his weapon, but instead touched skin. His fingers fumbled with the buttons of his shirt, trying to pull the gap closed.

"That's okay Soldier, we got it," a male voice said from somewhere above Rod's head. As he drifted in and out of clarity, he tried to focus on the nearest face but it became a blurred brown oval behind glasses. His thoughts whirred as information tried to find its rightful order in his brain.

"Mike?" he screamed, thrashing against strong hands holding him. "Where's Mike?"

The voice above his head began to speak again, yelling over the roar of the helicopter. Rod watched the man's lips move, desperately trying to hear, then shook his head.

Brown Oval leaned close to Rod's ear. "Hang on Soldier, we're landing, you'll be in the ER in minutes. They'll fix you up right away," he said reaching across Rod's body to steady the litter.

An updraft of dust clouded the figures of the medics who jumped out when the Black Hawk touched down. They gently lifted Rod's litter then ran toward a long tent that housed the Army Hospital in Bagram. A windstorm threatening the perilous landing of the helicopter hit with force and followed the medics into the ER spitting sand into the open tent.

Through a fog of drugs, Rod heard one of the Blackhawk medics explaining an injury. *Is it me they're talking about? Maybe it's Mike. Maybe Murphy? Sgt. Devore?*

"Pretty bad...took a mortar. The knee...cold packs," a voice explained. "Hanging by skin...tourniquet in the field. They don't know if it helped."

"Good luck, buddy," Brown Oval said leaning over Rod, bright light fracturing off his glasses before he disappeared from view.

Seconds later, Rod was engulfed in a sea of green scrubs. He felt his clothes being cut off. Then a new IV line clamped into the needle port taped to his arm began to empty fluid into his vein and he felt the coldness of his left knee as a man with graying hair lifted the medic's bandage off and peered closely at the knee.

"Can you move your toes Soldier?" Gray Hair asked.

Rod wiggled the toes of his right foot, but felt strangely detached from his left. His brain said: *move*, but his foot remained still.

"Move. Won't move," he mumbled and turned his head away from the bright light shining into his eyes.

"Let's get him out of here," Gray Hair said as the swarm of green scrubs descended once again like a cloak of protection around Rod, tucking warmed blankets tightly around him.

"What's happening? Where'm I going?" Rod struggled to say. A Navy corpsman leaned in close.

"We're headed to Landstuhl in Germany, Soldier," he said. "Now you rest."

Troubled dreams accompanied him on the flight. Beth stood smiling, her yellow hair flying around her face. Bigger and Tango sat quietly looking up at him, waiting for instructions. Mike bent near. Rod could smell the Juicy Fruit gum he chewed. Then running ahead of the squad, leading, kicking up dirt, his fist gripped the handle of a litter bearing a bloodied soldier. Calling his name, the soldier beckoned him close and Rod looked down at his own face. Behind him Mom wept. She held out a damp balled-up tissue. He felt Murphy at his side, Sergeant Devore, yelling, the explosion, Haji running, running, then Captain Moreno asking "Are you ready?"

CHAPTER THIRTY-ONE

Rod ran his right hand over his chest feeling coarse cotton beneath his palm. *Wrong*, his mind signaled. His fingers reached for his stomach and thigh, then stopped. Where his left knee should be, the cotton surface bumped up into a huge mound. His eyes flew open.

He pushed up from the hospital bed and looked down at the space beyond his knee where nothing existed. Frantic, he pulled the blanket and sheet away, his fingers exploring the huge bandage. *Get up, get up, gotta get away!* Rod heaved his body over the side of the bed and stood up, blood leaving his head. His right leg crumpled beneath his weight as he hit the floor. Spasms of pain shot through his body and his anguished scream reverberated down the hallway.

"ORDERLY! I need help here!" a petite Navy nurse shouted.

"Shh, Soldier, you're going to be okay," she said, scrambling to his side then crouching to grab him beneath his arms.

Sweat drenched Rod's armpits and he felt his heart slamming against his chest. At once strong hands lifted him and settled him back onto his bed.

Blood oozed fresh and pink from the bandage on his leg.

"The pain," he panted, his lungs burning, depleted of air.

The nurse quickly inserted a needle into his IV then nodded to the orderly who'd come to her rescue.

The pain began to subside immediately. Just then a man in blue scrubs with a stethoscope hooked around his neck appeared and began to remove the dressing swaddling Rod's thigh. The badge on the man's pocket read: MJR Hooks, MD Royal Navy.

"Good morning, Rod," the major said, his deft hands making short work of replacing the tape and gauze.

Hooks pulled off his latex gloves then dipped his head to study the clipboard he grabbed from the foot of Rod's bed.

"Feeling better, yes?" he said.

Rod turned his wild and bewildered gaze to the man whose eyes were huge behind round wire-rimmed glasses. The doctor's scrubs smelled of bleach and clean cotton as he bent over him.

"Just where am I?" Rod asked. The subsiding pain did nothing but confuse him more. He reached up to feel the top of his head touching a bandage and a prickle of stiff hair.

"Landstuhl. You've been here a week." Major Hooks placed his fingertips on Rod's wrist, glanced at his watch, then scribbled briefly on the clipboard.

"Fuck that! What's wrong that I've been here so long and don't remember?" Rod asked.

His tongue felt thick. As he tried to wrench away from the man's touch his muscles refused to obey.

"Nasty bump on your head, and then there's the surgery on your leg," the major said calmly.

Then a brief recollection pierced Rod's thoughts and he yanked the blankets away to reveal his freshly bandaged left thigh and right leg.

"Where's my leg!" he screamed. "My leg, where's my leg...?" He struggled to sit up, but a pounding surge of blood to his head spun the room off kilter.

"It's there, I can feel it! What's going on here? What are you doing to me?"

The doctor grabbed Rod's shoulders and wrestled him onto his back again.

"Nurse!" Hooks shouted, and at once, a man in green scrubs appeared, slipped a blood pressure cuff on Rod's arm and touched his wrist.

"Pain meds, Sir?" he asked looking at Major Hooks for direction.

The doctor shook his head. "Not yet."

"Sorry, son I thought you knew," Hooks said. "The field medic did a brilliant job stopping the blood and keeping you alive, but there was nothing left of it. We amputated below the knee."

"No, no, no..., you don't understand. I shouldn't have been there."

Rod felt frantic as a specter of disbelief began to rise. "I'm 3rd Infantry. I'm supposed to be a Sentinel."

His face screwed up, and long heavy sobs erupted. Through the fog of pain and fear another image surfaced.

"Oh, my God...where's my brother?"

Major Hooks reached for Rod's hand and held it, then shook his head.

"I'm sorry..." He nodded at the nurse who at once slipped a needle into Rod's IV and his world went black.

———

For the next two days when he made rounds, Major Hooks came to see Rod, always pleasant and encouraging. He explained matter-of-factly, his British voice carefully articulating that his staff would keep the wound debrided. The next step in his recovery would take place at Walter Reed where the wound would be closed, Hooks told him.

Each time the cheerful nurse and corpsman appeared beside his bed laden with bandages and gauze, Rod knew to steel himself against the inevitable ordeal. For all their care and assurances, peeling away the dressings from the mangled bloody stump, the cleansing steps, including trimming away dying flesh and re-bandaging caused excruciating pain. At first he tried not to look, then grew fascinated with the task, confused when it seemed he could still feel his amputated lower leg and foot.

After the nursing team would leave, having freshened the narcotic drip into his vein, he'd dreamily welcome the night descending as his muscles relaxed and sleep came. Even then, nausea from the pain medication cramped his stomach. He'd awaken thrashing on the bed, sweating and tangled in sheets, reliving the fire fight. Once again Rod saw relief and recognition on Mike's face.

"Where's my brother?" he'd moan quietly in the dark.

For all the doctor's attempts to assure Rod his healing was on track, his mood remained black. Rod knew the field docs tried their best, but here in the sleek Army hospital with every medical innovation possible, why hadn't his leg been saved? How did he let this happen?

What of Murphy and Bigger and his missions with the 25th? And, Sergeant Devore? He tried to reconstruct the events that got him here, but huge gaps of time filled with nothing became barricades. A cold dark thought began to plague him. Could Dad have been saved if a better doctor treated him?

The morning of the tenth day, as the pain meds wore off, he lie wakeful in the darkness, anger bubbling up acid in his gut. When the fluorescent light flickered on and Major Hooks pulled the curtain aside, Rod set his jaw set against the sharp pain throbbing up his left thigh and stared at the doctor. He ignored the tired lines around the Major's eyes and the faint shadow of a beard on the man's face.

"Why'd you take my leg off? You coulda sewed it back on, you son-of-a-bitch!" he yelled, feeling his breath come in short spurts, panting with rage.

"Do you know what you've done to me? I can't soldier! Being a Tomb Guard is all I ever wanted. Damn you!"

The power of his outburst welled up and poured out of him like scalding water.

Watching Major Hooks quietly listening, stoic in the face of his fury, deflated Rod's anger. When the tears came, unexpected, the major gently rested his hand on Rod's arm and waited for the sobs to subside. Once Rod's shaking shoulders grew still, Hooks busied himself with the information on Rod's chart then explained his early arrival before rounds.

"You're off to Walter Reed this morning," he said. "I asked staff to make inquiries about your brother, but so far, nothing. Sorry. Keep asking, yes?"

He held up Rod's transport orders, then signed the top sheet and handed it off to the nurse standing by.

"Get this soldier ready to roll, will you?" Rod heard him say. "The lad turned twenty yesterday. Brilliant celebration," Hooks added with a sigh and headed for the door.

"Sir?" Rod called out.

Hooks turned back, a questioning look on his face.

Rod reached out to grasp the doctor's hand.

"I'm sorry, Sir, it's just...I'll be good to go when I'm back on my feet, right?" Rod asked, watching the doctor's expression carefully for signs of truth.

"It's up to you. A lot of men coming through here go back. You do what they tell you at Walter Reed, and make that decision yourself," Major Hooks said turning toward the door again. "I don't want to see you back here either, yes?"

CHAPTER THIRTY-TWO

Rod struggled to look around at other troops making the journey like him, strapped down in the huge hold of the C-17 transport aircraft. Tucked into racks against the metal sides of the plane with a maze of tubes and lines running from their limbs, many appeared more grievously injured than him. Some men thrashed against their restraints, threatening to dislodge the intubation machines balanced on their chests. Others lay unconscious swaddled in bandages and blankets. Army medics, Air Force doctors and corpsman relentlessly patrolled the drafty steel grid covering the floor keeping an eye on the vitals of their patients and monitoring the various fluids that dripped into their veins.

His teeth began to chatter and the bandage covering the stump of his left leg felt strangely wet. He tried wiggling the toes on his right foot, but couldn't feel them and panicked.

"Cold!" he mumbled against the roar of the giant engines, then tried to sit up, but the webbed band strapped across his chest held secure. He felt the vibration of the aircraft rumble through his stomach.

"Please doc, I'm cold," he pleaded, this time louder.

A corpsman hanging an IV bag over the head of the man in the narrow bunk above Rod looked down.

"Hang on soldier, I gotcha," the corpsman said then pushed off toward the back of the aircraft.

"Gonna be fuckin' sick," Rod cried, tossing his head from side to side, desperately trying to keep the contents of his gut from spewing out onto his pillow.

"Here, here," the corpsman said, suddenly back at Rod's side, shoving a plastic basin beneath his lips as Rod's stomach convulsed and yellow bile rolled from his mouth.

A moment later, strong hands tucked a heated blanket around him and the corpsman wiped the vomit from Rod's face.

Slipping in and out of painkiller-induced fog as the flight droned on, Rod fumbled for bits of illusive and confounding information. Missing pieces of a puzzle he continually tried to reconstruct tumbled through his dreams. He would wake suddenly drenched in sweat, believing he was standing beside his bed, looking down at some poor son-of-bitch with his leg blown off. He worried about his mother getting the news of his injury. And Beth! He pictured her sweet face crumpled in fear. Then, what happened to Mike? Mom would want to know. And Murphy, and Sgt. Devore? No one knew, nor were they willing to find out. When he asked, he got blank stares of compassion, but not help with answers for the questions that remained as gaping holes in his memory.

When at last his body warmed, Rod lie still staring up at the bottom of the bunk above him, scant inches from his face. Its black metal mesh formed a grid. Fascinated by the regularity of the pattern, he began to count the squares. Soon the cries of pain and unintelligible moaning faded, replaced by the steady vibration of the aircraft's mighty engines and dreamless sleep that overtook him.

In less than 12 hours the aircraft pulled up to a ramp at Andrews Air Force Base in Maryland and medics began to ferry their charges into waiting ambulances headed for Walter Reed and Bethesda. Rod's pain medicine had begun to wear off. He felt every movement of the stretcher as the troops carrying it grunted and bumped down the gangway their boots thudding against the metal structure.

A chaplain waited at the foot of the gangplank. He reached for Rod's hands and drew them into his warm grasp.

"You're home Soldier, I'm Chaplain Garrity and God is with us," the man said, speaking close to Rod's ear.

"I'm not religious, chap," Rod protested through dry lips.

"That's okay son, our religion is relationships," the chaplain responded. "I'll be 'round to see you tomorrow. You get some rest, hear?"

Rod nodded then turned his head on the pillow to watch the chaplain's broad back as he moved on to the next injured man.

At Walter Reed, a new bevy of staff in ACUs and green scrubs closed in around him, chirping comments to each other and murmuring as they handed off charts and a portable IV stand Rod hadn't seen before. He watched it all, anxious and detached in some way, as if taking notes on this flurry of activity. *Three medics on the plane, now four here,* he counted, and felt calmer. From the vantage point of his gurney as it rolled quietly down the hallway, he saw a strip of blue near the ceiling and not recognizing it as paint, wondered how the sky could be so close.

A pretty nurse wearing the BDU uniform of the Air Force glided into his room with a tray in her hand.

"Welcome to Ward 57," she said leaning close, her brown eyes concerned and reassuring. "This will make you feel better pretty quick, Soldier."

The nurse inserted a syringe of clear liquid into the IV bag hanging by his bed then reached over him to straighten the blanket and adjust the pillow under his head. As she did, Rod smelled her perfume and struggled to read her name on the lanyard around her neck.

"Janine?" he mumbled, beginning to feel the delicious slide into darkness the pain medicine promised.

"It's Flo, Soldier."

Rod smiled. His eyes closed and he felt his muscles relax and the weight of the bandage on his leg lightened.

"Hey," Flo said, grabbing his chin and turning his face to hers. "Listen to me, your mother and fiancé are on their way, but it's storming like hell. Their flight's delayed. I'll tell you when they get here. Understand?"

Rod nodded. "Mom...Beth...'kay."

"You sleep now," the nurse said.

CHAPTER THIRTY-THREE

The next morning Rod woke to the rattle of carts bearing breakfast trays pushed through the hallways by aides. His mouth dry and when he swallowed, what little saliva responded tasted sour and rotten.

"Ah, shit, I threw up again," he said aloud, tentatively touching his fingertips to his lips then to the pillow. He lifted his head to tug at the pillowcase now stained orange and crusty. The effort sent a throbbing pain down his left side and he struggled to sit up.

"What do you think you are doing?" Flo said, as she bustled in.

Just then an aide placed a tray of food on Rod's bedside table.

"Get those fucking eggs away from me," he complained, feeling his stomach begin to heave.

Flo pushed the table out of his line of sight. She checked his chart then frowned.

"Morphine. You know if you're allergic?"

"No."

"I'm asking Doctor Higgins to check that out for you," she explained. "Now let's get you tidied up, okay?" Her expression turned from concern to pleasant as she pulled up a trolley piled with fresh towels, a basin of hot water, shampoo and a razor.

"Time for your bath," she said.

Rod started to relax as Flo began washing his body, then gently shampooed his hair.

"Stitches still up there?" he asked.

"Yep, but the laceration is closed. Your CT scan came back clean, so I imagine the doc'll be taking out those stitches pretty quick. Besides, you need a haircut!"

The warm shaving cream on his face felt luxurious as Flo carefully scraped away at his chin.

"You're going to look like a baby when I'm done," she joked.

"I'm twenty."

"Huh. You *are* a baby!" Her low chuckle sounded like music.

Rod winced as she began the last step in his morning ritual. Even though her practiced hands removed the bandages and dressing with care, the skin around the amputation tingled and felt raw. When she finished he was sweating against his fresh pillow.

"Thanks," he managed to murmur.

"Look here, Rod, it's time for meds, but I'm going to find Doctor Higgins first. You stay calm, now," Flo said then hurried away with her arms full of damp towels.

As she left, his bedside phone rang.

He fumbled for it, managing to murmur, "Specialist Strong."

A loud shriek reverberated from the earpiece.

"Hey, Mom."

"Roddie...I'm coming honey, bringing Beth." Her voice sounded thick. She'd been crying.

"S'okay, Mom, I'm all right."

"No, you're not," his mother protested. He heard the phone drop and she called out.

A male voice responded in a rustle of noise.

"Rod? Shit dude, what'd you go and do to yourself this time?" Rascal's unmistakable deep baritone boomed through the phone.

"I'm okay," Rod said.

"Beth called me. You mom's a mess, so's Beth. I'm taking them to the airport."

"Thanks man," Rod said, then felt a wave of pain surge through his left side. "Ugh," he muttered.

"What's that?"

"Nothing, just trying to get comfortable," Rod replied and squeezed his eyes shut to ward off the growing pain that threatened.

"Look, Rascal, I gotta go...and, thank you man...bye."

The receiver fell from his hand as he reached to clutch the sheet covering his chest.

Rod tried to relax, breathing deeply. He listened to the energy of Walter Reed Army Medical Center coming alive for the day. Orderlies pushed patients in wheelchairs past his doorway. Families of soldiers streamed down the hallway. The pain grew stronger, and he felt for the nurse's call button, but it flopped away from him dangling by the bed.

"Fuck, where's Flo?" he mumbled, trying to concentrate on the activity outside his door. Visitors passing by waved to him self-consciously. Some wept, others bore brave faces. NCOs and officers in immaculate boots tread the polished floors with purpose.

The bustle of the veritable institution began to grate on his nerves and he felt a scream rising in his chest. Outside his door he glimpsed an Army Heritage framed print that only served to remind him of his failure to stay safe. *God, where is she with the pain meds!*

"So no more morphine," Flo said, appearing back at the side of his bed. "This won't make you sick," she added, her hands busy with the IV.

Rod's muscles tensed, then seized again in pain. But as the drug took hold, a familiar warm wave began to pulse through his veins and the ever-present nausea vanished.

Flo was talking. "Your mom is on her way," she said, but her voice echoed and seemed to come from a long, deep tunnel. His eyes closed.

————

At evening rounds he stared mindlessly at the TV screen mounted in the ceiling of his room, listening to the voices of nearby soldiers in the ward ask the doctors when they could go back in-country. Later he recognized their sobs as the men fought for sleep.

Rod had been in Ward 57 three days.

Friday morning he awoke to see a soldier in trim ACUs at the foot of his bed holding his chart and staring at him.

"Hey there, ami, I gotta keep getting you out of trouble?" the soldier said.

Rod blinked his eyes and squinted.

"Shit! Rickie G! Where'd you come from?" Rod yelled, then winced as a stabbing pain ran down his left side and through the calf that no longer existed. He pushed up in bed, took a deep breath and stuck out his hand.

"Sarn't Goldman now, at your service...again."

"How'd you know I was here," Rod asked, his eyes going to the chevron patch on Goldman's uniform.

He licked his lips and glanced over at the tray and syringe on his bedside.

"I saw your name on the white board this morning when I got back from leave. I've been here six months. Transferred in from Fallujah when they made me a sergeant."

"Army found out about your EMT training, huh?"

"S'okay, ami. This is right where I want to be," the sergeant assured him.

Rod's eyes slid to the tray again.

"You here for my shot?"

Goldman hesitated. "Yeah, and more. I gotta clean your wound and get you ready for surgery. Doc's gonna close it today."

Rod looked away from Goldman's steady gaze.

"They're not going to put it back on?" he asked softly, his voice rising in hope that a miracle would occur.

"No ami, your leg is gone. I worked in a CASH in Iraq. I know how hard we tried to save guys' limbs. You took a *mortar* round! I know you don't want to hear it, but you coulda got killed. You didn't. You're lucky."

Goldman's voice grew tight as he turned away and busied his hands changing the IV, adding the contents of a fresh syringe. His friend's cool composure had been shaken. The drug took affect almost immediately and Rod watched the sergeant slip on surgical gloves, safety glasses, a mask and gown, then carefully begin to remove the bandages covering his thigh. He felt the cool saline solution as Goldman poured it over the wound then gently patted it dry.

"I can feel that. Like in my calf is still there," Rod said then he laughed. "Why?"

"Phantom sensation," Goldman responded. "It happens once in awhile," he added, as he bent to fix the gauze pads in place with strips of tape.

"Thanks, man...I'm going to sleep now," Rod said, his eyelids feeling heavy. "Come back?"

"You bet," Goldman assured him.

———

The next morning after breakfast, two soldiers Rod didn't recognize stood with Chaplain Garrity outside his door. Flo hovered nearby.

Rod looked her way, puzzled. "My mom here?"

The nurse shook her head.

Rod focused his gaze on the two soldiers.

"How ya doin' Strong? I'm Major Chuck Boston, Company B Commander, Warrior Transition Brigade," the senior officer said, striding into the room. "You report to me now. This here's Staff Sarn't Mortenson. He's in charge of you and eleven other guys in your squad."

Rod looked from the major to the staff sergeant then to Chaplain Garrity.

"Squad?"

The chaplain nodded.

"Remember I told you about relationships? This is one of them," he said.

"That's right. This is something new to make sure you guys get well and back to active lives as soon as possible," Major Boston said.

The man's gentle eyes held genuine compassion. He hadn't said *active duty* Rod noticed.

As the major spoke, Flo ministered to Rod's pain, adding a new syringe of medicine to the IV.

"There's Alpha Company, Bravo and Charlie. You're in Company B, because we have something in common," Boston continued. "We're both Old Guard."

Rod felt a rush of excitement and his heart began to pound.

"Sir, can you get me back in the Guard?" he asked, feeling like he glimpsed a sliver of light beneath a drawn shade.

Major Boston paused then looked closely into Rod's face before he spoke.

"You have a lot of work to do here. Let's talk about that another time."

The officer reached into his pocket and pulled out a small manila envelope.

"Meanwhile, your President sent you a token of his appreciation." He smiled and opened the flap.

"Me?" Rod said.

"Now this here's symbolic. You'll get the real thing when it catches up with you." Boston fumbled with a small crisp certificate.

"Your President authorizes me to present you with the Purple Heart for bravery under fire. Thank you for a job well done, Specialist."

The major held out the document for Rod to see, then placed it on the nightstand beside his bed.

"A medal for your uniform will be coming along soon, I promise," he said. "Staff Sarn't Mortenson, you stay here a bit and tell Specialist Strong how everything is going to work, then come find me."

"Roger, that Sir," Mortenson replied, turning to watch the officer leave.

Rod picked up the certificate, glanced at it and shook his head. He quickly folded the paper and poked it under his pillow.

After Major Boston left with the chaplain and Flo trailing behind him, the staff sergeant pulled up the leather armchair beside the bed and settled in.

"Good man, Boston. Saw combat in Iraq. He's here because he's been through Reed. Humvee ran over an IED. Got part of his ass blown off in Mosul. We're both combat Infantry. I came from Kabul."

"I didn't see a limp," Rod said.

"He's a tough son-of-a-bitch," Mortenson said.

Rod looked closely at the sergeant's weathered face noticing flecks of silver in the narrow strip of hair above his ears.

"I don't understand what I'm supposed to do," he said, beginning to rationalize the situation. "What's my mission?"

"Your mission is to get well. My mission is to help you do that. Anything you need. The paperwork, figure out where your family will be staying..."

"No one's here yet," Rod broke in.

"Oh, yeah..." Mortenson pulled a scrap of paper from his breast pocket, glanced at it, then resumed speaking. "I got word the flight your mom and fiancé took from San Diego got turned back in Chicago because of the weather. They should be here by Thursday or Friday."

"Thanks, Sarn't," Rod said.

He could hardly wait. But did he want Beth to see him? Instinctively his hand went for the bandage.

The sergeant cocked his head, then reached forward and pulled out the folded certificate Rod thought he concealed beneath his pillow.

"Why'd you hide this?" Mortenson asked, smoothing the paper with his fingertips.

"It's a fluke," Rod stammered. "For combat. Not me."

"Listen up. What you did was brave. You'd have done that for anyone. Don't tell me you don't deserve it."

"But, I..."

Sergeant Mortenson's hand flew up. "That's enough," he said.

Rod nodded. "Okay, Sarn't."

"Look, Strong, you take it easy. I'll be back to see you tomorrow sometime. Meanwhile, your case manager will be stopping by. If you think of anything you need, you call me. Here's the number." Mortenson dropped a card on Rod's bedside table and rose to leave.

"Anything else I can do for you?" he asked.

Flo returned to the room moments after Mortenson left. She held a tray with a covered bowl, a glass of milk and a package of crackers.

"Tempted?" she asked as she placed it on the side table and lifted the lid. The rich aroma of chicken noodle soup wafted up.

"I am," Rod said, pulling up by the handle hanging over his head.

The broth tasted salty and tangy, the chicken moist and tender. He gulped down the milk then bit into a cracker. The nurse glanced over at him as she got his evening meds ready and set out the dressing for his leg.

"I think you're getting better."

"Yes, ma'am!" Rod replied, feeling for the first time in days that actually might be the case.

CHAPTER THIRTY-FOUR

At 0700 the next morning, Flo returned.

"Up and at 'em, Rod!" she said, her voice as cheerful as the bright light she switched on over his bed. "I got good news, and better news."

"Yeah, what?" Rod grumbled. He still felt drowsy and warm beneath his blankets.

"Well, the really good news is your mom and fiancé will be here Friday for sure, and the better news? You're starting physical therapy this morning. You gotta be ready to work by 0800, so let's get going," Flo said.

"I'm not ready for that," Rod complained.

"Oh yes you are. Now hurry up, I gotta get you washed, and you have to shave and get dressed."

"I hurt."

Flo looked at Rod over the top of her glasses. "I know," she said softly.

"Shit!" Rod said.

Despite the sponge bath, shave and clean clothes, Rod didn't feel enthusiastic about starting therapy. When Flo motioned to him to sit up, he grunted with the effort of easing his body over the side of the bed. He flexed his right leg, then his left, and at once felt the illusive phantom pain below his knee. The swollen stump of his thigh looked huge covered in its tube-like sock. Doc Higgins and Flo had assured him its size would slowly shrink to resemble his healthy thigh.

"Take it easy," Flo cautioned, handing him crutches then grabbing the back of his sweatpants. "You just stand there a minute, okay?"

Rod gingerly stepped down on his right foot. His muscles felt weak and a sharp pain shot through his hip. He winced then balanced himself, leaning against the bed, the stump of his left thigh still resting on the mattress.

Flo reached into the pocket of her uniform then extended her hand.

"You missing this?" she asked, smiling broadly when Rod's face lit up.

"Where'd you find that?" he replied taking from her the small, dirty and torn reminder of his service thus far: the calendar.

"It was in your medical file. When you told me you'd lost it someplace, I remembered seeing it there."

"Thanks, Flo. For this and everything..." he started, but she broke in.

"You're welcome. You're not my favorite patient, but you're up there," she said using her standard retort, now familiar to the men in Ward 57; Rod knew it by heart.

Just then a lithe woman in tan corduroys and a blue polo shirt strode into the room pushing a wheelchair.

"Howdy, I'm Carrie," she said. "Come to take you to the MATC."

She brushed a shock of red hair from her eyes as she bent to lock the chair's brakes. Rod expected he'd see the two-story Military Advanced Training Center rehab gym sooner or later, but not this soon. Only ten days had passed since the insurgents' mortar.

Suddenly an urge to pee overcame him and he looked anxiously at the bathroom door.

"I see I'm just in time," Carrie said following his glance.

With practiced hands she guided Rod's hip over the side of the bed close to the wheelchair. At once a huge rush of blood filled the stump of his left leg in an exquisite flood of pain that throbbed like a hammer hitting his thumb.

"Aaaah," Rod cried, "I gotta lay back down!" He clutched the side of the mattress and tried to turn away.

"Bedpan", he muttered, franticly gesturing to Flo.

Carrie quickly put her arm around his waist to keep him upright while Flo slid the bedpan into place. A moment later he felt better, but looked longingly at the safety of his hospital bed.

"I do have to lay down, I can't do this," Rod exclaimed.

"Oh, no you don't. Little old ladies and football players overcome this. So will you," she said, leaving no doubt in Rod's mind she knew what was best.

Carrie kept up a cheerful conversation as she pushed his wheelchair, dodging visitors and ambulatory soldiers along with other wheelchair-bound patients.

"We're going to be fast friends, you and I, and as soon as your mom and fiancé get here, we'll be one happy family!"

"They're coming Friday," Rod said, recalling the morose thoughts beginning to fight for space in his mind.

Would Beth still love him with only one leg? Did Mom think he let her down?

Rod's thoughts rambled, shutting out much of Carrie's conversation until he heard Sergeant Mortenson's name.

"I hear Staff Sarn't Mortenson has some info on your brother and the guys with you when you got hurt. He's coming in this evening. I don't know what he found out, he just said to tell you he'd be dropping by," she said.

As he absorbed her words, Rod's heart began to beat faster. Carrie now hustled him along a long glassed-in corridor that looked out onto a huge gym.

"We're here!" Carrie said.

Natural light poured into the vast area, and although the sweltering June weather kept the hospital air-conditioning running full on inside the gym, soldiers in gym gear and shorts sweated.

Carrie pushed Rod through the sliding doors then stopped as a beefy soldier in a green Ranger tee shirt and baggy pants called her name.

"Wait one," she said, leaving Rod to look around at men and women working out.

Beyond a low banister at the far end, a rock-climbing wall extended from the bottom floor below to the ceiling above Rod's head. In the middle of the room, patients with missing limbs stretched out on padded tables, red-faced and grunting, trying to meet the demands of a physical therapist. Alongside a few, Rod heard people quietly offer encouragement. Nearby, a therapist examined dark red scars on a man's back. He grimaced when she touched him then joked with a person sitting beside him. A man in shorts stood shifting his weight back and forth onto a prosthetic leg as he tossed a medicine ball to a young girl whose face resembled his. Conversation flowed with laughter and an occasional loud explosive whoop of effort.

After days of pain and confinement to his bed, Rod viewed the activity with mixed feelings then realized his hands tightly gripped the arms of the chair. *Aren't they afraid? I am.*

Carrie returned to his side. "Well, what do you think?"

"I don't know if I can do this," he muttered, shifting in his chair.

"Oh, yeah? Hey, Sanders!" she called. The man in the green shirt looked her way.

"You ready to jump? I want to watch you."

He nodded and zipped off his sweat pants.

Rod watch in awe as the soldier jumped from the floor onto a knee-high metal platform, pushing off and landing easily on the feet of his healthy leg and his gleaming prosthetic one.

200

"All right!" Carrie enthused, then turned to Rod. "Now, what do you think?" she said, then motioned the man over to introduce them.

"Gary Sanders, 75th Rangers," he said, extending his sweaty hand to Rod. "Oops, sorry," he apologized, wiping his palm on the leg of his shorts.

"Rod Strong, 25th MPs for now," Rod said, his voice trailing off. "How long did it take you to do that?" he asked, nodding at the platform.

"Almost everyone thinks they can't do the things they like to do. I'm here to make sure they learn they can do everything," Carrie said.

"What you got is a *paper cut* like mine," Sanders said then lifted the leg of his shorts to reveal the top of the sleek metal apparatus attached to the stump of his leg. "Look, I'm your *been there* buddy. I'm going to help you through this, make sure you do what Carrie says...and more!"

Carrie smiled.

"But how long?" Rod persisted. He looked up into the soldier's face.

"I got injured in February last year, was running by May or June."

"Fuck that!" Rod exclaimed, impressed, then glanced at Carrie. "Sorry, Ma'am."

"Aaaah, I've heard it all," Carrie said then added, "Let's get you started."

She pushed Rod's chair over to a vacant table, locked the wheels then handed him the crutches.

"Stand up," she said.

Rod struggled with the crutches, moving them from hand to hand as he tried to push up on his right side.

"I can't," Rod protested. His right leg felt weak and rubbery. The pain of leaving his bed remained fresh in his mind.

Carrie stood beside him and put her left arm around his back, his right arm around her neck.

"Now on the count of three, shift your weight to your right leg and STAND UP!" she said. "One, two, three!"

Rod felt Carrie lean to her right taking his weight with her, and he stood up, balanced, with the crutch under his left arm. She slipped the remaining crutch under his right arm then stepped back.

"See! You can do it!"

At first, lying on the elevated table among other soldiers while Carrie gently began to stretch his legs felt relaxing.

"We have to do both legs," she explained, because he'd been immobile for nearly two weeks.

Rod shut his eyes to focus on the conversations flowing around him. When she grasped his left thigh, elevating it, then pressing it toward the ceiling, he gasped in pain.

"Carrie! Shit! That hurts!"

She smiled. "Yep," she said and kept on pushing. "If we don't do this, the muscles behind your knee will contract and you won't be able to bend it. It's the body's way of seeking a position of comfort. We can't let that happen."

Rod clenched his jaw and began counting the tiles in the ceiling. When she finished, she tossed him a white towel.

"Mop up the sweat," Carrie demanded.

"Are we done?" Rod asked. It seemed like he'd been on the table for an hour and the pain meds Flo gave him earlier were wearing off.

"Nah, we're just getting started," Carrie said then helped him back into his wheelchair. Rod slumped forward, his hands in his lap. He had never felt weaker.

"Hey, Strong, look at this," Sanders called from across the room. Rod's head snapped up to see the soldier jump into the air and hit the rim of a basketball hoop with his fingertips.

"Fucking showoff," Rod yelled.

Sanders laughed.

For the next fifteen minutes Rod sat in his wheelchair working his shoulders and arms in a *rickshaw* machine, pushing and pulling measured weight. Conditioning his upper body would make it easier to transfer to and from bed to wheelchair on his own, Carrie told him.

"You watching the Red Sox game tonight, Strong?" Sanders asked.

"Thought I would," Rod replied, then pushed up till his biceps burned. "Sox fan?" he managed to gasp.

"Yankees!"

"Sucker," Rod said.

"You got money on the game?"

"Yeah, right. All ten bucks!" Sweat began to run into Rod's eyes, and he paused to swipe at his face with a towel.

"We'll see, my man. I'm out of here. I'll catch up to you tomorrow to hear you cry," Sanders said.

When Carrie finally came to Rod's rescue she pushed him over to another table and then helped him ease his butt onto it. He thought they were done. He looked up at her and smiled expecting praise for his accomplishments.

"Massage?" he asked her.

"Uh, uh," Carrie replied, placing two wood blocks with handles on the table. She moved them to the outside of each of his thighs then pushed them close.

"I want you to grab those handles, and lift your body just like you'd call out pushups for a drill sergeant. Give me twenty and let's hear that count."

Rod rolled his eyes and grasped the handles.

"One, two, three, four, five, six..." he kept going, feeling the blood rush to his arms and shoulders and as his mind concentrated on the count, all thoughts of pain transferred to the effort of raising his hips off the tabletop.

"Breathe!" Carrie shouted, as he neared the end of the count.

"TWENTY!" Rod's tee shirt dripped with sweat and moisture ran down his arms and into his hands. His chest heaved and he sagged back on the table panting. At once a crisp white towel flopped on his face.

"We're done for now," Carrie said.

CHAPTER THIRTY-FIVE

That evening, tired and weak from his first day's efforts, Rod watched TV trying to focus on the Red Sox game. Throughout the ward, the hoots and yells of other patients tuned to the same channel reminded him of times before the Army. He concentrated on the exuberance, letting it take him away and didn't hear the rustle of uniform and footsteps as someone entered his room.

"Great game, huh?" Sergeant Mortenson stood beside Rod's bed.

"Sure is Sarn't," Rod replied, looking up at the sergeant's smiling face. "Who's your team?"

"Yankees. You?"

"Boston. Usually the Padres, but they're not doing so good."

Just then a loud cheer erupted throughout the ward.

"Sounds like you're not the only Sox fan," Mortenson said. He reached into a pocket and took out a folded piece of paper.

"What's that?" Rod asked. Then he remembered Carrie's comment about Mortenson dropping by.

"Got some news for you 'bout your brother," Mortenson said.

The sergeant looked down to read from his notes. "Medics patched him up in the same CASH where you were, then sent him back to the 82nd. He briefed his CO on what happened. Ambush. They told him it was you who pulled him out. He'll be calling you soon." The sergeant looked pointedly at Rod.

"Damn." Rod's eyes began to burn and he looked away from Mortenson's gaze. "Thanks, Sarn't," he said softly.

"You know a Sarn't Devore?" Mortenson rushed to ask.

"Sure do!"

"He says *Hooah*."

"Hooah," Rod whispered. Then, "My mom know?"

"Yeah, Red Cross called her."

Rod sighed, grateful for the flood of relief.

"What about Tuck and the two squad leaders?" Rod asked. He reached for the plastic tumbler of water on his night table and downed the liquid.

"Scratches and bruises. You're the only one sent stateside. Lucky you."

"Yeah, right," Rod replied. "Thanks, Sarn't," Rod added.

Knowing Mike had rejoined his outfit brightened Rod's spirits.

"S'all right. That's m'job," Mortenson responded.

For a long minute the two men focused on the baseball game.

But Rod's mind spun other thoughts to its surface.

"Sarn't. About Major Boston, why'd he leave The Old Guard to come here?"

"Hell, you know he didn't have no choice in that."

"He coulda gone back to the unit, right?" Rod asked.

"S'pose so. I guess the brass figured he'd be the right guy to lead you all since he'd been in the same situation."

"But you'd think he'd want to go back. It's the most honorable unit in the Army."

Mortenson laughed.

"You tell that to your Ranger buddies, Strong. Better yet? Don't mention it at all."

Rod felt embarrassed and realized how insensitive and smug his comments must have sounded.

"You think he can help me get back?" Rod finally ventured.

"He'll do what he can," the sergeant answered, but Rod thought his response sounded guarded.

"Sorry Sarn't, I didn't mean to come off like a whiner," Rod said.

"I know. I wish my tour had taken a different turn, too," Mortenson said a bit wistfully. Then his next comment confirmed it.

"I'd like to be back in-country. Now."

A loud roar resounded through the halls interrupting their conversation as the game ended.

"Those guys too," Rod added.

"Humph! I'll see you later, Strong. Gotta go find a brewski to drown my sorrows," Sgt. Mortenson said.

After the sergeant left, in spite of being exhausted from the day's events, Rod grabbed the now very worn calendar from his nightstand and looked back through the pages, then triumphantly wrote *Step 12* across June. He relaxed against his pillows and for the first time in weeks embraced the luxury of hope.

———

Rod hadn't realized he'd dozed off, until a hand on his shoulder woke him. Ricky G stood over the bed. He looked up, confused until he saw the silhouettes of two men standing outside in the hall. The sergeant turned away and waved them in.

"It's 1900, how come you're not up walking the shadow line?"

"Ortiz! Mathews! What the hell are you guys doing here?"

"They were hanging around outside your door, not knowing if they should come in," Sgt. Goldman said.

"We just found out you're back," Mathews explained, leaning over to grab Rod's arm in a brief hug.

Rod winced.

"Hey, I hurt you?" Mathews asked.

"No, just sore from therapy exercises. They're brutal."

"Sorry, Strong."

"It's good to see you guys!" Rod said quickly to cover his embarrassment, taking in the neat appearance of his friends. Their trim haircuts and clean-shaven jaws emphasized how grimy he felt. He knew he smelled bad.

"Well? Give. What happened?" Mathews said, resting his hands on the footboard of Rod's bed. Ortiz plopped down in the chair nearby.

Rod told them about the earthquake and its aftermath. He didn't tell them everything. Not how scared he was at the Taliban encampment, nor details about his injury. Most of that he couldn't remember anyway.

Sergeant Goldman moved about the room, getting Rod's meds ready and laying out the dressings to change his bandages.

"You meet my buddy, Ricky G here? We were in Ranger school together. Son-of-a-bitch saved my life."

Ortiz bumped Goldman's fist. Mathews shook his hand.

Rod gazed at the faces of his two friends, thinking except for Mike and Goldman, they were the most welcome sights he'd seen in months.

"What've you guys been up too?" Rod asked, eager for news of The Old Guard.

"Same old, same old," Ortiz said, then glanced at Mathews.

"That's okay, you tell 'im," Mathews said.

"We both made sergeant!" Ortiz said. "Cook's a Specialist and Jackson passed him up and is working on being a sergeant, too. Would you believe those two?"

"No. Alright! Good goin' you guys! Sarn't Ortiz, Sarn't Mathews...sounds kinda weird. Do I have to call you that here?"

"No, you dumb shit!" Ortiz said.

"But you better do it outside this room, or else...I'll *smoke* ya," Mathews insisted. Both men laughed loudly.

"You guys watch the game?" Rod asked.

"Who didn't?" Ortiz replied.

For a minute or two the three men traded comments about the Yankee's pitching and the Red Sox record win.

Ortiz stared at the mound of Rod's bandaged stump under the blanket, and as his expression shifted, he grew quiet.

"No yak, yak Ortiz?" Rod teased. In the excitement of the game, then seeing his buddies, the pain of the day vanished. He longed for the normalcy of his friend's incessant chatter.

"Yeah. Sorry. Thinking about that," he pointed to Rod's leg.

"This is nothing, there's guys here way worse than me," he said. For the first time in days, he felt something other than self-pity.

"I'm going to be back ready to compete for a spot," Rod said.

"Listen to you! Hooah!" Mathews said.

"You need help with that, let us know," Ortiz promised.

"Sure!" Mathews said. "We both got time off...Barton, too. Fuck, maybe Sarn't Owen would help."

"Not that tight ass," Ortiz said. "Sarn't complained about you leaving for weeks after," he added. "Thought you had friends in high places."

"I don't." Rod looked back and forth between the two men. "If I did, I'd sure like to see the SOBs right now."

"Okay, guys, that's it for now," Goldman said, coming to the side of the bed. "Rod's gotta get some rest. He has PT at 0700 tomorrow, then again at 1300."

"What?" Rod complained. "Twice a day? Ah, shit."

The good-natured banter of his friend's voices grew faint as they walked down the hallway and Rod yearned to be with them, headed back to Echo Company Barracks. Soon they'd be sitting in front of a TV shining their shoes. They'd be talking about Iraq and Afghanistan, the new guys, their plans for the weekend. Ortiz would be picking almost invisible bits of lint from his blues, concentrating on the appearance of his uniform. They'd go for a beer afterwards then hang around Mathews' room playing Poker. Rod counted their footsteps and sighed.

––––––––

By the time Donna and Beth arrived, Rod's attitude had soured. Neither Major Boston nor Sergeant Mortenson had been back to see him, and concerned that the stump of his thigh remained swollen, Doc Higgins' orders meant Flo and Goldman checked the incision on his leg for infection on each shift. Finally, the occupational therapist sent to retrain him to dress himself fled in frustration leaving him shivering and naked when he threw his pants across the room.

He no longer saw the brightness and beauty of the late summer landscape out the windows of the atrium. Instead he focused on the long cold corridors that protected him and kept the world at bay. His arms burned from the effort of pushing his body weight up from the wheel chair each morning. The excruciating pain of two-a-day rehabilitation wore on him, and for all Sanders' support, one day his spirits would be up, the next, down. In spite of Chaplain Garrity's comforting visits, on Friday night when Flo announced Beth and Donna would arrive Saturday morning, his comment was terse.

"I don't want to see them," Rod said, then turned his back on her.

CHAPTER THIRTY-SIX

"Sure you do," a gruff voice said. "They're about all you have right now, brother."

Rod looked up from his wheelchair to see a man standing in the doorway, arms crossed against his chest. No uniform, but his bearing hinted at command.

"May I?" the man said.

He gestured toward the chair in the room then ambled over and sat down, not waiting for Rod's approval. Lamplight spilled over his face, casting a shadow that hooded his eyes.

Gotta be another shrink, Rod thought, remembering the skinny doctor who'd walked him through the post-deployment health assessment interview a week or so after he got to Walter Reed. No soldier wanted to admit anything was wrong, especially a Ranger, or Old Guard, so he'd answered "fine" and "no" as many times as he could. He'd fooled the guy, for sure.

"What do you want?" Rod said.

He looked at the man's worn brown Nomex jacket and his blue ball cap squared neatly over cropped white hair.

Then Rod spotted the Master Army Aviator badge alongside a 1st Aviation Brigade medallion pinned to his cap and the unit patch on his sleeve.

"Vietnam?" Rod asked.

"Yep, that and more." The man stuck out his hand.

"Terence Taylor, former Chief Warrant Officer, now retired, and sometimes just *tired*." Taylor smiled, his lined face opening in an expressive gesture of welcome.

"How'd ya lose the leg?" he asked.

"I don't want to talk about it," Rod said.

"Sure you do. Just like you want to see your mom and your girlfriend. You just don't want to admit it."

"Fuck you! What do you know about me? You're sitting there all smug, *Mr. Vietnam Vet*, walking and talking like you know me, but you don't know shit about what happened to me."

Rod's blood pressure began to rise and the bandage on his stump started to itch.

"I do know, son," Taylor said reaching out to touch Rod's hand.

Rod snatched his hand back, as if the man's fingers had burned him.

"Keep your freakin' hands off me!"

He could feel the stump of his left leg starting to hurt, and reached for the call switch that would summon Goldman.

"Alright, alright...no problem," Taylor said, throwing up his hands, then sitting back in his chair.

Instead of Ricky G, the late shift nurse opened the door and hustled in, seeming more harried than usual. Her Army blouse hung outside her ACU trousers, barely hiding the baby bump preceding her.

"What's up, honey pie?" she asked, raising her eyebrows.

"Where's Sarn't Goldman?" Rod asked. *"And who are you?"* he griped.

"Oh, he went home hours ago," the nurse said, ignoring his tone of voice.

She massaged the small of her back then threw her shoulders back and stretched.

"I need meds. My leg hurts." Rod frowned at her.

The nurse turned her attention to Taylor.

"Oh, hellooo, Chief, I see you've made a new friend."

"Evening, Louise," the man said.

"Not my friend," Rod growled. "I said I need meds."

"Well, the Chief here's your friend whether you know it or not," Louise said, ignoring his request.

She bent her head to flip through the pages on Rod's chart.

Rod turned to look at the curious man who'd taken up residency in his bedside chair. The Chief leaned back and gazed at him then smiled. Fully relaxed and as if they'd known each other for years, he pulled out a paperback book and began to read.

"Do I get another shot?" Rod demanded, his voice angry.

He focused his attention on the nurse.

"No sweetie, you get Tylenol. I'll go get a couple of caps," Louise replied.

"So, you leaving?" Rod directed his terse question to the Chief then hoisted himself from the wheelchair to the edge of his bed.

"Nope, got nowhere to go right now."

When Louise returned with a small paper cup containing two white caplets, Rod downed them quickly and flopped back on his pillow. He tried counting the tiles in the ceiling over his bed to lull him to sleep. It always worked in the past, but his eyes kept straying to the pool of light falling on the Chief's book as the man turned the pages.

At last his eyelids grew heavy. He welcomed the familiar warmth and contentment of his pain receding and fell into a deep sleep.

In a dream it seemed as if a golden haired angel bending near his face brushed his cheek with her lips. He felt her feathery touch and breathed in the scent of lemonade. A voice called his name, first softly, then with urgent passion.

"Rod? Rod? Wake up baby! It's me!"

His eyes fluttered open banishing what seemed to be the mirage of translucent memory to see Beth sitting on the side of his bed, her slender hand grasping his.

It was morning and the Chief was gone.

"Hi!" he whispered, his expression relaxed and sweet. "Come here," he pleaded, pulling her to him.

Beth buried her face against his shoulder and her tears dampened his neck against the collar of his tee shirt.

"Hey, hey!" he said, pushing her back. "What's this? I'm okay!"

He reached up and brushed away the tears streaking her cheek.

"I am so happy to see you," Beth murmured, then dabbed at her eyes with a tissue she held tightly.

"Me, too," an unmistakable voice said.

Rod looked up to see his mom standing behind Beth.

"Come here, Mom," Rod said, opening his arms wide as Beth and his mother traded places.

Questions and answers flew back and forth until Rod had explained everything; at least what little he remembered. Finally, the room grew quiet.

Rod learned the two women made plans to help him before they arrived. Beth and Donna would stay at Mologne House where Rod could visit they explained. Donna put herself in charge of Rod's paperwork and scheduling while Beth took on the role of rehabilitation cheerleader.

"And who are these lovely ladies?" Flo asked.

She walked through the door with an armload of fresh towels for the bathroom and linens for his bed.

"Beth, my fiancé and my mom, Donna," Rod explained.

"Oh, really," Flo teased. "As if I didn't suspect."

"How's my boy doing?" Donna asked, adopting a professional tone, nurse to nurse, her tone serious.

"Well except for the complaining, I'd say he's doing just fine!" Flo assured her.

Donna beamed. "He's all Army," she said proudly.

"Oh, I heard all about his daddy and your other son. You must be very proud," Flo said, looking up as the clatter of trays knocking against a metal dolly echoed down the hallway. Each time the noise stopped, a male voice called out.

"Breakfast's here," Flo said, staring at Rod with a stern look.

"You eat everything on that tray, hear?"

"Yes, ma'am," Rod answered meekly, pulling the corners of his mouth down into a mock frown.

"See Mom, I'm taken care of just fine," he said, directing his expression at Donna.

After breakfast and Rod had proudly dressed himself, Donna and Beth walked alongside his wheelchair as he headed for the MATC.

Anxious to show them what he'd accomplished so far, he sought out Carrie. He found her helping a tough looking man tottering on two prosthetic legs hesitatingly along the parallel bars. The man's shirt clung to his back and beads of moisture dripped from his chin. White whiskers sprouted from his cheeks and chin.

"Rod!" Carrie called out. "Come here and meet Sergeant Major Wolf."

Rod rolled his chair close to the NCO, Beth trailing behind him.

"Please to meet you Sarn't Major," he said, smiling up at the man.

The sergeant major looked down at Rod and grunted, bowed his head, took a breath and stood straighter.

"Good to go, Soldier," he said.

By the time Rod and Beth returned to his room following the afternoon PT session, his energy had ebbed. The sutures closing the incision itched and deep aching pain that seemed to come from inside his bone, throbbed.

"I gotta take a nap, babe," he said to Beth.

A nurse's aide had dropped off two Tylenol capsules for him along with a fresh glass of ice water.

"Hand me that?" he said, gesturing to the medicine.

His arms were leaden from the overexertion of showing Beth how well he had progressed, and new blisters forming on his hands reminded him he forgot his gloves. As the two of them relaxed, the room became quiet and he didn't feel Beth's gentle kiss, nor hear her say she'd be back later.

CHAPTER THIRTY-SEVEN

Beth and Donna by his side every day soon wore thin. Since the day he enlisted, he'd been on his own for almost two years, and now Donna treated him like a child again. Beth would go from becoming quiet, twisting the engagement ring on her finger nervously, to vivacious and talkative. He needed to escape their smothering.

He sighed with relief when Chaplain Garrity and Staff Sergeant Mortenson finally convinced the two women to follow up on the help offered by the Soldier Family Assistance Center.

Two weeks after they arrived, when Beth told him she needed to do laundry and Donna had appointments with his patient care advocate, Rod zipped down to the MATC to get in an extra workout. With the rickshaw, free weights and parallel bars now seeming easy on one leg, his confidence had returned and he grew impatient for more improvement. The Walter Reed doctors assured him his target for recovery loomed close, but the next step, the mold for his stump seemed days away. Until that happened, his progress stopped.

"Hey, buddy, don't overdo it now," Sanders warned, glancing at a glassed in room where Carrie could be seen conducting a staff meeting.

Rod maneuvered himself onto the seat of a pull–down machine, and grunted through two sets.

"No problem," Rod wheezed, then pulled down the horizontal bar behind his head again.

Sweat poured down his red face and arms and into his hands. When his grip slipped, the heavy bar hit him on the back of his head and the pulley weight slammed down in a shuddering crash. Rod reached out to grab onto the bar, but it flew out of his grasp knocking him off the seat onto the floor. He landed on his left side.

"Aaaah," he screamed closing his eyes against the pounding pain. At the sound, a door banged open and Carrie ran to his side.

"What were you thinking?" she demanded. "Are you trying to get me fired?"

"I told you take it easy," Sanders said. He stood over Rod looking down at him, shaking his head.

Rod face had gone white and he felt weak and cold. A bead of perspiration lined his upper lip.

Carrie reached out and touched his hand. "Clammy!"

"I'm okay. I am really," Rod said, trying to sit up.

"Get me a blanket, quick," Carrie yelled to a therapist nearby.

"Sanders, go get his wheelchair and bring it over here."

Within seconds Rod sat slumped in his chair, wincing from fresh pain in his thigh. A warm blanket covered him. Carrie spun the chair around then wheeled him out of the busy gym taking the hallway back to his room in long strides.

"I told you to keep to the exercises on your chart. And not to do anything without my okay," she fumed. "How many times have you done this?"

"Just this once," Rod replied.

"Liar!" Carrie said, then stopped and came around to the front of the chair. "I know you feel better, and in your mind, everything is fine. But that", she said pointing at his stump, "takes longer to heal that you think."

"Oh, my God!" Carrie stared at the white sock pulled over his stump. A pink stain oozed fresh near the incision.

By the time he got back in bed, Doctor Higgins had been called and Flo began preparations to remove the bandages. Carrie stood by his side.

Doc Higgins entered the room at a run.

"What've we got here?" he asked, peering closely at the swollen pink incision on the stump of Rod's thigh now laid bare of bandages.

"It's infected, Strong", he said. "The mold for your leg can't be made until it's cleared up and the swelling is gone. It may be a week. Or longer. Sorry. Take your meds and keep your fingers crossed." Higgins turned to go but stopped. "Any questions?" he asked.

"Did I do this?"

"Probably not, but make sure the bandages stay in place and don't put any added stress on that area for a least a week. All right?"

"Yes, sir," Rod said then looked over at Carrie, who rolled her eyes.

"Okay, I got it," he said, feeling at that moment time had stopped.

After he'd taken his evening meds, he pointed the TV remote at the set mounted on the far wall and aimlessly clicked through the channels.

"Well, how you doin' tonight, hot shot?"

Terry Taylor lounged in the doorway. Without his blue ball cap, his white hair glowed in the light from the hallway. He had a book under his arm and a brown paper bag in his hand.

"Fine," Rod said, then wondered where the old guy had been for the past few days.

"Don't sound like you're fine," Taylor said moving to the chair beside Rod's bed.

"And you're here, why?" Rod asked.

"Brought you something," Taylor said, holding out the bag.

CHAPTER THIRTY-EIGHT

The aroma of the Big Mac made Rod's mouth water.

"Hey, all right!" he exclaimed, ripping the bag open to reveal the hefty hamburger and a pile of fries in the bottom.

"Just a little treat to keep your spirits up," Taylor said.

"Nothing wrong with my spirits a good leg wouldn't fix," Rod said through a mouthful of burger.

"I heard your mold got postponed. Flo told me."

"Me wanting to hurry things up made it worse," Rod admitted.

"Have you seen the big Swede in the prosthetics lab yet?"

"Nuh, uh, nobody's been by."

"I'm going to see if he'll drop in on you. Explain the steps. It might make you feel better. Like there's some progress."

"Whatever," Rod said. "French fry?" He offered the greasy sack.

Taylor shook his head. "Can't eat that stuff anymore."

The man leaned back in his chair watching Rod, and narrowed his eyes.

"What?" Rod asked.

"Are you glad your honey and mom are here after all?" Taylor asked.

Rod sighed. "Most of the time, yeah. But sometimes I catch Beth looking at me differently. And, my mom treats me like a kid! I gotta tell her to back off. Then she gets this sad look on her face. Oh, shit, I just wish all this could be over."

"I think I know how you feel," Taylor said.

"No you don't," Rod bristled. "You're sitting there with two good legs, a vet who volunteers to keep soldiers from going

221

over the edge. I didn't ask you to come in here you know," Rod said.

"I'm not a volunteer." Taylor said then pushed up from his chair.

"Then why are you here?" Rod demanded.

Taylor raised his pants leg to reveal a gleaming black prosthetic limb.

"To get a new one of these," he said quietly, releasing the fabric to crease neatly at the top of his shoe.

"So are you really a vet?" Rod asked.

"I am. And the boys here in the lab change my leg for me whenever a new version comes out."

"New version?" Rod asked. "I thought you got one and that was that."

"Nope, that's why I'll go talk to the Swede. Get him down here to see you."

"Hey, Chief, how're you doing tonight?" a familiar voice called from the open door. "They taking care of you okay?" Sergeant Goldman strode in with a tray of meds that he set on the bedside table.

"Just fine, thank you for asking," Taylor said heading for the door. "I'll send the Swede by, and I'll drop in again soon," he called over his shoulder.

"You know that guy?" Rod asked Goldman.

"Hell, yeah. Pretty tough, that one. Still working for Uncle Sam," Goldman replied.

"You mean in the Army?"

"Sort of. He's a contractor. He's a flight instructor for the Iraqi Army. Didn't he tell you he flew in Vietnam?"

"You mean he can fly an aircraft with a prosthetic leg?"

"Not only an aircraft, but a chopper," Goldman said. "He's famous."

"I'll be damned", Rod said, then tossed down the meds and crossed his arms behind his head against the pillows. "I'll be damned," he repeated softly.

After Sergeant Goldman left, Rod began to think of his own possibilities for the first time. He looked around his room at the Old Guard posters pinned to the wall and the layers of get well cards on the small dresser. He smiled and resolved to follow Doc Higgins' and Carrie's instructions without fail then began to plot his return to the Old Guard.

At that moment, his phone rang.

A deep male voice squawked in his ear. Rod's jaw dropped and he felt a rush of emotion so big he could barely speak.

"Mike! Where you been?"

CHAPTER THIRTY-NINE

Donna and Beth arrived the next morning laden with mail and a bouquet of daffodils.

Beth took a vase to the sink in his bathroom and Rod heard her humming as she tossed out dead flowers and arranged fresh ones.

His mother pulled a chair to the side of his bed and held up the brightly colored bunch of envelopes.

Donna sorted them neatly and put them on the blanket beside Rod's hand.

"Thanks Mom, I'll look at them later," he said. "Mike called last night. We talked for a half hour."

"I know," she said. "He called me too. I was so relieved just to hear his voice. He didn't give me any real details. Probably holding back so I won't worry. What did you two talk about?" Donna asked.

"Everything. He's coming home on leave soon, but I guess you know that," Rod said.

Actually, Mike shared more details with Rod than he expected. Capture by the Taliban scared him, he said. His injuries healed, but he gave up fighting the nightmares that kept him groggy and confessed he was seeing a shrink regularly. He made Rod promise not to tell Mom.

Donna smiled and nodded, her expression relaxed and happy. Her two sons were safe.

Then her prattle resumed. "Today's the day you get measured for your leg, right?" she said, her voice full of optimism.

"Can we go with you?" Beth asked.

"It's going to be another week," Rod told them. "The lab's backed up," he lied.

Donna's expression changed to resignation. "Well, I guess that's how it is with the war and all."

Rod changed the subject. "What's with your job, Mom? The hospital can't be letting you take off all this time with pay," he asked.

Donna looked over at Beth before she replied.

"I have two options. One, I go back to work next week, or two, I take a small second mortgage on the house to pay expenses there while I stay here."

"*No*, Mom. No second on the house," Rod said. "I'll be just fine here. The Army's taking care of me. No borrowing. You can't afford it!"

Rod looked up at Beth who'd come to stand behind his mother and drape her arm over her shoulders.

"And what about you?"

"Now don't get upset Rod, I'm taking off one semester. That's all. I can go back anytime. Right now my place is here with you."

"Oh, God, things are so out of control!" Rod cried, feeling guilt as the weight of their decisions closed in on him. He looked around franticly, "I gotta get out of this room. Bring the chair over here."

———

He'd forgotten August meant tourists in D.C. as Beth and Donna walked to the Atrium alongside him. More people than ever strolled the halls; some with a Public Affairs officer leading tours.

Leafy shade blanketed the hospital Atrium. Hidden in the shadows of the raised flowerbeds, Impatiens bloomed fiercely in hues of purple, lavender and pink. Rod rolled his chair to the center where sunshine illuminated a wooden table and warmed his face.

After an hour of reading cards and letters from friends and family, Donna looked over at him with a quizzical expression.

"No physical therapy today?"

"No, ma'am," Rod said, feeling the muscles in his jaw tense. "Carrie said to cut back a few days," he added.

"That's not like her," Beth commented.

"You don't know her!" Rod said, his voice loud in the tranquil setting.

"Why are you acting like this?" Donna asked him.

"I'll tell you!" He drew in a big breath. "My leg's infected. I can't get fitted until it's healed and shrunk back down. Maybe two weeks or more. Now you know!" he shouted, then wrenched his chair around and rolled out of the sunny garden room into the hallway.

"Rod!" Beth called, jumping up to run after him.

"Just leave me alone!" he cried, leaving Beth and his mother standing speechless.

———

When he got back to his room, he slammed the door then hoisted himself from the chair onto the edge of his bed to sit trembling. Tears welled in his eyes and he swiped the back of his hand across them.

His sobs echoed in the room and he flung himself face down on his pillow to muffle the sound. When he felt a warm hand on his back, he turned his face to the side to see Chaplain Garrity standing there.

"You okay?" the chaplain asked, holding out a glass of cold water. "Drink."

Rod sat up and downed the water, then smiled weakly.

"Thanks. Don't tell anyone, okay?" he pleaded. "I mean I don't usually cry about stuff you know."

"I know."

"Are my mom and fiancé still here?"

"They went back to Mologne House. Said to tell you they'd be back after dinner."

"Yeah, I got some explaining to do. And apologize..."

Chaplain Garrity interrupted. "Well, while you're thinking about that, there's someone out in the hall wants to see you. Chief sent him over. It's the guy who makes the prosthetic limbs," he explained. "He's busy, you want to see him or not?" The chaplain cocked his head, his winged eyebrows up in question.

Rod straightened his tee shirt. "You bet I do," he said. "Send him in!"

CHAPTER FORTY

"Good afternoon," a deep voice said from the doorway.

"I'm Nils Larsson. The Chief said you want to walk again and I'm your man."

The *Swede*'s six foot five inch frame seemed to fill the room. From Rod's limited vantage in his bed, the man's cropped blond hair and hawk-like nose gave him the look of a super hero. Starched tan chinos and a black polo shirt with an embroidered WRAMC logo on the breast pocket added to his imposing nature.

"You're the only official person who's come in to talk to me about it," Rod said.

"Usually one of the techs who works for me checks in first," Nils said. "But the Chief told me you have a special need, so I thought I'd stop in and see what it is."

"I do, but I'm waiting for an infection to clear up," Rod said. "After that I'm good to go," he added, trying to keep the disappointment out of his voice.

Nils took a thorough look at Rod's chart.

"Seems the swelling is already going down. That's promising."

"Maybe if I knew what's next, I'd heal faster," Rod said.

"You been down to the lab yet?"

Rod shook his head.

"Come on then, let's get you in your chair. I got something to show you," the Swede said.

Nils hit a button on the wall outside the lab. When the door slid open it revealed a long light-filled room set up with U-shaped workstations. A high stool and apparatus that resembled a vice for turning wood crowded each one. Instead of an ornate table leg on the vice, it clamped an odd-shaped plaster cast.

Nearby, large open drums held casts of limbs tagged with the names of the troops they belonged to. The lab buzzed with noisy conversation, the whine of machinery and uniformed men like Larsson coming and going.

"I saw a Marine walking up and down the hall when we came up here. He stopped every few feet or so to let one of your guys adjust the screws on his prosthetic knee. Why did he need to do that?" Rod asked, looking up at Nils.

The Swede smiled. "To match his gait. He wants to return to duty. Walking, marching. Needs to run to keep in shape."

"Running?"

A thought began to form in Rod's mind. "Do you have special feet?" he asked.

"Like how?"

"Feet that can roll out," Rod said.

"You mean when you step down, your foot rolls out?"

"Yeah, that's it!"

"Sure, Flex-Foot makes a model that will do that."

"Can I get that?" Rod asked.

He leaned forward in his chair, excited and eager.

"You know Tomb Guards have that special walk? With that foot I think I can do it!"

"The foot can mechanically do what you want, but it's up to you to make it happen," the man said.

229

Rod reached out to shake the Swede's hand enthusiastically. "Thanks!" he said, then wheeled his chair around toward the door.

"Hey, you want me to push you back?" Nils asked.

Instead of responding, Rod mentally ticked off step 14 on his calendar and sped out into the hall back toward Ward 57.

CHAPTER FORTY-ONE

His plan to regain his life began to crystallize after meeting Nils Larsson. First he had to apologize to his mother and Beth. He had everything planned out to say, but when Donna and his fiancé arrived in a cloud of perfume and bright summer dresses, he did little more than grab their hands tightly, his eyes glistening with tears.

"What's this?" Donna asked, immediately sinking onto the side of his bed, a worried expression knitting her brow.

He sniffed. "Sorry, Mom," he said, then smiled and took a deep breath.

"Honey, why are you crying," Beth murmured, leaning in to kiss his cheek.

Their concern increased his guilt. *I am so freakin' selfish.*

"I'm sorry for what I said earlier," he said, looking from Mom's face to Beth's. I know that both of you are in this with me. I'm grateful. Some of the guys have no one. I have the two most beautiful women in the world supporting me." His voice grew thick. "I love you both."

"Son, there was no doubt in my mind. Ever," Donna said. "We're your family. That's us, and Mike! By the way, he says to tell you *Hooah!*"

"You heard from Mike again?" Rod asked, brightening, his voice rising.

Donna smiled. "I did!" she said.

"He's with his unit. Still in Afghanistan and he's back in action," Beth said.

"He told me all that when I talked to him, but I thought he was holding something back."

"Apparently not," Beth assured him.

"Nothing permanent then?" Rod asked, remembering the limp form of his brother when he dragged him under fire across the clearing that night.

Donna shook her head.

"Mom, excuse me for changing the subject, but what's happening with you and Major General Shafter?" Rod asked.

"Well, we're still seeing each other, if that's what you mean." Donna's eyes lit up as she replied. "He's been following your progress. He likes you a lot, you know. Still thinking you might be interested in West Point." She pursed her lips and peered over her glasses.

Beth turned to look at him, a questioning expression on her face.

"Mom, I gotta get over this hurdle first," Rod said.

"I know, but don't be surprised if he pays you a visit one of these days. He comes to the Pentagon every so often for meetings."

"And what about Eric? Anyone hear from him?" Rod asked.

"He's still in-country," Beth said. "I got a call from his sister asking about you, and she told me he'd made Sergeant. Somewhere in Anbar Province running patrols along with trucks carrying supplies."

Rod flinched.

When Donna finally asked about the progress of the infection in his leg, Rod related the day's events and told them all about Nils and the crew in the prosthetic lab.

"Well then, since I'm leaving in a few hours, I guess Beth will have a lot more help getting you well," Donna said enthusiastically.

Just then Sergeant Goldman stuck his head through the doorway. "Hey Hotrod, you have space for more visitors?"

"Bring 'em on," he said.

Ortiz and Mathews crowded into the small room, trailing Cook and Jackson behind them.

"How's our boy tonight?" Ortiz said, his broad smile flashing.

"Hey, guys! Come on in! Meet my fiancé, Beth Gooding and my mom, Donna Strong."

Rod turned toward the women, feeling his face grow hot. Mathews laughed.

"These are my friends from the Guard," Rod explained.

"We know who they are," Donna said. "They've been here before. When you were out of it." Donna glanced at her watch. "Oh, my gosh, I gotta go. Beth, you want to go back with me while I check out?"

She looked pointedly at Rod's friends.

"My plane leaves in three hours."

Beth nodded.

Rod pulled his mom close. "You take care of yourself, okay? I'll be just fine, and I'll call you. I'm going to get out of here sooner than you expect. Don't worry."

Donna leaned over and hugged Rod almost as hard as she had the day he left for Basic Training.

With that, Donna and Beth said their goodbyes.

Mathews and Ortiz pulled chairs up to his bed and Cook and Jackson plopped down on either side.

"Okay, what gives?" Mathews demanded.

"Yeah, you called and said you had something to tell us. You needed our help," Cook said.

Rod looked at each of their earnest faces knowing the fifteenth step toward his goal would soon fall into place.

CHAPTER FORTY-TWO

"Guys, I want to come back to The Old Guard," Rod said.

"How?" Cook asked.

"What exactly do you want to do?" Ortiz asked.

"I'm going to be a Sentinel. Period." Rod said. He looked from face to face, his expression defiant. "And I want you guys to help me do it. What do you say?"

Mathews stood up. "What can we do to help you?"

Rod explained his plan to recover and return, telling them he wanted to set up a schedule once he had his prosthesis.

"Like a calendar when you guys can come here, or take me there, so I can practice walking."

The soldiers looked skeptical.

Finally, Mathews spoke up.

"Look Strong, that's going to take a lot of work on your part but I'll draw up a schedule like you want, with each of us slotted in when we're off duty. I'll e-mail it to you. Okay?"

Rod knew his friends weren't convinced, but alone he couldn't face the challenge. With their help he'd do it because he owed them and he owed it to his dad.

"That's great. Thanks!" Rod said, reaching out to grasp his friend's hand and shake it. "I really appreciate it. I really do."

The schedule arrived the next day. "We're ready when you are," Mathews wrote.

Rod scanned the names of soldiers who volunteered to help. Two stood out: Sergeants Owen and Hawkins.

While he waited, he worked out, using a walker to travel to the MATC and along the Ward 57 hallways until pain and fatigue forced him to a chair. He enlisted Carrie to help, explaining his goal and asking for specific exercises to accomplish it. With her eager supervision, his progress became defined. Yet, no matter how much endurance he believed he had, the preparation for learning to walk again turned out to be more difficult than he anticipated.

———

By mid-September, Rod regained strength in his upper body and right leg. The mold of his left leg had been made when Nils Larsson stopped by to report on the progress of the prosthetic. To celebrate Rod's achievements, Beth arranged a romantic night out for them, and he stood in the bathroom shaving, balanced against the sink.

"Hey Rod, you decent?" Nils asked, tapping on the half-open bathroom door.

"Sure, what's up?" He glanced up to see Nils' huge shoulders filling the doorway.

"Good news for you. Tomorrow we add the plate for your prosthetic and you'll get a temporary leg and foot. This time tomorrow, you'll be a two-legged soldier again."

"No shit! What time?" Rod asked, excited for the first time in weeks.

"Come on down at 0900. You're first up for the day," Nils said, then warned, "Now don't do anything stupid tonight."

"Yes, sir," Rod said. It was all he could do to finish shaving for the wide grin on his face.

On the way to the Old Ebbitt Grill for their first real night out, Rod related the details of Nils' visit, and explained how he wanted to start using the calendar Mathews sent as soon as possible.

Beth stayed strangely quiet.

CHAPTER FORTY-THREE

"Don't you want me to do this?" Rod asked once they'd been seated in the dining room.

"No, I'm glad and all, I just wonder where I fit into all this," she said, then looked up as their waiter flicked a lighter at the candle on their table and placed menus in front of them.

"Fit in? I don't understand."

"Well, to do this you will have to move out of the ward, and that means Mologne house or one of the dorms."

"So?"

Her attitude and comments flustered him.

Beth set aside the menu and looked into Rod's eyes.

"I can't move in with you. Mologne House is for married families and the dorms for single soldiers. What am I going to do?" Beth asked, her expressive blue eyes wide and questioning.

"Let's get married. Now," Rod blurted.

Beth stared at him then began to cry.

"What's wrong?" Rod asked, reaching across the table to grasp her hands.

"I've been wearing your ring for almost two years and this is the first time you've said anything about setting a date. I'm just surprised," Beth murmured.

"My fault," Rod said. "Since I lost my leg, all I've thought about is me."

"No, you're right, your getting well is the most important thing. I'm sorry Rod, you just surprised me."

She looked into his eyes. Rod saw compassion there, and love. If he ever doubted her feelings for him, no doubt existed now.

Back in his room after dinner, Rod and Beth sat on the side of his bed with their heads bent over a yellow lined pad making lists. One side held the names of his friends to invite. Beth's shorter list included her family and best friend from high school. At once serious, then silly, Rod believed he had never felt better.

"What the heck is going on in here?" Sergeant Goldman asked. He'd brought Rod's nightly caplets of Tylenol to help him sleep.

Rod looked up. "We're going to get married. Beth and I want Chaplain Garrity to perform the ceremony."

"Well, *laissez les bon temps roulez*! That is big news, Hotrod. 'Bout time you took care of that," the sergeant said.

"Goldman, I can't ever repay you for all you've done for me, except maybe this," Rod said, growing serious. "How about standing up with me?" he asked.

"Sure thing, ami! I'd be honored," the sergeant replied with a big smile lighting his face.

"What day?" Rod asked, turning to Beth.

"That depends on Chaplain Garrity and how soon I can pull this together," she responded. She stood up and grabbed her purse. "You get some sleep and leave the rest to me," she said. "I have to hurry and put in for a change of status at Mologne so they'll keep a place for us."

Rod leaned back against his pillows then held out his hand to Beth.

She bent to kiss him and whispered, "I love you."

CHAPTER FORTY-FOUR

On the day of their wedding Beth arrived early, dragging behind her a large suitcase for Rod's belongings. Within an hour, everything fit into it snugly and after Rod told everyone goodbye, the two of them began their slow walk to Mologne House.

Once on the broad sidewalk outside, Rod stopped and looked back.

Hues of red and yellow tinged the trees planted adjacent to Walter Reed and a brisk wind scattered dry leaves along the ground.

"What's the matter," Beth asked. "Did you forget something?"

Rod shook his head and turned back to her.

————

When Beth walked down the aisle of the chapel, with Donna beaming from her seat in the front row and his buddies from The Old Guard lined up beside Goldman, the realization that his life had changed once again came as a jolt. For a moment his expression grew somber.

"Are you all right?" Beth mouthed.

Rod nodded and smiled, then felt Goldman's hand under his elbow. The moment of uncertainty passed as Chaplain Garrity's words resonated in the intimate gathering.

"I now pronounce you man and wife!" Garrity announced moments later to the instant applause of the small wedding party.

Beth held Rod's hand tightly as they turned around to face tearful faces and a chorus of congratulations.

That night, Rod sat on the side of the double bed in their room, stripped to the waist, still wearing his uniform trousers. He stared at the closed door to the bathroom, listening to Beth's movements inside. When she emerged, wearing the short silk nightgown he'd help her choose, he gasped.

She came to the side of the bed and sat beside him. In the low light of the bedside lamp, her face looked soft and beautiful.

"Are you getting undressed?" she asked quietly. "I hope so."

"Beth, I...I wanted this marriage more than you know, but you didn't have to go through with it. I'm not the same man anymore," Rod stammered. "You didn't have to do this."

Beth kissed him gently on the cheek then touched his lips with her fingertips.

"Shhhh, honey, I love you." She dropped her hand to his belt and began to loosen it. "No matter what."

Three weeks later, Rod reported for the final fitting of his new walking limb.

Nils Larsson waved the Flex-Foot over his head as Rod entered the lab.

Rod leaned back in the hard metal chair and removed his prosthetic and handed it to Larsson. The shock of cold air hitting the damp sock covering his leg surprised him. Now so used to putting on one of his prosthetics each morning to work out in the MATC, or walk around the Walter Reed Medical Center for appointments, he felt naked and helpless without it.

"Brought my spits," Rod said, holding up the heavy black shoes he'd last worn the week before he flew to Afghanistan. He'd stayed up late last night polishing them, even went so far as to burnish the metal plates on the inside of the soles. While he rubbed the black wax into the leather he could almost hear the distinctive click of the Tomb Guard's turn he'd practiced so many months ago.

Immediately he substituted the sneaker on his right foot for one of the highly polished shoes. He eagerly slipped on the prosthetic, shoved the foot into the left shoe, quickly tied the laces, stood up and looked down at the identical feet of an Army Sentinel.

"Son of a gun," he whispered.

"Let's see you walk...normally. I gotta make sure the fit is perfect," Larsson instructed.

He pointed to the hallway beyond the door to the lab.

"Out there."

By 1800 Nils and Rod agreed no further adjustments were needed. He replaced his old prosthetic, tucked the new walking leg and foot under his arm, grabbed the shoe box containing his spits and headed home.

Sitting in the Metro car rumbling toward his stop, it dawned on Rob that of all the steps he'd taken so far, this one might just be the most significant on his way back to rejoining The Old Guard. On impulse, he opened his wallet and pulled out the tattered calendar.

CHAPTER FORTY-FIVE

Early the next morning, Rod shook Beth awake.

"I'm calling the guys," he said.

"Breakfast?" Beth said and giggled. She poked him in the back, and snuggled closer to him.

He looked at her tousled hair spread on the pillow, her pink cheeks still creased from sleep. She poked him again. It sure was tempting he thought, then sighed and stood up.

"Cereal and toast, babe. I gotta lot of work to do today."

"Okay," Beth said. "I'll get the coffee going." She yawned and walked to the window to pull the blinds open flooding the room with winter sunshine.

At 0800 he pushed open the doors to the MATC. The shadow line set up there by his friends ran along the windows at the back. The mat fit the description of the one in front of the Tomb exactly.

"Hold it!" Sergeant Cook yelled from the open doorway. "Do not step onto that mat without me watching," he called out and strode over to where Rod stood eyeing the long black strip of rubber.

"Thanks for coming so fast," Rod said, banging Cook on the back in a burst of enthusiasm.

"Yeah, well I'm the only one off today," Cook said. "With the funeral honors missions increasing and a lot of guys working on the Christmas party for the families it's kind of busy."

"I appreciate it, I really do," Rod said. He'd been so caught up in his own needs he'd pushed the toll of war far from his mind.

Cook brightened. "Ready"? He asked.

"You bet!"

"Walk for me," Cook demanded, pointing toward the opposite wall. "I want to see how you do with regular marching."

Rod obliged, then turned back to see a big smile on Cook's face and a thumbs up.

"I coulda told you I knew how to do that," Rod said. I've been practicing on the sidewalks around Walter Reed."

Completing the exacting steps on the shadow line mat took much more effort. Sergeant Cook demonstrated then Rod followed his instructions, duplicating them as closely as possible. Figuring out how to insure his left foot obeyed his brain's command as readily as the right foot took more effort than he expected. Soon sweat poured down his face, and his tee shirt grew wet across the chest and back.

"That's it for today," Cook finally said. "I gotta go, but Mathews will be here tomorrow. Get some rest and please don't practice this without one of us. Okay? We need to make sure you're executing the steps perfectly, and you don't know how to do that yet. Okay?" Cook asked again.

Rod nodded then raised his hand in goodbye. Walking back to Mologne House, he saw the faint glimmer of possibility that his goal might just be possible.

Later that month, Captain Boston called to tell him his transfer to The Old Guard had been approved. One step closer. He could pick up his packet the following Monday.

CHAPTER FORTY-SIX

"You're back", Captain Moreno said.

Rod snapped a salute and stood at attention.

"Yes, Sir."

"Welcome home," Moreno said, extending his hand.

"Thank you, Sir. Glad to be back, Sir." Rod reached for the officer's hand and shook it.

"Says here you're fit for duty, that right?"

"Yes, Sir, never been better," Rod replied, but he felt a trickle of sweat start to run down his cheek near his left ear. Mentally and physically his preparation had been extensive. But to reach his goal of walking the Tomb, the crucible remained.

"Corporal James? Call Master Sergeant Owen. Tell him to come see me. At ease, Strong," he said.

Rod pulled his patrol cap off, then carefully moved his legs apart and clasped his hands behind his back.

The thud of heavy boots down the hall announced Owen.

"Enter!" Captain Moreno called out in response to Owen's quick rap on his door.

"Sir," Owen said, saluting, then shifting his stance at Moreno's *at ease* command.

The master sergeant looked Rod up and down as if seeing him for the first time, even though he'd been on the crew readying him for the return. He'd been tougher than Hawkins.

"Well, well, well." Owen said. "Heard you might be coming back. Didn't think I'd ever see you again, Strong, not with your *special* talents and all."

"Yes, Master Sarn't, returning to duty," Rod said, careful not to betray the sergeant's involvement.

"Says he's got permission from Walter Reed to return," Captain Moreno said, holding out a file to Owen. "I'm thinking right after Christmas. How's that work for you?"

The master sergeant flipped the file open and began to read silently then closed the file and handed it back to Moreno.

"I don't know Sir," he said, shaking his head. "The cadence steps? Has to be right."

"Let's see you walk," Captain Moreno said.

As smoothly as possible, Rod began to walk, concentrating on keeping his steps even and measured.

"Not bad. Not great, either," Owen said, suppressing a tight-lipped smile. "Maybe with a couple of weeks with the squad...okay. If it's all right with you, Sir?" he added.

Moreno nodded.

"Thank you, Captain," Rod said.

He thrust out his hand. "Thank you Sarn't."

"Welcome back to The Old Guard," Owen said gruffly, grasping Rod's hand. "See you in January."

Within two weeks Rod had settled into the old routine, growing more comfortable every day. After the squad's organized marches and physical practices, he would work another hour or more in front of the narrow mirror in their room at Mologne House concentrating on the synchronized Sentinel steps until fatigue forced him to rest.

The day of the test, Rod woke early. He'd slept restlessly and had to rise before Beth to tend to his leg; cleaning, powdering, adjusting the cushion that rested between the stump below his left knee and the artificial limb that he depended on for its strength.

"You got everything?" Beth asked as he stood before the mirror in their room.

"Yep, ready. Now if I can just keep from freezing out there," he said glancing at the window where morning sun crackled the ice on the panes.

He turned and waved at Beth watching from the doorway of Mologne House as he walked toward the bus stop with his uniform in a plastic bag over his shoulder. At the Fort Myer gate, he flashed his ID at the guard and headed toward the Echo Company barracks.

He dressed carefully, pulling on the blue trousers with their gold stripe down the side, the shirt and the tie. He bent to lace up the black shoes he'd spit shined the night before. The previous day, the barber shaped up his haircut. He shrugged into the dark blue jacket, adjusted the lapels, hooked the webbed belt and then studied his image in the mirror. To calm himself, he visualized the numbers of steps on the mat and the practices he'd endured. He took a deep breath then grabbed his white gloves and cover.

A week of fresh snow had settled onto Summerall Field rendering the frozen sod like concrete. Sergeant Owen walked over to stand in a patch of weak sunlight near a huge oak tree.

"Let's go!" Sgt. Owen shouted at the waiting hopefuls. Rod's heart raced as Owen started the cadence.

"You ready for this Soldier?" Owen called out as Rod approached.

Rod nodded then snapped to attention shifting his weight fluidly from right to left leg as he'd learned to ease the effort of standing.

"Creed!" Owen barked.

Rod began softly, his breath coming in bursts of frost, "*My dedication to this sacred duty is total and wholehearted in the responsibility bestowed on me. Never will I falter and with dignity and perseverance my standard will remain perfection. Through the years of diligence and praise and the discomfort of the elements I will walk my tour in humble reference to the best of my ability."* At this moment Rod felt as though his dad fell into line beside him, and his voice grew stronger with pride. *"It is he who commands the respect I protect. His bravery, that made us so proud. Surrounded by well meaning crowds by day, alone in the thoughtful peace of night, this Solder will in honored glory rest under my eternal vigilance."*

When he finished, his eyes filled with tears and it was all he could do to resist brushing them away with one white-gloved hand.

"Manual of Arms. *Ready*, Port, Arms," Owen shouted.

Rod shouldered his M-14 and fluidly executed the movement. His gut churned, but not a flicker of expression crossed his face.

Beneath the cloudless sky Rod stood motionless. He dismissed the nagging pain he felt in his left hip, the cold that penetrated the top of his black cover, and the imperceptible weight shift from his left foot to his right, rolling onto the side of his right foot to do it.

He waited while Sergeant Owen conferred with Captain Moreno.

Finally, Moreno approached the waiting trainees holding a single sheet of paper in his hand.

"These men report to Sarn't Caldwell at the Sentinel platoon at 0500 tomorrow. Black, Jenkins, Martinez, Strong, Timmerman."

A flurry of movement around Rod ensued as the men broke ranks and disbursed. Centered like the eye of a storm a maelstrom of emotions swirled around Rod in a blur. At once the pain in his thigh he'd stubbornly pushed aside, throbbed fresh.

"Specialist Strong!" Captain Moreno's voice pierced the gray veil of pain banging at Rod's head.

"Strong! You hear me?" Moreno shouted, now inches from Rod's face.

Rod nodded, drawing the captain's expression into focus.

"Yes, Sir?"

"Don't make me regret this," Moreno said.

CHAPTER FORTY-SEVEN

"Am I ever going to see you again?" Beth groused from the depths of the down comforter that muffled her voice. She tossed the covers back from Rod's rumpled side of the bed and patted the mattress, still warm from his body.

"I told you once I got in, I'd work nine days in row. I'll be off Friday till Tuesday, then we can have fun," Rod said, looking down at Beth's face still nestled into her pillow. He settled back into the warmth of their bed and nuzzled her neck.

She threw her arms around him and locked her hands behind his back.

"Stay with me," she pouted. "This apartment is so lonely without you."

"Beth, babe...you knew what it would be like. We got this apartment in Arlington so I could get home faster. I'm doing everything I can to be with you more," he said, disengaging her embrace to sit on the edge of the bed.

Finally he sighed and opened the closet door to pull out a freshly ironed uniform.

"Can we do something Monday?" she asked.

"Sure," Rod said, but his mind had already forged ahead to his duties for the day.

When he joined the other trainees at the top of the stairs at 0500, sunrise layered the cemetery in shades of pink. Rod and the men went to work scanning the area for debris and removed bits of gum wrappers, soggy tissues and discarded water bottles left by careless tourists. Next, they checked all of the common areas in the museum rooms open to visitors. Rod rapidly rubbed clean a small set of fingerprints on the glass case holding commemorative swords.

"You guys done yet?" Sergeant Caldwell asked. He stood at the door to the New Man room with a key ring jangling in his hand. The five men crowded in and jumped to attention.

The training sergeant confronted each man in turn looking carefully for gigs.

He ripped off Martinez' name patch. "Crooked. One gig," he said then moved on.

"Corporal Timmerman, where is your Old Guard tab?" Caldwell yelled. "That's two gigs, Corporal. Go find it. NOW!" he said sending the soldier rushing from the room.

Rod stood next in line. Each time uniform inspection occurred, he'd had something wrong. Once, a small piece of lint on his Old Guard tab caught the sergeant's ire. Another time, the laces on his left boot were loose. This time, a scuff on the toe of his left shoe got caught. He hadn't felt it happen.

"Strong! *You* of all people. You know each and every piece of uniform attire you wear reflects on me."

Caldwell thrust his angry face inches from Rod's nose.

"Yes, Sarn't. Won't happen again," Rod replied quietly.

"It better *not*," Caldwell said, turning to the man behind Rod.

For all his practice, so far he hadn't earned a *Be On the Look Out* for the best uniform. Get it, and on that day the lucky soldier received a walk.

———

Weeks away from the final exam, to prepare for it, Rod and Beth traveled to Arlington Cemetery at least one day a week so he could run it and memorize the graves of dignitaries buried there.

"Why do you have to do this at night?" Beth asked. She perched on a bench alongside a path looking up at Rod. The sun had gone down hours before, and the moon created shifting images across the patches of snow that still dotted the dense forested greens with their white tombstones. She shivered and pulled her wool coat tighter.

"I just do," Rod said. "It's part of the training."

Beth sighed and leaned back, rewrapping her muffler to cover the bottom of her face.

"Which one is next?" Rod asked, bending over in front of her with his hands on his knees. His heart beat wildly as he gulped in air. Beth held out the list of names and locations for him to see.

"Let's stop," Beth pleaded. "I'm freezing."

"One more," Rod shouted, bounding off.

"But wait, you didn't look at the map," Beth cried, jumping to her feet, but Rod was gone.

The location of one grave needed no memorizing. Out of breath and panting, he skidded to a stop in front of the white marble cross.

"Hi, Dad," he said, leaning forward to touch the cold carved stone.

CHAPTER FORTY-EIGHT

"Strong, change to blues, three minutes, go", shouted Sergeant Caldwell.

Rod looked up, startled momentarily, and then sprinted down the hall from the New Man room to his locker, tearing at the Velcro fasteners on his ACUs. He'd rehearsed this hundreds of times by February, yet the immediacy of the command still spurred him.

Within seconds, his boots were off, the uniform a pile around his ankles. He sat to pull on the trousers and then tied the laces on his black shoes. He yanked the white shirt from its hanger and watched it fly through the air and the hanger clatter to the floor. He grabbed the shirt and thrust his arms into the sleeves, buttoning feverishly. His tie was knotted. Jacket on, brasses buttoned. He grabbed his cover, belt and gloves, ran back to the Ready Room and stood at attention in front of the mirrors his heart pounding. Sergeant Caldwell stepped up to fasten Rod's white webbed belt, pulling it tight.

Caldwell looked at his watch. "Not bad. Now back to greens, three minutes, no more. Go."

Back down the hall, open his locker then pull out the Class B uniform.

Sergeant Caldwell appeared beside him.

"You remember to breathe?" Caldwell asked.

"Yes, Sarn't" Rod managed to squeak out, gulping air.

"All right then, Strong. You've earned your first walk," the sergeant said.

Caldwell's stern expression softened and the NCO's smile betrayed his emotion.

"Thank you Sarn't" Rod said.

"There's a wreath in there from a school in Arizona, needs placing. You do that," the sergeant said, his voice gruff. Caldwell pointed to a small anteroom where three floral wreaths rested on stands.

"When Sarn't?" Rod asked.

"Now." Caldwell said. "Back to Blues, quick!"

Another dash down the hall and within minutes Rod returned, dressed once again in his sharp blue trousers and black coat.

Sergeant Caldwell handed Rod a pair of mirrored sunglasses then stepped back and looked at him.

"I'm watching you," he said.

Rod picked up the wreath and walked to the exterior door. The Old Guard bugler fell in place behind him. Concentrating on his gait, Rod moved toward the Tomb oblivious to the cold gusts of wind whipping the noisy tourists crowding the barrier rails and clustered in groups on the marble steps of the Memorial Amphitheater.

Immensely conscious of the beribboned wreath he carried, he felt the muscles in his arms tense. When he reached the center he turned toward the visitors and began to speak, hoping his mouth would not go dry from fear.

The ceremony you are about to witness is the Army wreath laying ceremony being conducted for Potter Junior High School. It is requested that everyone remain silent and standing during the ceremony. All military personnel in uniform will render the hand salute and it is appropriate for all others to place your right hand over your heart upon the command of Present Arms. Thank you.

Rod then executed a right face, walked back to retrieve the wreath and returned to the mat in front of the Tomb. Two boys and two girls from the school bundled in heavy coats descended the steps toward him accompanied by Sgt. Ortiz. Rod glanced at the two trembling students in front; girls with bright cheeks who smiled at him then stepped forward to steady the wreath as he guided it backward onto its resting place in front of the Tomb.

"Present *Arms!*" Ortiz shouted.

Rod solemnly walked back along the mat to stand behind the bugler and salute sharply. The bugler lifted his instrument to his lips and as the somber notes of Taps floated out over the cemetery, tears welled in Rod's eyes. It was all he could do to remain expressionless.

CHAPTER FORTY-NINE

One Year Later

The shrill ring of his alarm clock woke him from a troubling dream. His mouth was dry and he sat up trying to piece together the remnants of the dream. Somehow he was lost, trying to shoot an azimuth through a murky fog. A dog barked as if directing him but the sound reverberated off piles of broken concrete.

"Rod? You up?" Beth called from the kitchen.

He smelled coffee, glanced at the clock then headed for the bathroom.

He'd polished his shoes until two in the morning, making sure every bit of the leather gleamed, even the soles. On impulse he slipped the tattered calendar beneath the insole of his left shoe. When he finally crawled into bed, his mind continued to buzz with details and concern that he would fail no matter what.

Three last steps remained. *What if I forget?* He tried visualizing the seventeen pages of Tomb Guard details he'd committed to memory. It wasn't just the information he had to remember, but how the writer stated it in the documents: the spelling, the tenses, punctuation. Self-doubt pummeled him as it never had before. *I should have quit this, long ago. What was I thinking!*

Within hours, it would all be over. An hour and a half later he stood for inspection.

———

They all waited, their expressions stoic. Major Moreno, Owen, Sergeant Caldwell, the Sergeant of the Guard and several others, casual in khakis and Old Guard polos.

Rod knew they were looking for perfection, and he was going to give it to them.

Sweat escaped from the band of his cover and beaded on his brow. Without speaking, the Sergeant of the Guard and Sergeant Caldwell approached him to inspect his uniform. A white-gloved hand raised and a finger pointed at his shoulder.

"Lint, Specialist Strong, that's one gig!" Caldwell's voice rang out, and the perspiration under Rod's cover began to run down the side of his face. His wool jacket itched in the crook of his arms and a dull pain started in his hip. Yet he remained composed.

At 0700 Sergeant Caldwell called out the Manual of Arms orders.

As he stepped forward, Rod counted the cadence in his head, keeping his movements sharp. Finally, he began executing the last command. At a practiced cadence rate of 90 steps each minute, Rod marched 21 steps down the black mat past the white marble Tomb. He turned 90 degrees to face east, holding position for 21 seconds, then turned 90 degrees again to face north for 21 seconds. Each movement precise. As he executed the last step, Rod placed his rifle on his shoulder nearest the officers and NCOs. He then paced 21 steps north, turned and repeated the process.

Throughout the day at half hour intervals with little time to relax he repeated the process. Fixed on performing the movements perfectly, he barely noticed the crowds of tourists paying their respects; their voices hushed as they reached the Tomb. Once or twice he glanced at the steps as he turned and noticed the NCOs with clipboards watching him. By the end of the day his hip ached and his head pounded. Rod knew he neared exhaustion yet still faced a final hurdle.

When at last his turn at the mat ended, he stood at attention, waiting.

At a nod from Caldwell, Rod returned to the Tomb quarters for the last phase of his three-part examination: the written test.

––––––––

The smell of sweat and deodorant permeated the room. Caldwell pointed to a bare table with a single chair. Rod slid into the chair and felt his heart begin to beat fast. He counted, willing his breathing to slow down, trying to relax.

Master Sergeant Owen strode into the room, a folder of paper under his arm. He slapped a stack of blank paper and a pencil down in front of Rod.

"Once you begin this test, you must remain seated until I have given the order to dismiss. Any questions?"

"No, Sarn't," Rod responded.

"All right. Begin." At that, the rustle of paper and the sound of his scratching pencil became the only noise in the room.

Rod pictured the 17 pages of information he'd memorized verbatim and started to write. An hour later he shifted in his chair to ease the pressure of its wooden seat cutting into his left thigh. His right hand cramped up from holding the pencil and his thigh had begun to spasm from sitting so long.

When he began the task of proofreading his handwriting, worry contorted his face. If he missed a punctuation mark, left a word out or spelled it wrong the mistake earned a gig. Ten were allowed, but he didn't want any. He scanned the pages then leaned back in his chair. The afternoon sun had dropped behind the massive trees adjacent to the building, casting shadows in the quiet room. Behind him Rod heard the door open.

"That's it then," Owen announced. "Return to the New Man room, change to ACUs and await my call. Dismissed."

———

Sergeant Caldwell suddenly appeared in the doorway of the New Man room. An hour had passed.

Rod sat on a hard bench, fear of failure and dread growing stronger as each minute ticked away.

"Strong!" the sergeant yelled.

Rod looked up.

Caldwell jerked his head toward the corridor.

Outside the bright room, the hallway lights were extinguished rendering the passageway black. Rod stood a moment, puzzled, trying to orient himself to the area he knew so well.

"This way," a voice commanded as a calloused hand grabbed his wrist. Rod stumbled behind the dark figure leading him away, but he soon lost all track of where he might be.

"On your knees." the voice said, and Rod felt his hand being pulled downward. Blindly, he knelt and braced himself with his hands on a rough damp surface.

The stench of mold and what might be dead animals filled his nose. Cold slime oozed between his fingers and the knees of his ACU grew wet.

"Specialist Ramrod Strong," a voice began, "You have successfully passed all but one last test on your way to become an honorable Sentinel at the Tomb of the Unknown."

A second voice continued, "This final crucible will prove your persistence, strength and will to join your fellow Sentinels. Now listen carefully."

Voice one spoke again, "First, crawl through the tunnel you face here, retrieve your badge at the end, then return the same way you came. Second, once you have reached this exact location, run to the fountain below the Tomb and by swimming around its center column wash the New Man off of you. Further instructions await you there.

"Ready Strong?" a loud voice shouted.

"Hooah," Rod yelled back.

"Go!"

Rod scrambled forward, thrashing his way down the freezing tunnel through the blackness, the toes of his boots digging into what he hoped was only mud that lay slick and fetid on the floor. His outstretched hand touched wet fur that seemed to melt at the pressure of his fingers.

Liquids dripped from pipes above his head saturating his uniform. Far ahead at last, he saw a glimmer of light from a grate clogged with leaves. Beyond it the tunnel ended. A small paper bag lay centered on a pile of rotten moldering debris beneath the grate.

Rod reached for it, eagerly tearing the bag open. Inside, the coveted Sentinel badge gleamed. He ripped open the Velcro closing on his breast pocket, stuffed the badge and torn bag inside and started back, pushing hard against the tunnel's floor, oblivious to the muck. When he reached the open end of the tunnel, a door stood open. Rod jumped up and stumbled out in spite of the now pounding pain in his left thigh.

Orienting himself immediately, he realized he was in the amphitheater. Below, down flights of stairs, moonlight illuminated the white marble of the Tomb. The sound of water splashing in the fountain beyond it guided his path.

When he reached the fountain's wide basin, he climbed in and began lunging around its perimeter in long strides, splashing and throwing the cold water into the air yelling *Hooah* into the silence of the cemetery.

He was soaked, exhausted and somewhere in the recesses of his mind he knew there would be hell to pay for screwing up his leg, but at this moment Rod knew exhilaration he never imagined possible.

Panting and crying, he finally pulled himself onto the edge of the fountain and looked down at the lights of Washington, DC below. He turned to gaze back up the hill at the Tomb where a Sentinel stood guard. When he did, the sound of quiet applause reached him as a knot of men emerged from the shadows.

Master Sergeant Owen stood in front. He held out a blanket.

"Hooah, Strong. Welcome to the Sentinels."

CHAPTER FIFTY

Arlington, Virginia 2010

Rod awakened early, planning to grab the first Metro run to the post thinking he'd have an hour at least in the gym. But the quiet of the streets at 0600 drew him out for a run instead.

Now he stood alongside Ortiz, part of an eighteen soldier funeral escort. Early morning May sunshine illuminated the fresh green buds on the old trees surrounding Summerall Field. In the past two years Owen had been promoted to Sergeant of the Guard, and Moreno was now a major and the Officer in Charge. They had just completed their review of the men. Soon Moreno would retire and Owen deploy to Afghanistan as a Command Sergeant Major.

The night chill that settled into the ground permeated the sole of Rod's right shoe. Daring not to move his legs, he wiggled his toes to evade a cramp.

"Who's that?" Ortiz whispered, sliding his eyes toward a black sedan pulling to the curb behind the bus waiting to transport the funeral unit to the cemetery.

The vehicle stopped and its driver quickly ran around and opened the door for an individual seated in the back, then motioned for Major Moreno.

"Attention!" Moreno shouted then snapped a salute to the man who exited the sedan and now stood facing his men.

Rod's eyes widened.

Major General Longworth Shafter stood before them in his dress uniform with its impressing array of colorful battle ribbons, bars and medals.

"Sir!" Moreno said, saluting Shafter, then turning to face the men.

"Gentlemen, this is an amazing group of Old Guard soldiers. Sergeant of the Guard, they have you to thank," the Major General said and nodded at Owen.

"Thank you, Sir." Owen turned on his heel to face the men.

"Specialist Ramrod Strong, step forward," Owen said.

Rod walked to the front of the men.

The Major General strode over to Rod and stood in front of him. The man's driver stepped to his side and handed Shafter a small box, then opened it.

Major General Shafter lifted a glittering badge and turned once again to face Rod.

"Specialist, it is with extreme pleasure I present you with this permanent badge of The Old Guard," he said, affixing the silver laurel leaf wreath encircling the engraving of the Tomb's face.

Rod saluted. The Major General returned the salute and extended his hand.

"Thank you Sir," Rod said.

"Major General Shafter has another commendation for you, too, Specialist Strong," Major Moreno said. "It's a long time coming."

He handed Shafter a second box.

The officer lifted a medal from the velvet bed of the box and held it in his palm.

"Specialist Ramrod Strong, on behalf of the President of the United States, the commands at Fort Myer, the 25th Military Police, the 82nd Airborne and a grateful nation, I am honored to present to you this Purple Heart. Despite injuries inflicted by insurgents in Afghanistan on ten, December 2007, the bravery you demonstrated in the rescue of your brother Corporal Michael Strong saved his life. Thank you for your service."

The Major General reached forward and pinned the purple ribbon onto Rod's jacket beneath the laurel wreath.

"Thank you, Sir," Rod said again, saluting.

Behind Rod a smattering of applause caught his attention. When he turned he saw Beth and his mom, their faces beaming. Not only was this his last mission as a Sentinel, the timing proved bittersweet. The ceremony today honored Terry Taylor, the man who'd lifted his spirits at Walter Reed.

The soldiers' usual easy banter on the short ride to Arlington Cemetery seemed more subdued and Rod's thoughts were elsewhere. He wondered about his dad's funeral and how courageous his mom had been facing two sons to raise alone. Then he smiled as he remembered the good times he shared with the Chief; his late-night visits and the clink of longnecks shared while they talked. Indeed, that brave and decent man had become more than just a mentor when Rod needed help, but a stand-in for the father he barely remembered.

Chosen to stand vigil at the gravesite until the old soldier's coffin rested in the ground filled Rod with a sense of honor and finality. He glanced once at the bus containing the escort soldiers as it rolled away from the curb, leaving him behind as was the custom, then he turned toward the post chapel gate to begin his last walk, alone, and away from Arlington.

CPSIA information can be obtained
at www.ICGtesting.com
Printed in the USA
FFOW02n1950110817
38640FF